A DOUBLED-EDGED LOVE AFFAIR

"Luke," she whispered, and had no idea what to say next.

His lips met hers in a gentle joining of warmth against warmth. Hunger broke free within her. With a whimper, she wrapped her arms around his neck, standing on tiptoe to press herself against him, her mouth deepening the kiss of its own accord. With a groan, Luke's arms slid around her, holding her tight, as tight as she had fantasized, his sensual mouth moving hungrily over hers.

It was good, so good. It was the closest thing to heaven Tess had ever known.

And it ended in the next moment.

Because sanity and terror reawakened in her brain.

She jerked away, the back of one hand pressed hard against her mouth. "What the *hell* do you think you're doing?" she hissed.

His breath as ragged as her own, Luke stared down at her. Then anger blazed in his emerald eyes. "The same might be asked of you, *Elizabeth*," he said. "Just how far were you willing to go to win me over to your side?"

STOLEN HEARTS

MICHELLE MARTIN

FANFARE ™

Bantam Books

New York • Toronto • London • Sydney • Auckland

STOLEN HEARTS

A Bantam Fanfare Book/February 1997

FANFARE and the portrayal of a boxed "ff" are trademarks of
Bantam Books, a division of Bantam Doubleday Dell Publishing
Group, Inc.

ISBN 0-553-57648-8

Published simultaneously in the United States and Canada

Bantam Books are published by Bantam Books, a division of Bantam
Doubleday Dell Publishing Group, Inc. Its trademark, consisting of
the words "Bantam Books" and the portrayal of a rooster, is Regis-
tered in U.S. Patent and Trademark Office and in other countries.
Marca Registrada. Bantam Books, 1540 Broadway, New York, New
York 10036.

PRINTED IN THE UNITED STATES OF AMERICA
OPM   0   9   8   7   6   5   4   3   2   1

For current information on Bantam's women's fiction, visit our new web site *Isn't It Romantic* at the following address:

http://www.bdd.com/romance

CHAPTER

1

Tess popped another chocolate into her mouth and settled lower into her bubble bath, the newest issue of Vanity Fair in hand. How she loved reading about the rich and debauched, and here, right before another story about Hollywood shenanigans, was a Tiffany ad for a mouthwatering emerald necklace and earring set. Life, she thought, didn't get much better than this: she had Debussy on the CD player, chocolates close at hand, her work, her health, and emeralds to die for. Maybe it was time to visit Tiffany's again.

She added hot water to the huge garden tub twice before she finally decided she had wrinkled enough. Besides, she was running low on chocolates. They were her one and only vice—she considered jewel theft a pleasure, not a vice—and she shamelessly indulged herself at the least provocation.

With a contented sigh for an afternoon well spent, Tess stood up, dried off, pulled on a caftan, and went to replace Debussy with Ravel on the CD player, when the doorbell rang.

She padded barefoot across the hardwood

living room floor, her muscles still mush from the bath, and pulled open the door.

"You're busted, babe!"

Tess's knees nearly gave out on her. Clutching the mahogany door, she stared up at her past. "Bert?" she croaked.

Bert roared with laughter that echoed up and down the lushly carpeted outer hallway. "Oh, baby, if you could just see your face. You look like you've seen a cop!"

She felt like she'd been squashed by a Mack truck. Tess ordered herself to breathe again. "It's just that it's been seven years, Bert. I . . . heard you had left Australia and were working in South America."

"I'll give you my life story just as soon as you let me in."

Every synapse in her brain was frozen. In? He actually wanted to come in? "Um, sure, Bert. Of course. Sorry about that." Tess stumbled backward. She shuddered as the giant swept past her. God, he still wore the same cologne!

"Not bad," Bert said as he looked around at the Manhattan apartment's sunken living room, the eighteenth– and nineteenth–century French and English furniture, the Monet, Matisse, and Degas originals on the pale peach walls. "How'd you swing it?"

"The . . . uh . . . owners are on an extended vacation in Europe. I'm . . . house-sitting."

Bert's chuckle was downright affectionate. "That's my girl. You always knew how to work an angle. It looks like you've done well by yourself. I'm proud of you, babe. You were the only one of my girls who really had the gift."

"Thanks, Bert. Um . . . do you want a beer?"

"Now when have I ever turned down a beer? Just as long as it's none of that domestic soda pop this country calls beer," Bert said, strolling into the living room as if he owned it to sprawl on the delicate gold brocade Regency couch.

"Give me some credit," Tess said, heading for the kitchen. "Nothing but imported brew graces my fridge."

She let the kitchen door swing shut and then the spasms convulsed her. Shaking so badly she couldn't stand, she collapsed onto a white kitchen chair, wrapping her arms around herself. It didn't help. Her skin was ice. Nausea threatened to overwhelm her.

His girl.

It had been seven years since they had last worked together and Bert still considered her his girl.

And in a horrible way, wasn't that exactly what she was? Hadn't he made her the woman she was today?

The nausea overcame her and Tess dashed for the sink, praying Bert wouldn't hear the retching. She hurriedly turned the water on full blast, rinsed out her mouth, then numbly rinsed her entire face. It had never occurred to her that she would react this way to seeing Bert again.

Still shaking, she walked over to a cupboard, pulled down a beer glass, grabbed a bottle of beer from the refrigerator, and slowly poured it into the glass, careful not to make a head. Bert hated waste.

Watching the beer, Tess reminded herself that she was a professional and it was time she started acting like one. She was not eighteen or fifteen or eleven anymore. Things had changed. She had changed. Bert was no longer in control of her life. Bert knew nothing about her life. He couldn't. She had been fanatically devoted to shrouding every moment of her existence these last seven years.

So why had he decided to reenter her life now?

Nothing pleasant came to mind. It never had where Bert was concerned. What did he want from her?

Why had he tracked her down? Why had he suddenly appeared *now*? The trembling started again.

"Enough!" Tess muttered with self-disgust. She slammed a fist into her thigh. The pain was a shock, but it worked. It pushed the fear back into the recesses of her heart so she could concentrate on thinking like a rational adult, even though Bert was lounging in her living room. It was time to see what game he wanted to play now.

She carried the beer out to him, sat in the green striped brocade chair opposite him and, with enforced cheerfulness, asked what he had been up to. Bert needed no further prompting. He had always liked to talk about himself. Really, there wasn't anything else that interested him.

Leaning back in her chair, her breathing calm, her nerves taut but steady, one half of Tess's mind listened to Bert's account of the many illegal activities that had kept him happily occupied these last seven years, while the other half of her mind studied him as if her life depended on it . . . and perhaps it did.

It hadn't been her childish imagination, he really was huge, at least six and a half feet tall. All of the muscles were still there, but now they were covered by a layer of fat that, while not making him obese, made him seem a bit slower, a bit less sharp. Looks, however, could be deceiving where Bert was concerned. Tess had learned that lesson long ago.

His pale brown hair had thinned, disappearing completely from the top of his head. His clothes and shoes were Italian, his watch Rolex, his silk shirt open to his navel. Twenty-four-carat gold chains dangled on his massive, hairy chest. South America, as Bert's stories and his appearance informed Tess, had been good to him. But then, cocaine had done so much for so many people, why not Bert?

"So why come back to the States if South

America was doing so well by you?" she asked when he paused to take a long swallow of beer.

"I was a little fish in a large, lucrative pond, babe," Bert said with a sad sigh.

"The locals took over your operation?"

"With a vengeance. But that's ancient history," Bert said, his massive hand waving away the past as if it were a dying mosquito. "I've come back to my homeland and to the best, the brightest of my girls for one final job that will set us up for life. You working on anything?"

Tess smiled. "There are some emeralds I'm considering, but they can wait. What's up?"

"It's a honey of a deal. I thought of you the minute it fell into my lap. It'll make us rich beyond even the wildest of *my* dreams, and I always dream big, babe."

It was, Tess thought, typical of Bert that he had not asked her about her life these last seven years. Typical that his reason for seeing her was mercenary. Typical that she was expected to eagerly launch herself into another foray against the law.

It had never been wise to disappoint Bert, so she asked about the honey of a deal.

"Ever hear of a kid named Elizabeth Cushman?" he asked and, when she shook her head, he continued. "She disappeared about twenty years ago, kidnapping, never turned up. She was the heiress to the Cushman Auction House. Ever hear of *that*?"

Tess crossed her legs, wholly at ease now. This was just like old times and she knew what was expected of her, how to think, how to act. "Who hasn't? They handle the best goods in the world. Lots of money, lots of prestige, lots of power, though they prefer to call it influence."

Bert uttered what was, for him, an affectionate

chuckle. "That's my girl. You got it in one. But don't forget the Farleigh necklace."

Tess's surprise and interest were genuine. "You mean *these* Cushmans are *the* Cushmans with the most valuable emerald necklace in the western world?"

"Thought that would catch your interest," Bert said with a leer. "The old Cushman patriarch died about eight months ago. His son, Elizabeth Cushman's father, killed himself about a year after Elizabeth disappeared. Couldn't handle the guilt, I suppose. You know what these snotty-nosed rich kids are like. The mother died in a riding accident a few years back and that leaves no direct heir to the Cushman millions. And we're talking hundreds of millions."

"And the Farleigh necklace."

"Exactly," Bert said, stroking his gold chains. "The grandmother is still alive and should hang on for a few more years. By all accounts she's a tough old bird. She's running things for now and trying to figure out how to pass on the empire and the Farleigh. That's where you come in. The eldest Cushman daughter always collects the Farleigh necklace on her twenty-first birthday and hands it back into the family coffers on her death. So, with my help you'll pass yourself off as the old lady's long-lost granddaughter Elizabeth and collect the Farleigh as your due."

Tess's mouth fell open, and then she burst out laughing. She couldn't help it. This was just the sort of preposterous, grandiose scheme Bert *would* think of.

"What is this, *Candid Camera*?" she said.

"I have come here with a serious business proposition, Tess, and I expect you to treat it accordingly."

His voice was cold steel and Tess sobered instantly. She had the crescent scar on her right temple to remind her how dangerous it was to disobey Bert when he had that tone in his voice.

"Sorry, Bert, you just surprised me," she said in

an appropriately abashed tone. "This wasn't what I was expecting. I mean, how on earth am I supposed to pass myself off as some long-dead rich kid? You and I both know my blood is the farthest thing from blue."

Bert looked her up and down, as if for the first time, inventorying her, dissecting her. Tess felt the bile rise in her throat. Then he relaxed back onto the gold couch. "Mongrels fake it all the time, babe. You'll do just fine after I've coached you. You always were the best actress of the lot. Now, I've got some pictures of this Cushman kid and her family and you've got enough resemblance to them to pass yourself off without any telltale surgery or hair dyes or contact lenses. You've got the coloring and the height and the age. You've even got that appendix scar. That's what first made me think of you. Nothing faked. I'm going to give the Cushmans the genuine article."

"After a sufficient amount of coaching," Tess said dryly.

Bert smiled with immense self-satisfaction. "I've done some digging on the Cushmans and that kid. I know stuff that, when used properly, will convince them you're Elizabeth. Then it's only a matter of getting the old lady to fork over forty-three point five million dollars' worth of necklace, we disappear like a head-on with the Bermuda Triangle, sell the necklace to a collector I know, and split the proceeds. What do you say?"

"What's the cut?"

Bert shrugged his massive shoulders. "The usual."

Tess smiled and shook her head. "Uh-uh. I'm older and wiser now, Bert, and I'll be the one in the trenches on this job. No ten–ninety split for your best girl. Let's make it fifty–fifty."

Bert's gray eyes narrowed to slate. "I don't

bargain with my girls, Tess. You know that. The split is ten–ninety. Take it or leave it."

Tess was undismayed. "But I'm the good actress with the appendix scar, remember? You need me, Bert. That's why you're here."

His eyes bored into her. "Don't play games with me, little girl. I taught you everything you know. There isn't a dodge you can make that I can't see."

"True enough," Tess said quietly. "But I'm not a kid anymore, Bert. I've been independent for seven long years and, while I may not be your equal, I am no longer your . . . property. The way you've described this job, I'm going to be your partner. A junior partner, sure, but your partner nevertheless."

He was silent a moment. "You know," he said at last, "if you play your part well, you'll earn more than a ten–ninety split on a necklace. You'll earn an empire worth hundreds of millions of dollars."

Tess ruthlessly held back her smile. She had seen this one coming from a mile off. In the six years he had owned her—and he had reminded her of that status daily—Bert had taught her almost everything she knew about being a thief and a con. But in those six years, she had also learned Bert inside and out. How lovely that she could still follow his thought processes after all these years. "You mean . . . keep up the con until the old lady croaks?" she said with feigned surprise.

"Exactly."

"I admit it's an intriguing idea," Tess said, crossing her legs. "But what happens when I give you the necklace and go on being Elizabeth? The old lady will be sore when the Farleigh turns up missing."

"We'll replace it with a paste job."

"Okay. And what happens if you sell the necklace to your collector and a year later the old lady takes it into her head to call me a fraud and kick me out?"

"Then you're out in the cold, babe. The choice

is yours: a ten–ninety split or a couple of years of hard work for the empire. Which do you want?"

"Ah, Bert, how can you ask?" Tess said with a grin. "You trained me. I think I'd make a great empress."

He smiled at her. "Didn't I say you were my best girl?"

"So, tell me how I inherit an empire."

Bert spent the next hour going over his plans for the Cushman con and Tess couldn't hold back her open admiration. He hadn't lost his touch. As far-fetched as it seemed, she began to think the con really would work. And if it did, Tess suspected that Bert had no intention of settling for the Farleigh. He probably meant to walk off with a good chunk of the empire as well. Bert never took less when he could take more.

He handed her pictures of the Cushmans so she could begin to familiarize herself with her soon-to-be family. Tomorrow, she and Bert would begin an intensive training program for her newest role. In a few weeks, she would be ready to stroll into the Cushman mansion and claim what was unrightfully hers.

"This is the one you'll have to convince," Bert said, handing her the last of the pictures.

Tess stared at a man in his mid–thirties. Thick chestnut hair brushed an Oxford shirt collar. His green eyes were grim, his mouth tightly set. The sharp planes of his face denoted strength and, Tess thought, cynicism. It was just a head-and-shoulders shot, but she could easily imagine the rest of him. He would be tall and strong. Those shoulders hardly belonged to a ninety-pound weakling.

"Who is he?" she asked.

"Luke Mansfield, the Cushman family lawyer."

This surprised Tess. "Mansfield? Of Mansfield and Roper?"

"Yep."

"Oh, come on, Bert! He's just some rich kid keeping other rich kids out of jail and dallying on the side with every tall debutante in the pack."

Bert's narrowed gaze pinned her to her chair. "Don't start thinking you know more than me, little girl, and don't underestimate Mansfield. He's your worst enemy. He's tough, he's smart, and he's the one who has to believe you're Elizabeth before we're in."

Tess frowned at the picture in her hand. She had seen his name in the social columns innumerable times. How could a social butterfly threaten her? True, he didn't look like a barrel of laughs, but she figured she could handle him with both hands tied behind her back . . . and hopping on one foot.

"If you say so," she murmured, placing the picture on the table beside her.

"I say so and you'll know so soon enough. You seem to have forgotten some of the basic facts of life, babe." Bert's steel-gray eyes drilled into her. "You don't question my decisions, you don't second-guess me, you don't follow anyone's script but mine. Got it?"

He stood up, looming over her. God, he was a behemoth! "Got it, Bert," Tess said softly, staring up at him, feeling like she was eleven years old again.

When he finally left, Tess closed the door slowly behind him and turned to stare at the apartment. It looked like the rest of her world felt: tilted crazily on its axis, foreign, unreal.

It had actually happened! She was really going to work with Bert again. They weren't going to relieve Cartier of a major portion of its diamonds. They weren't going to remove a supposedly lost Rubens from the secret gallery of a private collector. They were going to con an emerald necklace from the doyenne of the western world's oldest and greatest auction house.

And she, the mongrel who didn't even know her own name, was going to become Elizabeth Cushman, a long-dead heiress with the right connections and the rarefied blue blood of New York's old money.

"Far freaking out," Tess murmured.

She walked over to the large gilt framed mirror above the marble fireplace and stared at herself. She was still five feet nothing and unbeautiful. Ah, well. Jane Cushman wasn't demanding beauty, just an heiress. Her coloring would link her to John Cushman and, while she had no physical feature that really resembled Eugenie Cushman, Tess had an abundance of strength that would more than link her by character. Then, of course, there was her appendix scar. Tess silently blessed her fishy forebears for endowing her with a malfunctional appendix. It had given her a job. The biggest job of her life.

She turned slightly, her fingers drumming on the cool pink marble of the mantel, the hardness settling in her as it always did when she began to work. True, this job in no way resembled how she had fantasized working with Bert again. But he had named the game and Tess had been waiting for years for just such a honey of a deal. She would play his game to win.

A grim smile tightened her mouth as Tess headed for the phone. Gladys and Cyril were not going to believe her luck.

CHAPTER

2

"I cannot believe you're doing this!" Luke Mansfield said for the tenth time in as many minutes. "I can't believe you're making *me* do this! I had a deposition at nine, I have a lunch appointment at one, a hearing at three, I have to prepare for another hearing tomorrow, and what am I doing instead? Watching my oldest client go off the deep end!"

"You should relax more, Luke," Jane Cushman said soothingly. "You'll break into hives."

Luke crossed one long leg over the other and glared at her. "I am going to charge you double for this little goose chase. Make that triple. How many impostors have traipsed through here in the last twenty years?"

"Thirty-two," Jane calmly replied, refilling her cup from a delicate porcelain teapot. "I do not see the harm in interviewing one more."

"*You don't see . . . !* What about my schedule? What about my sanity? You're a masochist, that's what you are. And a sadist. You think nothing of breaking your heart once again or of ruining my entire day!"

"I have no real hope about this one, Luke,

merely curiosity," Jane replied, taking a sip of tea. "The approach these people have used is unique and I am interested to see how they carry it off. Aren't you even the least bit intrigued by Dr. Weinstein and his protégée?"

"No, just disgusted," Luke retorted. "All you're going to get is another bleached blonde throwing herself into your arms and crying 'Grandmother!' and sobbing how she recognizes this vase and that painting. I'd think you'd have had enough of such bad melodrama by now."

"A little variety in my days—however badly enacted—is always welcome," Jane replied with an amused smile. "I'm not at all concerned. After all, I have you to look after me . . . at triple your normal hourly rate. You have your people checking into Dr. Weinstein's credentials?"

"With a fine-tooth comb," Luke pronounced with grim satisfaction. "I'll have him arrested for fraud by the end of the week . . . along with his *Elizabeth*."

Jane sighed. "You've become such a cynical young man. Do try for once, Luke, to keep an open mind. What if Dr. Weinstein really has stumbled upon my granddaughter?"

"Then I will stand nude outside your bedroom window and serenade you with a superior rendition of 'La Cucaracha.' "

Jane's laughter was interrupted by her estimable butler, Hodgkins, who gravely entered the sitting room to announce the appearance of Dr. Weinstein and Company.

"Marvelous! The bad melodrama is about to begin," Jane said, standing up. She glanced down at her attorney. "For shame, Luke Mansfield! Where are your manners? Rise and greet our guests with all the pomp and circumstance that is their due."

With a weary sigh, Luke stood up. Jane Cushman might be the shrewdest thing on two feet, but she
was only human and she had occasional lapses of
common sense. This was a prime example. She was
wasting his extremely valuable time this morning and
Luke bitterly resented it. Elizabeth was dead. Everyone
had accepted that long ago, even Eugenie. But Jane had
not. Well, Luke thought with another sigh, at seventy-
four she was allowed to have a few eccentricities. He
just wished they didn't have to impinge on his workday.

"Dr. Weinstein and Miss Alcott," Hodgkins
intoned before withdrawing.

A massive man strode into the small, feminine
sitting room, almost engulfing it. He had a leonine mane
of salt-and-pepper hair of which he was undoubtedly
vain. He was dressed in a conservative gray business suit,
a red carnation in his boutonniere, tortoiseshell glasses
on his face, a gold wedding band his only jewelry. Quiet,
sophisticated power and affluence was the impression
created. Deliberately created, in Luke's opinion. It was
just the sort of effect a good con would choose.

The woman who had made a wreck of Luke's
schedule then followed the good doctor into the room.

Luke forgot to breathe.

She was lovely. Riotous blond curls, pulled
back into a ponytail, were springing gleefully around
her forehead and temples. Her eyes were a blue so deep
they were nearly violet. Her lips were full and tempting.

She was small and delicate, her hips and
breasts gently flaring her emerald-green silk jumpsuit.
She held herself with calm and assurance, her blue eyes
widening slightly when they met his gaze, her expression unreadable.

Jane moved forward to greet the newest players
in a very old game, giving Luke a chance to jump-start
his respiratory system.

"Dr. Weinstein, how good of you to come,"

Jane said, shaking the massive hand of the alleged psychiatrist who towered over her.

"It is good of you to see me, Mrs. Cushman," Dr. Weinstein replied in a deep basso voice. "This is the young woman I mentioned to you: Tess Alcott. Tess, this is Mrs. Cushman, your grandmother."

"That has yet to be proved to my satisfaction, Dr. Weinstein," Jane said sharply in the voice she used to quell obstreperous collectors. Then she turned to the young woman with a smile. "My dear, I am very glad to meet you."

"I don't know why," Tess Alcott said, her voice frank and amused. "You don't really believe this lost-granddaughter routine, do you?"

Luke, Jane, and Dr. Weinstein stared at her.

"Look," Tess continued, "you seem like a very nice lady, Mrs. Cushman. You shouldn't be encouraging some shrink who dabbles in hypnosis and some woman who doesn't even know her own name. People will begin to say rude and embarrassing things about you."

"Oh, you mustn't worry about me. I've got very tough skin," Jane replied, her pale blue eyes shuttered. "And I tend to give better than I get."

"I'll just bet you do," Tess said, an appreciative smile tugging at her full mouth. Then she shrugged. "It's your call. I'm game if you are."

"I believe," Dr. Weinstein said stiffly, "that I may have mentioned to you during our phone call yesterday, Mrs. Cushman, that Miss Alcott is in denial about the truth of her identity. This is often the case when dealing with traumatic amnesia."

"I see," Jane said and then called Luke to her side and introduced him.

Having brought himself back into some semblance of order, Luke met Weinstein's gray eyes, which oozed benign disinterest, and kept his hands behind his back, avoiding the large hand extended to him. Luke never touched slime when he could avoid it. Then he turned to Tess, meeting her direct gaze with one of his own.

It was a mistake.

His brain short-circuited.

Jane led them to the small tea table, she and Tess sitting opposite each other, the men on either side. Luke caught a faint, tantalizing scent that was pure Tess Alcott.

Get a grip, Mansfield, he ordered himself.

He spent the next minute insulting himself. He was a lawyer, dammit, one of the best around, and he would by God start acting like one! If Tess Alcott thought she could win him over with her big blue eyes and sexy hair, she was in for a shock.

Hodgkins brought in a fresh pot of tea, filled their cups, and gravely withdrew. Jane ignored her teacup to lean back in her chair, critically studying Tess, who cheerfully returned the scrutiny.

"In the letter I received last week," she said coolly, "Dr. Weinstein informed me that you have led a rather adventurous life, Miss Alcott."

Tess grinned.

Luke groaned inwardly. Dimples. She had dimples.

"Well, that's one way of describing my disreputable past," Tess said wryly. "I was a thief, Mrs. Cushman. The best around. I may be on the straight and narrow now, but I still take pride in that earlier career."

"How very forthright, Ms. Alcott," Luke sneered. "What, may I ask, do you consider the highlight of your *career*? Forcing insurance companies to shell out millions of dollars to recompense the people you stole from? Wasting the valuable time of our police forces? Having Jane invite you into this house?"

"Actually," Tess said after a sip of tea, the tip of her tongue catching a drop on her full upper lip, "the best job I ever pulled off was conning a university education out of Oxford. The paperwork and footwork were horrendous, but the free education was worth it."

"Fascinating," Jane said and, to Luke's disgust, she meant it. "What was your major?"

"Art history. Impractical, I know, but I figured I already had a career, so why not enjoy myself at school?"

"About your so-called career," Luke grimly broke in, "have you ever tried to scam an inheritance from a wealthy family?"

"Luke!" Jane said disapprovingly.

"No, no I never tried that one," Tess replied, her blue gaze calmly meeting his. "I always figured the lost-heir dodge was just too risky, too many unknown factors. No, jewel and art theft were the mainstays of my career. Stealing beautiful things provides the greatest satisfaction, you see. Anything else just isn't worth the effort."

"Very sensible," Jane said. "And what made you reform such a successful career?"

"A sudden, blazing enlightenment," Tess said dryly. "I was twenty-one years old and I had half the police forces of Europe and all of Interpol on my tail. It came to me that crime simply wasn't worth it anymore. So, I turned myself in to the World Enforcement Bureau."

"How very commendable," Jane said.

"No, just practical. It's no fun having to look over your shoulder all the time. Besides, I had enough money socked away to keep me in Godiva chocolates for life."

A dry, appreciative laugh escaped Jane. Luke glared at her. She was not supposed to be enjoying herself! She was supposed to be having her heart broken by yet another impostor. *Women,* Luke thought with disgust.

"And in what prison did you pay your immodest debt to society?" he demanded, skewering Tess with the gaze prosecuting attorneys had learned to dread.

"No prison, I worked a deal with WEB," Tess replied, leaning back in her chair, unperturbed. "They'd been after me for years, but they could never come up with any hard evidence against me. Not that they didn't try. I was just too good for them and they knew it. So, they agreed to have me work for them gratis for three years and made me return whatever ill-gotten goods I still had on hand. There was this one emerald ring I dearly wish I'd kept. It . . . Ah, well. In exchange, WEB wiped my record clean. I've been working freelance this last year."

"As what?" Luke demanded.

Tess grinned. "You might call me a consultant. WEB is actually very fond of me now that I'm no longer making them look like incompetent fools."

"For a young woman of only twenty-five, you have led a remarkable life," Jane said, her eyes veiled as she studied Tess. "Tell me, Miss Alcott, what lured you into the criminal milieu?"

For a brief second, Tess's face hardened with a bitterness that shocked Luke. It was replaced by an amused smile so quickly that he couldn't be sure he had really had that brief glimpse behind the mask.

"I fell in with wrong crowd," she replied.

"I believe," Dr. Weinstein interposed, setting down his teacup, "that I mentioned the Carswells to you? They were infamous, prior to their incarceration, for their use of children to execute their crimes."

Alarm bells began clanging in Luke's head. This was all wrong. Every aspect of Tess's life that she and Weinstein had provided thus far could be checked and double-checked. What kind of a con were they running?

He caught his breath, *Elizabeth*. Where was Elizabeth in all of this? He studied Tess with growing admiration. She really was very good at what she did.

"Tell me, Ms. Alcott," he said mildly, "do you ride?"

"Sure," she replied. "I've got a great ten-speed at home."

"I did not mean bicycles, Ms. Alcott, I meant horses."

Tess gaped at him. "Are you nuts? And get myself killed? Thank you, no. Horses terrify me."

It was, Luke thought, an intricate maze she had constructed. What was at the heart of it? "Terrify you?" he said. "How odd. Elizabeth, the *real* Elizabeth, was raised on horseback. Her mother, Eugenie, was a renowned equestrian and horse breeder."

"Then Eugenie had more guts than sense," Tess retorted.

It was all Luke could do to hold back a laugh. *Damn* the woman!

"I prefer to think my daughter-in-law had an abundant supply of both guts and sense," Jane broke in.

"You know, I'm puzzled, Jane," Luke said. "I couldn't help but notice that Ms. Alcott has a crescent scar on her right temple. Elizabeth didn't have a scar like that, did she?"

"No," Jane calmly replied, "she did not."

"How do you explain this discrepancy, Ms. Alcott?"

"I got the scar when I was sixteen," Tess replied with equal calm.

"Might one ask how?"

Tess glanced at Weinstein and then smiled at Luke. "I said no."

"To whom?" Jane inquired.

Again that glance at Weinstein. "To my mentor in crime," Tess replied. "He took it badly."

Jane paused before taking a sip of tea. "You have no memory of your family, Miss Alcott?"

"None," Tess replied, crossing her legs. "Well, nothing linear and nothing concrete. My first real memories begin with the Carswells and I must have been four or five when they got me."

"Then you don't remember this house," Luke demanded, "or your *grandmother*?"

Tess's blue eyes met his squarely. "Max, here, says I should, but I don't. And I don't want to. The police are no longer after my hide. I've got a nice, steady, honest life for myself: a lovely home, a good job, and plenty of chocolates. I don't want some unknown family unsettling what I've built. I don't remember Mrs. Cushman or this house and I thank God for it."

"Now Tess," Dr. Weinstein remonstrated as Luke turned this unusual declaration over in his mind, "you know that is not entirely accurate. You have recalled a few fragments of your early childhood in our hypnosis sessions and they mesh remarkably well with what I have been able to learn about the Cushmans and what we have already seen of this house."

"They would, of course," Luke murmured and was surprised to see Tess suddenly grin at him. He found himself smiling back. Double damn the woman! What on earth was wrong with him today? "You realize, Ms. Alcott," he said coldly, "that I believe none of this fairy tale you and *Doctor* Weinstein are spinning?"

"You'd be a fool if you did, Mr. Mansfield," Tess replied.

"You will soon find that I am the farthest thing from a fool," Luke retorted. "Let's put those hypnotic memory fragments of yours to the test, shall we? The pictures first, I think, Jane."

"Very well," Jane replied. She pulled a large manila folder out from under the table and took from it five eight-by-ten color photographs, each of a different, well-groomed pony. "Do you recognize any of these, Miss Alcott?"

Tess glanced at them and then looked up at Jane. "Those are horses. I told you, I don't like horses."

"They are ponies," Jane corrected, handing the pictures to Tess, "and Elizabeth adored one of them. Which one?"

Tess thumbed through the pictures quickly and then tossed them back on the table. "How on earth should I know?" she demanded and then turned to Weinstein. "I told you this was pointless, Max. Come on, let's go."

She was already out of her chair.

"Now, now, Miss Alcott," Jane said soothingly, "you scarcely looked at those photographs. Why don't you try again?"

"Because it's useless," Tess said, rounding on the elderly woman. "I have no memory of horses or ponies except the ones I saw in Westerns on television. You show me a pony that swishes its tail when you say 'Howdy' and *that* pony I'll remember for you!"

There was a moment of silence.

"This one," Jane said calmly, pulling out the photo of a palomino pony with a long mane, "belonged to the Mansfields. Luke trained her to swish her tail when anyone said 'Howdy.' It used to make Elizabeth hiccup with laughter."

"Oh," Tess said. She sat back down in her chair.

And again there was silence.

She seemed, Luke thought, uncomfortable, as if she really didn't want to believe that she might have one of Elizabeth's memories. He began to understand why she had been so successful in her criminal career. The performance was masterful. Performance it had to be. Luke refused to believe that he really could be looking at Elizabeth Cushman.

"Do you speak any foreign languages, Miss Alcott?" Jane said, breaking into the silence.

"Six."

Luke and Jane stared at Tess. "Including French?" Jane asked.

"Oh, sure," Tess replied, her assurance back in full sway. "French is vital. It's spoken by some of the richest people in the world. I speak any language that will profit me, Mrs. Cushman."

"French was Elizabeth's second language," Jane said. "My daughter-in-law, Eugenie, was French, you see."

"With that name? I should hope so. American kids would have ragged her silly otherwise."

"This hard-boiled persona is all very amusing, Ms. Alcott," Luke said, "but it occurs to me that a successful jewel and art thief would have to adopt a somewhat softer façade to successfully ply her trade, to appear before the social elite in possession of said jewels and art either as intellectual and sophisticated, or at the least innocent and forthright . . . somewhat like the character you've adopted today."

"Absolutely," Tess blithely replied. She seemed to have a remarkably thick skin. "A good thief has to be a good con. I've been everything from a virgin shop clerk to a jaded computer analyst to a European princess." A fond smile touched her lips. "I quite liked having people bow and scrape whenever I went by. It's amazing what you can get people to believe in a few hours or a few days. You see, a successful con is like a blitzkrieg: in and out so fast that no one has a chance to question your credentials."

"And is the hardened criminal sitting before us today a con?" Jane inquired.

Tess stared at her a moment and then a grin curled across her full lips, bringing out her dimples in all their glory. "Only a little one," she confessed. "I really am hardened, but I am a bit more sophisticated."

Jane laughed and reached over to pat her hand. "My dear, I am so glad you came to tea today. I have enjoyed our conversation enormously. You and Dr. Weinstein must stay to lunch if you have no other plans."

"We would be delighted," the alleged psychiatrist replied.

It would have shocked Luke if he had said anything else. "Why don't you ring for Hodgkins to bring in those other items?" he said to Jane.

"Certainly, Luke," Jane replied, her amused glance assuring him she was fully aware of his impatience and growing temper.

Hodgkins was summoned. He entered the sitting room like a glacier slowly sliding into the ocean. Luke had never seen him with any expression other than that of frozen self-effacement. He placed a full silver tray on the table, collected their tea things on a smaller tray, and stolidly withdrew.

Jane took a silver cup from the tray and held it out to Tess. "Do you recognize this, Miss Alcott?"

Tess took the cup and turned it over in her hands. She suddenly shivered and hurriedly handed it back to Jane. She didn't look at Weinstein. "It doesn't ring any bells," she said.

Luke stared at her. What sort of game was she playing now?

"No?" Jane said. "How very odd. It was Elizabeth's favorite. What about this?" she said, holding up a gold bracelet.

Tess took it and turned it over in her hands a

moment. Then she gave it back to Jane. "It's sweet, but I've never seen it before."

It would have surprised Luke if she had. The bracelet belonged to his sister Hannah. The white teddy bear, which Tess also negatived, had been his brother Joshua's. Luke sighed inwardly as he settled back in his chair to watch the rest of the performance. He had hoped to trip up this newest impostor with these fake mementos, but Tess Alcott was too surefooted for such a trap. It would take more than a bogus teddy bear to catch this thief.

"What about this one?" Jane said, handing her a brown teddy bear.

Tess grasped the bear in both hands, its feet resting on the table. She suddenly smiled, as if entranced. "Hello, Fred," she murmured.

Jane leaned across the small table. "Why do you call it Fred?"

Tess blinked at the older woman. "I don't know. It just seemed to fit. He's a cute little guy."

"Elizabeth named that bear after Fred Flintstone."

"She was a perceptive kid," Tess said, setting it back on the tray. "The resemblance is uncanny."

Luke bit his lower lip.

Jane had been winding a brightly painted carousel music box. Now it began to turn and the tinkling music of "All the Pretty Little Horses" filled the room.

The color drained from Tess's face. She jerked herself to her feet, shaking violently. "Turn that damned thing off or so help me I'll smash it with my bare hands!"

Luke, Jane, and Weinstein stared at her.

"Turn it off!"

Her gaze never leaving the impostor's stricken face, Jane reached out and turned the carousel off. The minute the music stopped, Tess took a great gulp of air and then turned on her heel to stalk to the French doors looking out on the back terrace. She stared out the windows, her arms wrapped around herself.

"Dr. Weinstein?" Jane said.

The alleged psychiatrist pushed back his chair and stood up. "I'll see what has upset her." He went across the room to Tess and spoke to her quietly, as if trying to calm her.

"What just happened?" Jane said in a low voice.

"I don't know," Luke replied, staring at Tess's rigid back, "but I don't like it."

"What? Not knowing? Or Miss Alcott's unexpected reaction?"

"Both."

Tess turned to them, looped her arm through Weinstein's, and walked back to the table.

"Sorry about the high flights of drama," she said ruefully. "I told you I don't like horses."

"That's quite all right, my dear," Jane replied. "It must be stressful for you having Dr. Weinstein telling you one thing and Luke and me challenging you for all you're worth. I daresay a nice long walk around the grounds will do your nerves a world of good. Luke, be a gentleman and give Miss Alcott a tour of the estate. I'm no longer as spry as I was in my youth," she said to Tess, "so I shall remain seated here in quiet splendor and engage Dr. Weinstein in conversation. Psychiatry has always fascinated me, you know, Doctor."

Luke smiled inwardly. Jane had very neatly boxed up Weinstein, leaving Tess in his clutches to be interrogated within an inch of her life. The day was improving. He rose from his chair.

"Shall we?" he said to Tess.

She shrugged. "Why not?"

CHAPTER

3

Luke led Tess out the French doors, across the brick terrace, and down the terrace steps to a broad, closely cropped expanse of blue-green lawn. A multitude of birds calling to each other was the only sound beneath a clear blue sky. To their right and left rose an ancient wood, dark branches arching toward the sun.

"Lovely, isn't it?" Luke said, stopping beside a magnificent oak that towered above the center of the lawn.

"I always like to see old money put to good use," Tess replied.

"This must all seem achingly familiar."

Tess's smile was wry. "You wouldn't believe me if I agreed with you, Mr. Mansfield, so why even pose the question?"

"Just trying to find a pattern, Ms. Alcott, in what you do and do not choose to remember," he said, leaning against the tree and folding his arms across his chest. "Take this mighty oak, for example. It's been here for centuries. Elizabeth would have seen it every day of her childhood. Did you?"

"I told you, I don't remember my childhood. So, where's the swing?"

"Why do you ask?"

Tess grinned knowingly at him and pointed to one of the lower, thicker branches. "The metal rings suggest there used to be a swing here."

Luke gave her a lazy salute. He had to hand it to her, she was the first worthy opponent he had met in a long time. "As it happens, there was a swing here. Elizabeth loved it. John Cushman had it removed after she was kidnapped. He couldn't bear looking at it."

"Understandable," Tess murmured.

"Yes. So tell me, Ms. Alcott, just how much of this Return of the Lost Heiress story do you believe?"

Tess chuckled. "None of it."

Luke's arms fell to his sides, his hands curling into fists. "Then what the *hell* are you doing here?"

Tess cheerfully held up her hands as if to ward off an imminent attack. "Hey, Dr. Weinstein is my *psychiatrist*. The guy's a genius, everyone says so, including him. Who am I to argue with genius? If he says I'm Elizabeth Cushman, what the hell? I'll play along. My story is that I'm here trying to find my past, and I'm sticking to it."

"Even though it means hurting an old woman who never did you a moment's harm?"

"Mr. Mansfield, give the woman some credit," Tess said in disgust. "Jane Cushman doesn't believe me any more than you do. She's tough, she's sharp, and she's enjoying herself. So back off."

Luke could not recall any woman ever telling him to back off before. "Do you always come across so strong?" he inquired mildly.

"You're a big boy, Mansfield. You can take it. Look, let's cut the polite chatter," Tess said, her hands on her gently rounded hips. "You and I are adversaries, you've made that clear from the start. You and Jane

Cushman are trying to rout me with every teddy bear and cup in my path, Max is pushing me to accept a family I don't believe in, and I'm standing in the middle feeling very much under attack. When I feel like this, I fight back. If you can't take a fair punch to the midsection now and then, you're in the wrong business."

Luke stalked to within a foot of her. "You will soon find, to your everlasting regret, that I am very much in the *right* business, Ms. Alcott."

"Pride goeth before a fall," she murmured, staring up at him.

Her blue eyes were short-circuiting his brain again. "That cuts both ways, Ms. Alcott," he managed. She barely reached his shoulder. She had to tilt her head back to meet his gaze, her slim throat arched. "You know, I'm curious," he said. "What is a tough, talented, and successful thief like yourself doing with a psychiatrist?"

Tess stiffened under his gaze and took a step back. "I loathe not remembering the first five years of my life," she snapped.

"Ah, yes, your alleged amnesia," he said, grateful for the safety of his job. "Tell me, Ms. Alcott, what *do* you remember thanks to those convenient little hypnosis sessions with Dr. Weinstein?"

"Such skepticism! Don't you believe in hypnosis, Mr. Mansfield?"

"Actually, I do. I just don't believe in you. So trot out some memories. Impress me. Convince me. Drench the lawn with your tears."

"I haven't cried since I was five, Mansfield," Tess retorted with an angry edge to her voice, "so put your handkerchief away. I keep telling you that I remember next to nothing of my childhood. All I have is a vague recollection of an overly fond Great Dane about three times my size and weight who couldn't see me without bathing me with his tongue. And I remember a woman with red hair calling me Beth."

She stared out across the lawn and thickly wooded park. "I remember being on a sailboat with a man, although I can't tell you what that man looked like. And I remember being awakened in the dead of night by a man who had his hand over my mouth. That, Mr. Mansfield, is it for five years of living. If you want to know how and when I got my appendix scar, I can't tell you. If you want to know why I called that teddy bear Fred, I can't tell you. If you want to know why I keep seeing a playhouse on this lawn when one doesn't exist, I can't tell you."

Luke stiffened. "Where do you see the playhouse?"

Tess pointed to their left. "Over there. It's a miniature Cape Cod cottage with lace curtains and a white picket fence. All I can say is, thank God I'm already seeing Max, otherwise I'd have to find a therapist fast."

"Not necessarily," Luke said, gazing at the wide, immaculate expanse of lawn. "Elizabeth had a miniature Cape Cod cottage playhouse with lace curtains and a white picket fence."

And the Cushmans had taken care to keep details of their daughter's life hidden from the public, both before and after her kidnapping. Only the Cushman family and close friends had known about the playhouse, a fifth-year birthday gift to Elizabeth three months before she was kidnapped. It had been demolished after her disappearance, on John Cushman's orders.

"Are you serious, or just humoring me?" Tess demanded.

"Of course," Luke said mildly, glancing down at her, "*Weinstein* could have found out about the playhouse and described it to you."

"Yes, there is that," Tess cheerfully agreed. "Now, as I recall, you are under orders to give me a tour along with the interrogation."

"You know, you're absolutely right. Let's go visit the horses," Luke said with malicious delight as he began striding toward the stables.

Tess trotted up to his side. "You don't usually walk with short women, do you?"

He glanced down at her and couldn't help but smile. "Was I doing my Paul Bunyan routine again? Sorry. Everyone in my family is tall and, yes, most of the women I date are tall as well."

"Tall?" Tess scoffed. "That Franklin debutante is a giantess!"

Luke nearly tripped. "How do you know about Maria?"

Her smile was serene. "Ah, Mr. Mansfield, I know far more about you than you could ever suspect." Tess climbed gracefully through a white board fence to reach an empty paddock. "When Max told me last week I'd probably be meeting you, I checked you out. The report kept putting me to sleep. You've had the easiest life I've ever studied, Mansfield: the right family, more money than God, the right schools, the right connections, the right jobs, the right clients. Nothing ever seems to go wrong for you. I'm amazed you haven't died of boredom."

"I like boredom."

Tess grimaced. "You would."

"And why would you want to study such a bland life?"

"I like to know everything I can about an adversary. Keeps me from getting blown out of the water."

"So this is war?" Luke inquired, climbing over the fence.

"Oh no, this is merely an interesting little

boxing match that will leave one of us with our head bashed in."

"Not me. I'm very light on my feet."

"Yes, Mr. Mansfield, but so am I."

Luke stared down at her, blond curls springing to freedom around her face, blue eyes calm and forthright beneath his scrutiny. Light? Oh yes, small and light. He could lift her easily in his arms and . . . *Don't even think it,* Luke ordered himself. Tess Alcott was a fraud bent on hurting his friend and client and Luke had just made it his life's goal to prove it. His back stiff, his face expressionless, he led her to the stables.

"And what did your night-table reading tell you about me?" he demanded.

"Oh, let's see," Tess said, looking around the shadowed stable with an excellent imitation of nonchalance, "you are thirty-five and the eldest of four tall children. Your family tree goes back to the Garden of Eden. You took your undergraduate degree at Columbia and your law degree at Harvard, with honors up the wazoo. You were the captain of the Harvard rowing team and might even have made it into the Olympics if you hadn't broken your wrist playing handball. Bad judgment call on your part, if you ask me. Trading handball for the Olympics. Shame on you! You let the team down.

"You ride well, play a mean game of chess, and carefully avoid any and all romantic entanglements since you ended your engagement to Jennifer Eire twelve years ago. Hence the Giantess. You bowed to family pressure and entered the family law firm to defend the rich and useless against the mighty arm of the law. Prosecuting attorneys have been known to quake in their Hush Puppies when they learn you're the defending attorney. They call you the Grim Reaper." She looked him up and down. "Suitable," she commented. "Last, but not least, you adore Jane Cushman and would willingly slay any and all dragons that come to her door, even half-pints like me."

"Phew!" Luke said, duly impressed. "How on earth did you come up with so much information?"

"Mr. Mansfield," Tess intoned, "I am a professional thief. I never reveal my sources. That is why I have known such success in my checkered career."

"I beg your pardon," Luke said with a reluctant smile.

They walked down a row of empty box stalls. Only the last two stalls on their right were occupied, one with a chestnut Morgan, the other with a dapple-gray half-Arabian. Each thrust their heads toward Luke, eager for attention and any tidbit he might have brought them. Luke stroked first one and then the other while Tess kept a good five feet away from the stall doors.

"Eugenie had twenty horses here," Luke said. "Some think she had the best string on the East Coast. When she died, Jane didn't want to maintain such a large stable, so she sold most of the horses and kept these two for her private use."

"She *rides*?"

Luke grinned. "With a passion, despite doctor's orders and Board hysterics, Jane rides." He turned to Tess and laughed. She was looking green about the gills and that reaction couldn't be faked. "You weren't kidding about not liking horses, were you?"

"I never joke about death, Mr. Mansfield, and those hairy, four-legged monsters behind you are instruments of destruction. I have had a vision and been saved, Hallelujah!"

Luke could afford to be amused. Since Ms. Alcott didn't like horses, she couldn't be Elizabeth. End of story. He took Tess's elbow and led her away from the stalls. It was the first time he had touched her, the first time he had stood so close to her. It did not seem wise.

Fortunately, Tess casually pulled herself free to admire a flower bed planted beside the barn and Luke moved several feet in the opposite direction. What in the name of everything holy was wrong with him today? Why, when she stood six feet away, was he inundated with her scent? Had she doctored his tea? Was this some weird conspiracy between Tess Alcott, his brain, and his hormones to keep him from protecting Jane long enough so Tess could steal her blind?

Keeping a good three feet between them, Luke grimly led Tess on a circular path that provided views of meadows and woods and formal gardens as he ruthlessly grilled her on everything from her criminal career to her French, which she spoke fluently, damn her. The impostor had an answer, a quip, or a solid punch to the midsection for every question he fired at her. By the time they returned to the brick terrace, Luke knew he had a much tougher fight on his hands to protect Jane than he had originally anticipated. He revised his opinion accordingly. Tess Alcott was *the* most talented and dangerous opponent he had ever faced.

"Ah, there you are," Jane said, beaming as they returned to the sitting room. "Dr. Weinstein and I have been having the most marvelous chat. My dear Ms. Alcott, would you be so kind as to stay with me for an extended visit, say for two weeks."

Luke glared at Jane throughout lunch, but it did no good. She chatted with Tess and Weinstein as if they were treasured old friends, warmly pressing their hands when they finally said their good-byes and walked from the house to the doctor's silver Lincoln Town Car.

"Damnit, Jane, have you lost your mind?" Luke exploded when they were finally alone. "Are you deliberately courting the nice men with white coats and butterfly nets? Inviting Tess Alcott to stay!" He paced the black and white tiles of the Grand Hall with barely controlled fury. "How can you encourage that heartless little fraud?"

"I think having Miss Alcott here for two weeks will give us an excellent opportunity to study her in more depth," Jane replied mildly, her pale blue eyes lit with amusement as she led him into the living room. She sat down on the white sofa, Luke pacing before her.

"She will steal you blind!"

"Nonsense," Jane said. "She's given up that line of work. Weren't you listening?"

"She may not be stealing art and jewels, but I swear to you, Jane, that she is dead set on stealing Elizabeth's rightful place in your heart, in this house, and in the Cushman fortune!"

"Actually, thus far she has done everything possible to convince us that she is *not* Elizabeth, a strategy that I find most fascinating. Now do sit down, Luke, and stop striding about like a lion in heat."

Luke was startled into a laugh and unbent so far as to sit beside Jane. He took her aged hands in his and forced her to meet his gaze. "I want you to listen very closely, Mrs. Cushman, and pay strict attention to what I am saying: Tess Alcott is a cold-blooded impostor."

"No, dear, she is almost certainly my grand-daughter, Elizabeth."

Luke's hands clenched Jane's as he stared down into her heavily lined face. "No," he ground out. "You can't be serious. You can't have been won over by a pair of big blue eyes and dimples!"

"Only partially, dear," Jane replied.

"My God!" Luke exploded, surging to his feet to pace the floor once again. "Has the world gone mad today? However fascinated you may be by her representation of herself, Tess Alcott is *not* Elizabeth! She is afraid of horses, she hates the sight and sound of the carousel, she didn't recognize the silver cup, and I strongly doubt that she recognized Fred!"

"True enough," Jane replied. "But if you were a five-year-old child suddenly and brutally torn from everything safe and loving, would not you do everything in your power to forget that happy past? Memories of that former life could only remind a child—who desperately needs to feel secure—how unsafe her new world really is. It seems to me that any touchstone to that past would trigger either fear or anger, not happy recognition. Miss Alcott exhibited the first two emotions today."

Arms akimbo, Luke stopped pacing to glare down at his client. "How did you ever miss a career in the law?"

"My father wanted me to be a poet. He thought it a more suitable activity for a woman."

Luke had to smile. Jane Cushman's father had probably been the only person to underestimate her. "Jane," he said in his most reasonable manner, "I agree that Tess Alcott is very good at what she does. She's had twenty-five years of training to be this clever, this convincing. She gave a masterful performance today to hide her despicable fraud and I intend to prove it!"

"Excellent," Jane retorted. "Dig up everything you can on Miss Alcott. I suspect you'll be coming up with just the evidence we need to conclusively prove that she is Elizabeth."

Luke ran his hands down his face, struggling for calm. "All right, let's leave Ms. Alcott out of this for a moment. We are also confronted with Dr. Maxwell Weinstein, a charlatan if ever there was one."

"Undoubtedly. Mind you, he's very good. He sidestepped every trap I laid for him in our little tête-à-tête. Still, I don't believe *his* performance."

"But Jane, if Weinstein is a fraud, then Tess must be as well!"

"Not necessarily," Jane retorted. "Whoever Weinstein is, he may have stumbled upon some knowledge linking Miss Alcott to Elizabeth. He could have contacted her and either convinced her of the truth of that link, or of his ability to sell her to us. In either case, Miss Alcott is not precluded from being my true granddaughter."

"Yes, but—"

Jane began to laugh. "Oh Luke, why do you fight Miss Alcott so when you are so clearly attracted to her?"

Luke's jaw dropped, which sent Jane off into peals of laughter.

"Poor boy," she gasped, wiping her eyes, "did you really think your surly demeanor could hide your true feelings from a woman who has known you since you were in diapers? Oh, don't worry, no one else would have guessed. But I must say it did my old heart good to watch you being so rude to the poor girl. You haven't done anything socially unacceptable since you were twelve."

"I am simply trying to protect you from *the poor girl*," Luke stiffly retorted.

"Oh, I know. You're doing a wonderful job of protecting me—and yourself—from Miss Alcott. Still, I've been taking care of myself for over seventy years now and I think I've got the hang of it."

"Jane—"

"Of course this girl may not be Elizabeth," Jane pressed on. "The stakes are high. It makes sense that only the best con would try to win this game. I know you think I've got a blind spot where Elizabeth is concerned, but I've still got my wits about me, Luke, and I know to be on my guard. I will be studying Miss

Alcott under a microscope these next two weeks. Why else do you think I invited her?"

"Temporary insanity?"

Jane frowned at Luke. "I prefer to regard it as a canny trap to catch a thief or reclaim my grand-daughter."

"Then you'll be needing someone to guard that trap," Luke grimly stated. "When Ms. Alcott moves in tomorrow, I move in, too, and the moment she takes the smallest misstep, I'll have her pert little fanny tossed so deep in jail they'll never get her out!"

"Why, of course, Luke," Jane said with a smile. "If you think it best."

CHAPTER

4

Tess sat beside Bert in the Lincoln Town Car, her fingernails digging into the palms of her hands. She knew that Bert wanted to rip her head off, but that wasn't what was worrying her. It should have, of course. She should have been very, very worried about Bert. Instead, all she could worry about was herself.

Why had Luke Mansfield's green eyes set her heart pounding? Why had she been distracted every minute she was with him? Why couldn't she get the image of his tall, lean body out of her mind?

Was this lust? Oh, it couldn't be! She had met many far more handsome men in her life, many much more willing to take her at face value. None of them had created this shock to her system.

Was this passion, then? No, that was impossible, because she was constitutionally incapable of feeling passion. Bert and Dennis Foucher had seen to that when she was only sixteen.

What was wrong with her, then? Why, when she had been with Luke, had she forgotten the most basic facts of her existence? How could her whole body be humming because of a man who would toss her into the eager arms of the law at the first opportunity? She was on a job, the most important job of her life. She couldn't let some man distract her.

Bert jerked the Lincoln to a stop in the underground garage of Weinstein's Manhattan apartment building, jumped out of the car, and slammed the door so hard the car shook.

She couldn't let Bert know that somehow a man *had* distracted her.

Cautiously, she slid out of the car and started for the bank of elevators. Bert grabbed her elbow in a painful vise far different from when Luke had held just that elbow. He almost threw her into the elevator. With his free hand he punched the button for Weinstein's floor. The elevator began to soar upward, Bert's huge hand cutting off the circulation in her arm.

The doors opened and he jerked her down the hall to Weinstein's apartment. He unlocked the door and dragged her inside, slamming the door shut behind them.

"Bert—" she began.

He knotted her ponytail around his free hand, snapping her head back.

"What the hell did you think you were doing?" he shouted. "You nearly ruined us before we got our feet in the door!"

He threw her across the room. Fortunately, the brown leather sofa broke her fall. Tess scrambled to her feet as Bert began to stalk toward her.

"A change of strategy was called for and I made it," she said quickly, praying she could break through his anger before he broke her in two.

"You are not on this job to think!" Bert screamed, smashing the lamp on the end table to her left. "*I* plan the roles, *I* plan the timing, *I* plan the strategy! *You* are nothing! You are only a tool *I* am using to hide the biggest robbery of my career!"

"I know, Bert," Tess said soothingly. "You're in charge, you always have been, you always will be. But I'm the one in the trenches and we had a grenade thrown at us right at the start. I had to adjust."

"What in hell are you babbling about?"

"Mrs. Cushman wasn't what we expected," Tess said, easing around the sofa so that it stood between them. She began to breathe again. "We knew she's a tough businesswoman, but we thought she had a blind spot when it came to Elizabeth. Why else would she cling to the hope that the kid's still alive? But Jane Cushman is nobody's fool, even when her heart is involved. One look in her eyes, and I knew she had heard every angle, had seen every ploy, knew of cons that we haven't even thought of. Being the weepy amnesiac tearfully searching for her past wasn't the right angle to use on her, you must have seen that. So, I decided to expand your script, figuring that the best way to disarm her was to make her determined to prove to *me* that I really am Elizabeth Cushman."

Some of the fury left Bert's face, his hands unclenched as he turned this over in his head. He nodded slowly. "You may be right," he said at last. Tess let out a silent sigh of relief. "In fact, it's just the shift I would have made if I could have gotten you alone for a minute. That Cushman woman has probably endured dozens of young women fawning and sobbing all over her. You're doing something different. You're piquing her interest. Is that why you denied recognizing the Tiffany cup?"

Tess forced a nonchalant shrug. "I wanted to throw her off balance," she replied.

"Fair enough," Bert conceded. "But what the hell happened with that damned carousel?"

What had happened? The carousel music had started playing and she had been crushed beneath an avalanche of rock and mud. She hadn't been able to breathe. Her lungs had completely shut down. What in the heavenly name of Monet *had* happened? Were her childhood asthma attacks coming back to haunt her? Tess prayed not, because they would not go down well with Jane. Elizabeth had been as healthy as a horse. There were no lung problems on either side of the family.

"Was it too dramatic?" she asked casually. "I thought the interview needed a few histrionics."

"It worked out okay," Bert conceded, "but don't ever ad-lib on me again. I've got this job planned down to the newspaper stories announcing the return of Elizabeth Cushman to the family fold. I don't want to have to start cleaning up after you because you suddenly decide to get creative. Which reminds me: why in *hell* did you mention WEB to them? Now I'll have to scramble to cover your story."

"Relax, Bert. I haven't been idle these last seven years. I've got a few friends at WEB and they'll cover me no matter what kind of inquiry comes their way."

Bert gazed appreciatively at her. "I trained you *very* well."

"You made me what I am today, Bert."

"I'll get you your empire yet, babe, Mansfield notwithstanding." Bert chuckled with grim amusement. "*He* does not seem to like you."

"He'd toss me into a torture chamber if he could find one," Tess agreed.

Bert laughed. "I told you he was trouble and he is. But I figure with your charm and my brains, we'll make him come around in the end. I'm gonna love this job, babe. It'll be my masterpiece."

"I don't know, Bert," Tess said, slowly moving from around the leather couch to sit on the matching chair beside it, "I've always thought the Cartier job was the best work you ever did."

"Now that *was* beautiful," Bert said with a happy sigh as he sat on the couch and kicked off his shoes.

For the next hour, Tess gratefully guided him through happy reminiscences of the many successful jobs he had planned in the past and she had helped execute. That led to his further tales of adventure in South America and a sudden recollection that he really ought to check his Swiss bank accounts. Then he ordered her into the kitchen to make him a mid-afternoon snack.

Until Tess could get safely inside the Cushman mansion, she was more than happy to play the kitchen drudge. It was best to avoid Bert's company whenever possible. There was no telling when it would suddenly occur to him that she was no longer the thin, small child who had been so adept at stealing for him, but a woman with all the appropriate features to keep a man entertained.

She had no desire, no intention, and no stomach for entertaining Bert, or any other man for that matter. Far better to make his omelet than to risk any advances he might make. If it came to a battle for physical supremacy, she had no illusions as to who would win.

So, she feigned cheerfulness and walked into Maxwell Weinstein's kitchen. She opened a cupboard, pulled out her box of Godiva chocolates, and popped one into her mouth. Thank God for chocolates! They made anything bearable.

Reaching into the refrigerator for the eggs, she finally felt the dull throbbing in her elbow. She pushed up the green sleeve of her jumpsuit and swore when she saw the large purple bruise encircling her arm. Damn Bert! There was no way to explain away the bruise to Jane Cushman, which meant long sleeves for the next week. Sighing, she grabbed the eggs, green onions, mushrooms, and cheese and set them on the counter to her left, directly below the photographs she had taped to the wall. There were the Cushmans, all in a row. A family.

"Good afternoon, Grandmother," she said to the snapshot of Jane Cushman. "And how do you like your eggs?" Jane's regal face regarded her with a somewhat quelling expression in her pale blue eyes. She was not a woman to be easily deceived. Well, Tess had always liked a challenge.

Beside that snapshot was a picture of John Cushman. "Yo, Dad-ems," Tess said, pulling a bowl down from the cupboard, "what's new?" He was a handsome man, even beautiful. His dark blond hair was thick and teased by a sea breeze. He stood at no more than medium height beside his yacht, the *Lizzy Dawn*, named for his daughter, Elizabeth Aurora Cushman. He smiled engagingly into the camera. Handsome, yes, and undoubtedly charming, but his dark blue eyes lacked the strength of character to be found in Jane's eyes.

"*Regardes, Maman,*" Tess said as she used one hand to deftly crack the three eggs into the bowl, one after another. Eugenie Danon Cushman was beautiful, even in her fifties when this picture had been taken. Her hair, a brilliant red in her youth, was here a vibrant white, shocking in contrast to the depth of color in her violet eyes, eyes that had her mother-in-law's strength and determination. She would have to have been a remarkably strong woman, Tess thought, to survive not only her daughter's disappearance and death, but her husband's suicide as well. She had been a worthy daughter-in-law to Jane.

Beside the picture of Eugenie was a photo of Tess's newest role. Elizabeth Cushman's small face was alive with laughter as one of the family Great Danes bathed her face with its huge tongue. At five, she had a small, athletic body, thick braids of blond hair, and eyes the blue of her father. If she had survived, Tess thought, she would have become a beautiful woman with the charm and happiness of her father and perhaps the strength of her mother.

Chopping the vegetables automatically, Tess looked again at the sturdy little arms holding most of the Great Dane, which easily outweighed her, at bay. There was laughter at the dog's antics, but a slight frown creased Elizabeth's brow directed, not at the dog, but at the photographer who had dared to intrude on this affectionate scene. Yes, she might well have grown up to be a strong woman, one well able to take on the Cushman empire. It was a pity, Tess thought, that that would never happen.

Her eyes turned reluctantly to the last snapshot taped below this family row. Luke Mansfield stared grimly at her.

This picture had in no way prepared her for the sheer animal power of the man, for the charm of his smile, for the sensual lure he cast simply standing in a room. She hadn't known. And if she had, could she have protected herself any better?

"My God," she whispered, "I'm attracted to the man!"

This was incredible.

This was disastrous. Too much hinged on this job for her to suddenly discover she really was a woman after all these years of faking it.

Fear sliced into her. So much for handling him with both hands tied behind her back and hopping on one foot. What a fool she had been.

She had just walked into a minefield with no warning flags in sight. Luke Mansfield was more than she could handle. She had no experience of lust. No training in fending off her own desires, because she had never desired anyone before. Still, she couldn't just give up on the job when she'd managed to get a foot in the

Cushman door. When it came down to choosing between her incomprehensible feelings and this job, it was no contest.

She dumped the chopped vegetables into an omelet pan and began to murderously beat the eggs in the bowl. She had just uncovered a heretofore unknown weakness in herself. For whatever reason, she was more susceptible to the opposite sex than she had thought. Fine. She would act accordingly, boarding up that defect and plastering it over so that no one, including her, would ever be able to find it again.

Fortunately, she and Luke wouldn't be at such close quarters again. He would undoubtedly turn up now and then during the next two weeks to protect Jane Cushman's interests, but Tess could handle that. She knew her enemy now and it was herself. Luke Mansfield would not be able to catch her off guard again. She would avoid him as she would a jail cell.

Late the next morning, wearing a simple (long-sleeved) lavender shirt dress and sandals, Bert at her side, Tess once again walked into the Cushman mansion. Hodgkins icily led them into the huge living room which boasted fireplaces on opposite sides of the room, two walls of windows, and a beamed ceiling. Jane and Luke were seated on a huge white sofa, a pitcher of lemonade before them on the glass coffee table.

Dimly Tess was aware that she was staring at Luke and knew she should not, but how could she help it? The sunlight from the windows set his thick chestnut hair aflame. His dark charcoal business suit was molded to his lean body. His emerald-green eyes were hooded, unreadable, intoxicating.

Which is more important, dammit? With a wrench that was painful, Tess tore her gaze from Luke to regard Jane Cushman, who had risen at their entrance.

"Ah, Dr. Weinstein, Miss Alcott, how good of you to come so promptly," Jane said, taking each of their hands in turn. "Come sit down and have some lemonade."

"None for me, thank you, Mrs. Cushman," Bert said. "I just wanted to make sure Tess got here safely and to thank you once again for your extraordinary generosity in taking her in with you. I'm sure you can do for her what years of therapy could not. Now Tess," Bert said, looking down at her with a wry smile, "try to keep an open mind while you're here, won't you? There are worse things than being reunited with your family."

"Whatever you say, Max," Tess said.

Bert sighed and smiled at Jane as if to say, what can you do with a truculent child? "I'll be in my office on a regular basis, if either of you feel a need to talk," he said. Then, with a nod at Luke, he left.

Tess was on her own.

"Well, my dear," Jane said, putting an arm around her waist and leading her to the sofa. Tess carefully kept the surprise at this intimacy from her face, "I am so glad that you have come. Luke, be a gentleman and pour Miss Alcott a glass of lemonade."

"If I'm going to be staying with you for two weeks, provided you can stand me that long," Tess said, "don't you think we ought to forgo the formalities? You can't keep calling me Miss Alcott all the time. I'll start to feel like I'm in court."

"Very well," Jane said with a smile as she sat on the couch, "we shall advance to a first-name basis."

Luke handed Tess a tall, frosty glass of lemonade, his fingers accidentally brushing against hers. She nearly dropped the glass. Ruthlessly forcing herself to retain her façade of calm good cheer, Tess smiled blandly up into Luke's hooded green eyes, sat in the chair to Jane's right, crossed her legs, and ordered her heartbeat to return to a normal pace.

Her heart mutinied.

"From what you've said," Jane continued, "Tess Alcott is not your real name?"

"Hardly," Tess replied and even managed a grin. "At Oxford I used Preen, Wentworth, Finch, Harley, and Charles. After I graduated I used . . . let's see . . . Marshall, Woodcock, Danby, Clark, Brugger, Horst . . . oh, and Jeanne-Marie St. Juste. No one was more surprised than me when I came up with that one."

Jane laughed. "Just how many names have you had?"

"Dozens. I keep a log so I don't reuse a name that the authorities might remember in quite the wrong way. Usually I've kept Tess, but I've also used Julia, Suzanne, Marguerite, Sophia, and a few less colorful others. As for the last names, I've been through the alphabet three times now."

"Hence the *A* for Alcott?"

"Yes, and no. When I turned myself in to WEB, I was only up to *T* for Tyler, but I figured a new start and a new life required the first letter of the alphabet, so I went back to *A*."

"And how did you choose Alcott?"

Tess grinned. Her heartbeat was back to normal. She could breathe easily. Relief washed over her. It looked like this was going to work after all. "I was rereading *Little Women* for the umpteenth time and the name just sort of came to me."

Jane returned her smile. "And so you've been Alcott ever since?"

"I like it. It's such down-to-earth, honest Americana that most marks can't help but trust it."

"I thought," Luke politely put in, "that you had reformed your career and that marks were no longer of interest to you."

"Old habits die hard," Tess retorted, forcing herself to meet his challenging green gaze.

"I must say, it will be nice having young people to stay for a few weeks," Jane said brightly. "This house is just too big for one old woman."

"People?" Tess said, trying not to choke on a sip of lemonade.

"Yes. Luke will be staying, too. We should have some fine times together."

"I'm having my apartment redecorated," Luke said as he settled back against the sofa, his smile almost malicious, "and Jane graciously asked me to stay with her until it's done."

"How kind of her," Tess murmured.

So, he meant to be Jane's watchdog, did he? And he didn't give a damn if she believed his lie or not? Fine. She preferred open warfare to hidden animosity any day of the week. Every job required some readjustment of tactics, even of tactics forged the day before. She had lived without a libido for years before this, she could hide it away for the next two weeks. Really she could. She raised her glass of lemonade in toast, once again forcing herself to look directly at Luke. She would have to get used to it.

"The more the merrier," she said lightly.

"I'm looking forward to hearing more about your colorful past," Luke said with equal lightness. "It just fascinates me. I've even been doing a little checking up on your exploits."

"Oh, now there's a shock," Tess said. "I trust WEB was forthcoming about my exemplary work?"

"They gave you a glowing review."

"What a swell bunch of people. I love them like family. Who have you got checking up on me?"

"Baldwin Security."

His poker face didn't fool her. "Very good," Tess said, keeping every single one of the expletives raging in her brain from showing on her face. "It's one of the best."

"I'll tell Leroy you said so."

"That's enough fencing for now, children," Jane said.

"On the contrary," Luke grimly retorted, "Ms. Alcott is going to be living with you for two weeks, Jane. I think you should know more than her phony name, if only to sleep well at night, don't you?"

"Luke—"

"So, tell me, *Ms. Alcott*," he said, "what was it like growing up as a female Oliver to a pair of modern-day Fagins?"

Tess's stomach turned over. She could see Barbara Carswell's tight, furious face, feel her hand slapping her again and again as Ernie Carswell looked on, bored. She had been free of those monsters for more than fourteen years and still—

"The Carswells were all right, I suppose," she said with a shrug, forcing back the nausea. "They never had fewer than ten kids working for them at any one time. We tended to look out for each other, and the Carswells kept us all clothed and fed. I even acquired a rudimentary understanding of reading, writing, and arithmetic. That's more than a lot of kids in this country can claim."

"It sounds like you knew some of those others," Jane said quietly.

Tess shrugged again. "The Carswells never chose anything remotely palatial to work from. It's hard to hide ten kids in a middle-class suburb. So we mostly hung out on the wrong side of the Miami barrio and learned about the realities of life. The barrio wasn't exactly clean, or safe for that matter. But oh my, the food when you got it was great."

"Did the Carswells ever tell you how they . . .

acquired you?" Luke demanded, his face as frozen as that iceberg Jane called a butler.

"Sure. They bought me."

Luke and Jane stared at her. "I beg your pardon?" he said.

"You've lived too long in your ivory tower, Mansfield," Tess said, unable to keep all the bitterness from her voice. "There are people who snatch kids all the time and sell them to people like the Carswells, or to porn rings, or to people who want a child so badly they have no problem in not asking questions when a kid is suddenly placed in their arms. It's sort of like cattle rustling. Just change the brand and who's to know the difference?"

"The children, to start," Jane said grimly.

"Wrong. Most of us couldn't have told you where we came from if you put a gun to our heads. The shrinks call it traumatic amnesia. The information just simply wasn't there for us. It was as if we had suddenly landed on a new and terrifying planet."

Tess heard the anger in her voice and inwardly cringed. *Keep it light!* she ordered herself. Just because they were treading perilously close to her greatest vulnerability—her amnesia—was no reason to lose sight of the role she was playing.

Luke regarded her a moment with an odd expression she couldn't decipher. "Did you ever wonder about your parents?"

"Oh, sure. I decided long ago they had probably sold me to the Carswells for drug money. Don't look so shocked! It happens all the time. And in the end, it didn't matter. I was with the Carswells and there was nowhere else to go."

Jane looked a little pale. "You're very ... adaptable, Tess. You don't think your parents might have been John and Eugenie Cushman?"

"I've seen my blood. It's the farthest thing from blue."

"But you fit in very well amidst all this luxury and wealth," Luke observed with a mocking smile.

Tess allowed herself to skewer him with one of her own killing gazes. "Like Jane said, I'm adaptable."

"A necessary skill in your career, I'm sure," Luke said, unrattled. "So, you claim to have no family. What about friends who can vouch for your sterling character?"

"None."

"No family, no friends?" Jane said. "What *do* you have?"

"My work."

"Ah yes, your career," Luke said. "Tell me all about your humble beginnings, Ms. Alcott. How old were you when you first started to work for the Carswells?"

"Maybe four, probably five. I was small for my age. Still am."

"That makes it twenty years ago, then. Another big surprise in your résumé. What time of year was it?"

"Who could tell? It was *Miami*! I'd never been to Miami before."

Tess stopped. How on earth did she know she had never been to Miami prior to the Carswells buying her?

"But you lived there for five or six years, you got used to the seasons. Compare them. When did the Carswells buy you?" Luke demanded.

"Hot," she muttered, still nonplussed by this sudden piece of her childhood surfacing. She *hadn't* been to Miami before! "It was real hot. Maybe late summer. July, August, I don't know."

"Luke, I know you have to get back to your office," Jane said firmly. "I will expect you for dinner. I shall do my poor best to entertain Tess while you are gone."

Tess hid her smile by taking another sip of lemonade. It seemed Mr. Mansfield could be as neatly trapped as she. Luke had no choice but to glower at Jane, bid Tess a curt good-bye, and decamp.

"It should be an interesting two weeks," Tess said, watching him stride from the room.

"Yes, I think so, too," Jane said, mischief lighting her eyes.

Tess turned to her and grinned. "Do you get some kind of weird kick putting two Siamese Fighting Fish in the same aquarium?"

"This wasn't my idea," Jane said guilelessly.

"No doubt. But you're going to love every minute of it."

Jane laughed. "Yes, I am. Come along, let me show you your room."

Standing up together, Jane looped Tess's arm through hers and led her from the living room. Tess had to force herself not to pull free. Physical contact bred security and Jane had to become secure in the belief that she was trustworthy. That she was Elizabeth. Instead, Tess wanted to recoil from the old woman's touch, to fend off this casual intimacy as they walked up the stairs to the second floor.

"Impressive little shack you've got here, Jane."

Jane smiled blandly at her. "I like it."

Tess's brain kicked in. Jane knew what she was doing! She was using the same intimacy tactic Tess was using on her! Why, the old she-devil! Jane was probably lulling her into a false sense of security just before she released a steel-toothed trap. Luke Mansfield wasn't the only danger in this house.

Remember, she said to herself, repeating a life-long mantra, *nothing and no one is safe.*

Jane opened a bedroom door and pulled Tess

inside. "This was Elizabeth's room," she said simply. "I thought you might like it."

Tess loathed it on sight. It had been kept very much a child's bedroom. A sky mural with thick, cushy clouds covered three walls. The large bay window and window seat invited an afternoon spent gazing down at the park. There was a large toy box along the side wall. Her suitcase rested on the twin bed. Her garment bag hung in a walk-in closet. Opposite the bed were a tiny table and chairs fit for any five-year-old's tea parties.

It was a perfect child's haven and all that Tess could think about was a terrified five-year-old girl being torn from the room twenty years earlier. She had known children who had been kidnapped. She had pulled jobs with them. Even now, she could feel their terror, their confusion, their shock at living in a world that wasn't safe. She prayed that Elizabeth had died quickly, easily, after the kidnapping. No child should have to live through the aftermath of such violence.

"This . . . isn't what I expected," she managed. She wanted to get out of this hellish room *now* and away from the memories and feelings of her own nightmarish past that this perfect child's room was dredging up.

"I'm sure there will be lots of little surprises in the next two weeks," Jane said.

Tess glanced at her suspiciously. If the coming surprises were anything like what she had already endured today, she should probably just pack it in right now.

But no, she was being childish. Nothing was more important than this con. Nothing.

Forcing a smile to her lips, Tess looped her arm through Jane's. "Come on and show me the rest of your stately manor."

Having memorized the house plans two weeks ago, along with the secret nooks and crannies that had been added over the years, Tess was free to study Jane and to wonder yet again who Bert's informant had been. The wealth of detail he had passed on to her had to have come from an intimate of the household. But who?

It sure wasn't the matriarch. Tess hid her amusement when Jane failed to point out the safe hidden in the ballroom sidebar. Instead, she uttered her real appreciation of the large, oak-floored ballroom with its huge crystal chandeliers and ceiling frescoes of emerald-green dragons frolicking amidst painted clouds.

From everything she had studied of them and had seen today, the Cushmans not only exalted real beauty, they knew how to incorporate it into every level of their lives. She had to fight off a growing admiration for the family. Admiration led to friendship, even intimacy. She could afford none of them. Intimacy on a job always blew up in your face. Bert had drummed that little lesson into her head by the time she was twelve. She could not afford to admire or like Jane Cushman. Jane was a mark, end of story. Anything else put the job in jeopardy.

She had to convince Jane of a fantasy—that she was Elizabeth—and Jane had to believe in that fantasy strongly enough to convince Bert that she was convinced. Papers had to be signed, promises made, a necklace obtained, and it was up to Tess to make sure that all of that happened.

So she giggled like a schoolgirl at some of Jane's sillier stories, smiled and laughed and told silly stories in turn, forced herself to keep her arm looped through Jane's, and kept her heart carefully hidden away.

"Who is that elegant gentleman?" she asked, pointing to a life-sized portrait of an elderly man which hung in the library opposite an extensive gun collection in a glass case with a pitiful lock.

"My late husband, Edward," Jane replied.

Tess studied him with interest. The portrait

must have been painted in the last years of his life. Even in his eighties, Edward Cushman had been a handsome, vigorous man. He looked, Tess thought with a grin, like he could give Jane a good deal of trouble if pressed to it, and she said so.

Jane smiled fondly up at her late husband. "He was a rascal," she stated. "He loved arguing with me just to get my dander up. He could tease me into a fury and then kiss me into a pool of butter. He was . . . incomparable."

"You must miss him very much," Tess said quietly.

"It hurts like hell," Jane said frankly, turning from the portrait and back to her. "I absolutely forbade him to die before me, but Edward always was an independent beast. I intend to give him a good piece of my mind when I finally join him."

"I hope that's not for years and years yet," Tess said, looping her arm through Jane's once again and forcing herself not to cringe. She had meant it, dammit. She had meant it!

Having been warned beforehand that Jane maintained the old-fashioned habit of dressing for dinner, Tess appeared in the family dining room that evening in a simple blue sheath dress, a strand of pearls at her throat, her hair pulled back in a bun that was doing a poor job of holding it in one place. Jane was already seated at the head of the oak table. Luke sat at the foot of the table. He, too, wore evening clothes. And wore them well.

Luke raised one sardonic brow, his green eyes sweeping over her with an approval she hadn't sought, and was desperately glad to have received.

She mechanically took her place at the middle of the table. Oh yes, she was attracted to Luke Mansfield. She was feeling like a woman for the first time in her life and it was terrifying. Fortunately, Jane began a conversation about the upcoming sale of some important pieces from an even more important English estate and Tess was knowledgeable enough about art and the current market to keep the conversation lively and directed very much away from herself. Luke spoke little, but his gaze seemed to be on her throughout the meal, slowly shredding her façade.

"I think the Monet will bring an excellent price, don't you?" Jane said.

"Hm?" Tess said and then quickly marshaled her thoughts. "Oh, as far as I'm concerned, the Monet should bring a fabulous price. I'm a slave to Monet."

"I enjoy his work as well," Jane said, "but I'm not what you would call a groupie."

Tess laughed. "I am. I stole six of his pieces while I was active, and now I own three, with my eye on future purchases. Maybe I should attend the auction and do a bit of bidding myself. Assuming, of course, there would be no conflict of interest."

"Not yet, at any rate," Jane calmly replied. "Why are you so devoted to Monet?"

Tess sighed in happy memory. "When I worked for the Carswells, my main turf was the museums: the Bass Museum of Art, the Lowe Art Museum, the South Florida Art Center."

"Museums?" Luke said. "My, you *were* precocious."

"Hardly," Tess retorted. "I was just very savvy. Museums offer a wealth of opportunity for a talented pickpocket. Surely you've seen the signs warning visitors to guard their wallets and purses? Most people don't pay much attention, which was fortunate for me. I almost never failed to make my quota."

"The Carswells had you on a quota system?" Luke demanded with surprise.

"Of course," Tess said. "It was the best way to get kids to work. Tell them they have to steal at least a hundred dollars' worth of goods or money a day, or they don't eat, and those kids will steal a hundred dollars' worth of goods a day. I picked up the trade well enough so I didn't go hungry too often. Some of the others weren't so lucky. Either you've got a knack for stealing or you don't, and some of them didn't."

"So you learned to steal out of necessity?" Jane said.

"I'm a firm believer in survival."

"At any cost?" Luke demanded.

She looked him square in the eye. "Yes."

"But I don't understand," Jane broke in quietly, "how working the museums to make your daily quota made you a Monet devotee."

Tess turned from Luke to Jane with relief. "I discovered his work in the Bass Museum of Art when I was nine. They have a lovely collection of old masters, even Rococo and Baroque, a few Impressionists. Only at nine, I wasn't very impressed. It was a weekday, and it was raining, and the pickings were slim. I was getting pretty desperate because it was almost closing time and I'd only made about half my quota for the day. The day before had been equally dismal, so I was hungry." Tess stared into her crystal water goblet for a moment. "Anyway," she said, giving herself a mental shake, "there I was, desperate, depressed, convinced there was no good and no beauty in life, and I turned a corner and there, on the wall, was one of Monet's huge water lilies canvases. Suddenly I felt myself immersed in the painting. I was gliding through the water, lilies brushing gently against me. It was absolutely one of the most beautiful experiences of my life. I've been addicted ever since."

"And did you make your quota?" Luke asked quietly.

"No," Tess said with a shrug. "But because of Monet, I didn't mind so much."

Jane turned the conversation to a less personal discussion of some of the jewelry that would soon be up for auction, and Tess kept the conversational ball rolling with the utmost relief. Remembering Miami and the Carswells, let alone talking about them, always set her nerves on edge.

The stress of maintaining her con and surviving Luke's hooded gaze left her exhausted by the end of the meal. She couldn't help but yawn over her hot chocolate, while Jane and Luke sipped their coffee as they chatted away about Luke's sister Miriam and her penchant for attracting over-the-hill athletes.

"Good heavens, child," Jane said, interrupting Luke to turn on Tess. "Stop yawning away like a hippopotamus and go to bed."

"You're tired of my scintillating company?" Tess inquired.

"You ceased being scintillating twenty minutes ago. Why else have I engaged Luke in gossip? Go to bed, Tess."

"Yes, ma'am."

Tess saluted and gratefully escaped the dining room and Luke Mansfield. It had been a long, stressful day, she told herself as she slowly climbed the stairs to the second floor. That was why her defenses had been so weak tonight. That was why it was safer to turn tail and run rather than slug it out. A good night's rest and old memories or Luke Mansfield wouldn't be able to disconcert or distract her again.

She opened the door to Elizabeth's room and held back a groan. It was just as awful as she remembered it. She had unpacked before dinner and in her absence someone had turned down the bed and left the bedside lamp on. If she had been a five-year-old child, she might have felt peace and contentment entering such a haven.

But Tess was a twenty-five-year-old woman

who had worked hard to create her own haven these last seven years and she wanted none of Elizabeth's. Still, maybe she could put it to some use. The room could be blamed for the return of some of Elizabeth's "memories."

Slowly she undressed and pulled on her oversized white cotton pajamas. She ran a brush through her hair and then looked around for a book to lull her to sleep. Her gaze fell on the toy box. Slowly, reluctantly, she walked across the room and lifted up the wooden lid. Dozens of toys, books, games, and stuffed animals, including Fred, were carefully arranged inside. She needed no one to tell her they had belonged to Elizabeth. The books, of course, were children's books: several by Dr. Seuss, a Winnie the Pooh collection, *The Wizard of Oz*. Having never read them in her youth, Tess didn't intend to start reading them now. Jane had given her carte blanche of the Cushman library and she would use it.

She padded down the back stairs in her bare feet, to avoid Jane and Luke, and walked into the library. Luke stood at the river-rock fireplace, a snifter of brandy balanced in his long fingers. He stared into it as if seeking the answers to the universe.

"Oops! Sorry," she said, striding briskly into the room as if her very being were not centered on the green-eyed monster from Hell. "I didn't mean to disturb you. I just came for a book. Something like Richardson's *Pamela*. Guaranteed to knock you out cold inside of two minutes."

Luke's emerald gaze stopped her half way across the room. "You're looking for *Pamela*?" he said. "You nearly fell asleep over your cup of after-dinner hot chocolate."

Tess forced herself to look away from Luke. She walked toward the bookshelves, hoping to find a book and escape quickly. "Hodgkins laced the hot chocolate with caffeine," she said calmly, "I'm convinced of it."

"His dislike of heartless cons exceeds even my own. But then, he's known Jane longer."

"Fortunately," Tess said lightly, "Jane relies on her own opinion, not on that of her butler or watchdog, I mean lawyer."

"This *watchdog* will protect Jane from your machinations with the last breath in his body."

"I expected nothing less," Tess said, scanning the shelves for *Pamela*.

"Who are you really, Tess Alcott?"

"You got me. I'll let you know when I find out."

"So, you intend to play this amnesia story for all it's worth?"

Rage erupted in Tess and spun her around to face her enemy. "Do you remember your fifth birthday party?" she demanded.

Luke looked surprised at suddenly being under attack. "Sure."

"Do you remember what your childhood bedroom looked like?"

"Of course."

"Do you remember what your favorite food was?"

"Yes."

"Well, I don't!" Tess said bitterly. "You're supposed to be such a hotshot lawyer, Mansfield, but you're batting less than a hundred when it comes to knowing what the truth is about me!"

She spun back to the bookshelves, trying to get her temper and her pain under control. The library was silent for what seemed a very long moment.

"I'm beginning to think you're right," Luke said gently. "But still, even with my lousy batting average, you can't win."

"There's that male arrogance, rearing its ugly head again," Tess said, standing on tiptoe to read the titles on the upper shelves, wanting to relax into Luke's quiet, and not daring to. "But in a way you're right, Mansfield. I can't really win because I don't have anything to lose. I'm looking for my past, remember? If Jane isn't there, it's no skin off my nose. I'll eventually find someone who was there and I'll be able to conduct my own little 'Up Close and Personal' interview. So yap away, Mansfield, you can only give yourself a sore throat."

His chuckle rumbled up and down her spine. Without looking, she knew that Luke had leaned his back against the fireplace mantel and was studying her from head to toe.

"Love your negligee," he said.

Tess forced herself to laugh as she grabbed *Pamela* and turned to him. The brandy snifter was resting on the mantel. His hands were free. He seemed more dangerous that way. "I think it's best to choose function over form," she said a little breathlessly, tension coiling within her. "In my line of work, it's often necessary to make a quick, and unscheduled, exit and that means no time to grab your clothes if you're sleeping in the nude . . . as I found out the hard way in my youth."

Luke's grin broadened, lightening his face, eroding the cynical mask. "Now that is something I dearly would have loved to see."

"Six French *gendarmes* had the dubious pleasure instead," Tess said, walking back across the room. It seemed to stretch on for miles before her. "Fortunately, the shock of seeing a naked girl running across the rooftops of the Left Bank kept them from firing their guns and I was able to make my getaway unscathed. Later, I heard about an American bank robber who pulled all of his jobs in the nude because, I am told on the greatest authority, if you've only seen someone naked, you can't recognize them dressed."

"That wouldn't work where you're concerned," Luke murmured, his gaze forcing her to a stop directly in front of him. "It's a good thing you didn't meet those *gendarmes* the next day."

A blush flooded Tess's cheeks. "Why, Mr. Mansfield, I do believe you're actually paying me a compliment."

"It has been known to happen," Luke said, sounding a bit surprised himself. "I once made some very nice remarks about a racing skiff I was assigned at Harvard."

"Careful, Mansfield. Such unbridled enthusiasm will have you running amok."

"Running amok sounds wonderful just now," Luke said with a sigh, his hand reaching out and brushing against her cheek, lingering there, stilling her breath.

She had never known a man's touch could be so lovely.

The world tilted crazily beneath Tess's feet as he slowly lowered his head to hers. "Luke," she whispered and had no idea what to say next.

His lips met hers in a gentle joining of warmth against warmth. Hunger broke free within her. She wrapped her arms around his neck, standing on tiptoe to press herself against him, her mouth deepening the kiss of its own accord. With a groan, Luke slid his arms around her, holding her tight, his sensual mouth moving hungrily over hers.

It was good, so good. It was the closest thing to heaven Tess had ever known.

And it ended in the next moment as sanity abruptly returned.

She jerked away, her book clutched to her

chest, the back of one hand pressed against her mouth. "What the *hell* do you think you're doing?" she hissed.

His breath as ragged as her own, Luke stared down at her. Then anger blazed in his eyes. "The same might be asked of you, *Elizabeth*," he sneered. "Just how far were you willing to go to win me over to your side?"

Something in Tess, newly born, died in that moment. Oh God, he had been using her, testing her. And she had fallen for it. Her hand ached to strike the superiority from Luke's handsome face. Instead, she gripped her book even harder.

"Don't think you can use your masculine charms to seduce me out of this house," she snapped. "I am neither that stupid nor that desperate!"

She stalked from the room, slamming the library door shut behind her.

CHAPTER

5

Still dripping from his shower, Luke wrapped a towel around his hips and headed for the bedside phone. He punched in a Boston number, gave his name, and was quickly put through to the head of Baldwin Security.

"Leroy? Luke Mansfield," he said. "Any word on Weinstein?"

"Luke," Leroy Baldwin said with an exasperated sigh, "you asked me that same question, four times, yesterday, and five times the day before that. If you would just stay off the phone, I might get some work done."

"You mean you haven't found anything?"

Leroy sighed again. "Give me a break, man. When have I had the time? If you would just stop hassling me—"

"Haven't you found out *anything*?"

Another, heavier sigh. "Weinstein's story continues to check out, Luke. Degrees, clinical practice, articles in reputable journals, everything. We've traced him back to high school and everything still checks out."

Luke's fist slammed into the wall. "But this guy is a fraud!"

"Hey, I trust your instincts on this. The man may well be a fraud. The problem is that he's a *good* fraud and that takes a bit more time to prove."

Luke began to pace, his towel slipping dangerously down his hips. "You are supposedly the best in the business, Leroy, but all I've gotten from you so far are excuses!"

"You know, no man is ever this hot and bothered unless there's a woman involved. Who is she?"

"I don't know!" Luke shouted.

"It's Tess Alcott, then. I'd watch my back with that one, Luke. According to my initial report from WEB, she's a tiger with barely sheathed claws. I'd hate to see what you'll look like if she ever goes after you."

"I can take care of myself."

"Yeah, right. That's why you are at this very moment pacing around like a caged lion in heat."

Luke stopped in mid-pace and stared at his phone. "Have you been talking to Jane Cushman lately?"

"Heard that one before, have you?" Leroy said, chuckling. "This Jane sounds like my kind of woman."

"She would eat you for breakfast. What else did your WEB contacts tell you about Tess?"

"Not a whole helluva lot. A very private person, your Ms. Alcott. She doesn't fraternize with her co-workers. In fact, she has to be threatened with vivisection before she'll agree to take on partners for whatever job she's working. She refuses to carry anything resembling a gun on the job, or off the job for that matter. She's brilliant at adapting to any situation that gets thrown at her, and she's a sucker for *Joe Versus the Volcano*."

"What?"

"A middling flick with Tom Hanks and Meg Ryan."

"I know what the movie is. I *own* the movie," Luke retorted. "How does WEB know she's a sucker for that film?"

"Whenever she watches it at home—and a very nice home it is, too—she turns on her answering machine that has the basic message of 'Hi, I'm watching *Joe Versus the Volcano*, so buzz off.'"

Luke laughed. "You should see it sometime, Leroy. It does a great job contrasting survival with living your dreams." Luke stopped a moment. Tess believed in survival at any cost. Did she even have a dream she wanted to live? Did he? "But we're getting off track," he said hastily. "Weinstein's story should be the easier one to crack. Why haven't you?"

"Look, Luke, I've never let you down in the past and I'm not going to start now. I've got my best people working on Weinstein. I'll have what you want by the end of the week, I promise. Now relax!"

Sighing, Luke hung up the phone. Relax? Laugh and be merry? Dance with the Giantess . . . um . . . Maria Franklin? Put Tess Alcott out of his mind when he could still taste her sweet lips on his mouth? Fat chance.

With an oath, Luke used the towel to dry himself and then began to get dressed.

All right, he was attracted to Tess Alcott. He was feeling alive and excited for the first time in years. Despite her tough exterior, there was a haunted look he had glimpsed occasionally in the darkest depths of her blue eyes that touched a chord in Luke. Tess, like him, seemed to know human deception and betrayal firsthand. The human need to trust had been aborted in her by experience. He had never expected to find that he had anything in common with a thief, let alone that that thief could reignite a flame within him he thought had died long ago.

With any other woman at any other time he would have been amazed that she had so easily scaled his walls, let alone leapt over the moat with the snapping crocodiles. But this was Tess Alcott and her sweet mouth here and now sabotaging his prime objective: protecting Jane . . . and himself.

Luke was not amazed. He was horrified. He was in so much trouble he didn't know where to begin to dig himself out. How could he have been so stupid, so incredibly asinine as to kiss Tess last night? It wasn't as if she had been dressed for seduction or had done anything, said anything, to provoke him.

Yet she had been so lovely. Her baggy pajamas had only emphasized her femininity. Toughness had warred with sadness in her blue eyes. She had given him a glimpse of the terrified and terrorized child she had been and the sad woman she was today. He had forgotten why she was in this house. He had forgotten in that moment that they were enemies.

He had had to touch her. He had had to touch her and once touching, he had had to kiss her. The need had been greater than sanity, greater than his job, greater than protecting Jane.

That kiss had been, for Luke, a revelation of a self he had forgotten. Fortunately, anger had come to his rescue, returned reason to his brain, brought sanity back into his universe. How he wished Tess *had* slapped him, as she clearly wanted to do, because then he could have shaken her until her teeth rattled and the truth came out about Elizabeth, and Weinstein, and what the hell an acknowledged con artist and thief was doing at the Cushman estate, and what maddening game she was playing with his brain and his hormones.

"I am losing my mind," Luke said aloud. He sat down hard on the side of his bed. He was feeling—

feeling!—things that had his brain tied up in knots. He had been skating the emotional surface for such a long time, that this sudden plunge into the emotional depths had knocked the wind out of him. Emotion superseding reason? It couldn't be. But it was.

Luke took a deep breath. "Get a grip, Mansfield," he ordered himself. This was just his hormones getting in his way, that was all. His hormones were mucking up his brain and he was going to put a stop to it. He would protect Jane Cushman from this charlatan no matter how desirable that charlatan might be. Jane would not be hurt, she would not be duped, and he would return to his sane, uneventful path through life the minute Tess Alcott was booked for fraud.

Luke swore bitterly and barged out of his room—and right into Tess, his hands automatically going around her to steady them both. Her skin was warm and soft, her scent stealing over him. Into him. He jerked himself back from her as if he'd been burned. She swayed a moment before finding her balance.

"I want to talk to you," he said brusquely.

"Really?" Tess said, her voice arctic. "How odd. I can't think of a thing we could say to each other that wouldn't be insulting." She tried to sidestep him, but he blocked her path.

"About last night—"

"Going to apologize?"

"Hardly," Luke retorted.

"I didn't think so. You didn't say anything last night that you didn't mean. It amazes me that Jane can enjoy the company of such a foul-minded, unscrupulous man."

"You know, I'd be shocked to discover that you've ever been this bitchy with Jane."

Anger flared in Tess's blue eyes. "My conversations with Jane Cushman are none of your business!"

"On the contrary, they *are* my business, a business that I value."

"Oh yes," Tess scoffed. "The ever-loyal watchdog. Or should I say lapdog?" She succeeded in getting past Luke, but his hand caught her arm and spun her back around.

"I'm going to find out what game you're playing," he growled, "and when I do, you're going to wish you'd never heard of the Cushman millions."

Blue eyes blazed up at him. "Such honor, such integrity! They must impress Jane very much. How impressed do you think she'd be if she knew you tried to prostitute yourself last night in defense of her millions?"

Luke grasped Tess's arms, knowing he was hurting her and in his fury not caring. "If we're going to discuss prostitution, you never answered my question last night. Just how far *would* you go to win me over to your side? You know, it might be fun to find out. My bed is just in here."

"You bastard!" Tess seethed, wrenching herself free and backing from Luke. "I have never sold my body to any man for any price and I certainly wouldn't begin with some two-bit shyster lawyer dangling from an old woman's purse strings!"

Luke stared after her as she stormed down the stairs.

What had just happened? Had that been *him* manhandling a woman whose head barely reached his shoulders? Had he really said such vile things?

For the first time in his life, Luke felt dirty, ugly. If Tess was a fraud, she was playing a gentleman's game of it and he had trespassed badly. All she had done was make Jane laugh. All she had done was make him forget who he was, what he was, and where he was going.

Right now, he was going to apologize. There was no other option.

He searched the entire house and half the grounds before he found Tess methodically swimming laps in the outdoor pool, her body slicing neatly through the water, her strokes never varying, her turns crisp and clean.

She had strength and stamina and grace ... important attributes for her line of work, Luke ruthlessly told himself, trying to ignore the sudden need to feel her wet body pressed hard against him.

She levered herself out of the water, dragged a towel over herself a few times, pulled the green caftan she'd been wearing back over her head, and started for the house. Luke walked around the pool, meeting her halfway.

"Ms. Alcott, I'd like to speak with you."

"Oh, not again," she said disgustedly.

He couldn't help but smile. It was one of her more annoying habits: no matter how damn mad he was, she could make him smile. "I'm afraid so," he said. "I owe you an apology and I intend to make it."

Apparently puzzled, she peered up at the blue sky and then looked at him. "You've been out in the sun too long, Mansfield. Better get inside before your hallucinations get worse."

She started to walk around him, but Luke had no intention of starting that old dance again. He grabbed her arm—gently.

"Hold it right there," he said. "I am bigger and stronger than you, so forget any ideas about walking away from this. I am going to apologize to you and you are going to listen!"

She shifted most of her weight onto one leg and sighed heavily. "All right, all right. Just get it over with."

This was not a helpful attitude, particularly

when Luke was not precisely in the habit of apologizing to anyone. Remembering what he was apologizing for, he hurriedly released her arm.

"I'm sorry for using Brute Squad tactics on you this morning," he said, forcing himself to be sincere rather than relying on the safety of anger. "I should never have manhandled you like that. Nor should I have thought, let alone said, such horrible things to you. You're an acknowledged con and thief, but you would no more prostitute yourself to win your case than I would. So I apologize for every insulting thing I said to you . . . last night and this morning."

"Are you done yet?" Tess asked in a bored voice.

Every good intention flew out of his head. "You are the most infuriating woman I have ever met! Has your life of crime so completely corrupted you that you can't even accept an honest apology?"

"It's a free country, Mansfield. I can accept, or refuse, what I choose. I don't like your bullying tactics, I don't like your filthy mind, and I don't like *you*. Now if you'll excuse me, I have to change."

"Change? That's a good one," Luke sneered. "What role are you going to play now? Abandoned waif? Pollyanna? Lucrezia Borgia?"

"I am a thief, not a murderess, Mansfield!"

"And so proud of being a thief."

"Yes, I am!" she said, blue eyes blazing up at him. "Why shouldn't I be proud of doing a difficult job and doing it well?"

"Do you even know what a moral or an ethic is?" Luke demanded.

"Oh, give me a break," Tess said, arms akimbo as she glared at him. "This whole country is based on the fine art of highway robbery! First we stole the land from the Indians, then we started stealing it from each other. There isn't a family fortune in this country that wasn't built on piracy, bootlegging, or creative doctoring of the accounts. Look at your own noble house. The Mansfield fortune really took off when your illustrious great-grandfather stole an entire railroad from his stockholders!"

"Now that is a deliberate skewing of the facts—"

"Bullshit," Tess snapped. "He wanted to run the railroad his way and when the stockholders balked, he hijacked the company. Your illustrious *grandfather* happily bought up company after company while their former owners were jumping out of windows in 1929. Your great-uncle was a very successful bootlegger. Do you even *know* what half the Mansfield companies *do*?"

"My brother Joshua runs the family business—" Luke began.

"And you keep your pristine hands off all that ill-gotten lucre. How noble of you. Aren't you even now defending that beloved millionaire Jesse Wallingham in a very nasty extortion case?"

"I'm his attorney, certainly. But Wallingham is my father's friend and he is innocent and I resent—"

"And what's your fee for taking on this headline-making case? Two hundred dollars an hour? Three?"

"Four hundred," Luke muttered.

"And consoling his young trophy wife while poor Jesse cools his heels in jail, no doubt."

"I have met Gloria Wallingham exactly *twice* in my life!"

"What about that little affair of public record with Linda Collier?"

"How on earth do you know about Linda?"

"Hey, I read the gossip rags, just like any redblooded grocery-shopping woman. So, was Linda as good as her press suggests?"

"Better!" Luke barked.

"That *must* have been fun. However did the very tall Maria Franklin win you away from the double-jointed Ms. Collier?"

Luke couldn't help himself. The image was so ludicrous that he burst out laughing. Just as suddenly, he stopped and stared down at Tess. "Hey, wait a minute!" he breathed. "Just who is interrogating whom here?"

Tess smiled sunnily up at him.

Luke, in spite of himself, was amused. "My hypothetical hat is off to you, Ms. Alcott. You are *very* good at what you do."

"Aren't I, though?" Tess said serenely as she started for the house.

He let her go this time, watching her walk away with a jaunty lilt in her step. She was so damned . . . irritating. And challenging. And fun. And lovely.

He drove to his office at Rockefeller Plaza, alternately insulting himself, remembering Tess's sweet kiss and worrying about what was happening to his self-control, his good sense, his moat with the ferocious crocodiles.

He immersed himself in work to chase away all thoughts of Tess Alcott. He spent two hours on the phone, developing a cauliflower ear that demanded a break. So he spent forty-five minutes discussing with Carol, his paralegal, the precedents he wanted her to find for the Wallingham case. He revamped his calendar with Harriet, his secretary, dictated five letters, three court motions, and a demand for payment. Then he began returning his phone calls.

He was in the middle of trying to refer an old acquaintance to a renowned divorce lawyer when it finally hit him.

If Tess wouldn't sell herself to win an ally— and she wouldn't, he knew that now as surely as he knew his own name—why had she kissed him? Why had she arched into him and practically melted into his arms?

"My God," Luke breathed. She might very well be trying to con Jane's millions, but her reaction to him, from her anger to her kisses, had been honest from the start.

"What did you say?"

Luke dazedly returned to the phone call. "Sorry, Jeff. Call Apodaca, that's the best advice I can give you."

"Yeah, you're probably right," Jeff said with a sigh. "I've heard she's the best."

A moment later, Luke hung up his phone and stared straight ahead. How could an acknowledged thief who knew how to plant a punishing blow to the midsection be heart honest in the midst of a cold-blooded con?

Suddenly a familiar voice from the reception area pierced his consciousness.

Startled, he looked at his calendar and then his watch. With a groan, he dragged his hands down his face. Then he stood up, put on his coat, and walked to the door. She was the last person he wanted to see right now, but he had no choice. A Mansfield did not stand up his steady date.

"Luke, darling, there you are!" Maria Franklin said in her silky voice. "Ready for lunch?"

"Sure. Sorry I'm late, Maria. I got caught up in some work."

"You always get caught up in work, darling," Maria said as she looped her arm through his.

Startled, he glanced at her. Good heavens, she *was* tall! Her chin topped his shoulder. It actually made him uncomfortable.

She made him uncomfortable. Her black hair was piled on her head in a seemingly careless fashion that must have taken her hairdresser hours to arrange.

Her glossy red lipstick was perfectly applied to her slender lips, her makeup artfully hiding all signs of natural beauty. Her black eyes were coy as she looked up at him.

"I've just been shopping," she said as they stopped at the bank of elevators. "What do you think?"

She turned in a slow, slinky circle before him, the red Italian minidress molded to her voluptuous body, the dark stockings emphasizing her shapely legs.

"Gorgeous as always, Maria. That dress was made for you, what there is of it."

Maria laughed with pleasure as they stepped into the elevator. She tilted her face up and kissed him for a moment on the mouth.

He stared at her. Nothing. He had felt nothing.

"I just wanted to make sure you only had eyes for me at lunch," Maria said.

"Guaranteed," Luke automatically replied. Had he ever felt anything when they had kissed these last two months?

They walked to their usual restaurant where his secretary had made their usual lunch reservations. They followed the maître d' to their usual, secluded table, people turning in their chairs to watch them.

"I just love being the center of attention," Maria whispered in his ear as she leaned against him.

"I never knew you were an exhibitionist, Maria."

"Only in public, darling," Maria replied, laughing.

Sipping a glass of wine after ordering, Luke watched her as she chatted with him about the charity ball she had attended the night before, the scene thrown there by the wife of one of New York's more prominent stockbrokers and ladies' men, and the lunch Maria had had with Luke's mother the week before.

As she talked and laughed and teased, she

leaned invitingly across the table toward him, displaying her high breasts to best advantage, flashing her perfect teeth at him, her black eyes speaking sensual promises she had no intention of keeping.

He sat watching the performance and wondered who was the greater fraud: Tess Alcott or Maria Franklin?

Maria's musical laughter at one of her own jokes settled the matter. It really was no contest.

Whatever ulterior motives she might have, Luke realized he had met an honest woman, and it wasn't the Giantess.

When had he become so shallow, or so removed, that a woman like Maria could actually attract his interest? He thought he had done such a good job of protecting himself from further betrayals by burying himself in his work and keeping every relationship on the surface, far from his heart. Instead, it seemed that the women over the last twenty years who had wanted him for his money and his name had succeeded in making him value himself as little as they had valued him.

He had betrayed himself. Maria Franklin was proof of that.

What mirror had been uncovered, what door opened, that he should see his life so clearly?

Shaken, Luke stared at his wine glass. Had Tess Alcott's kiss done so much?

Forcing himself to refocus on lunch, he joined in Maria's laughter, offering up his own amusing anecdotes as they ate, while he silently planned the best way to break up with the Giantess without ruffling too much fur.

He went back to work, but he found it hard to concentrate. He kept feeling Tess's hot mouth on his lips, hearing her soft cry of pleasure, seeing her anguished face as they had backed away from each other.

This now painful reverie ended when his secretary buzzed him to say that Leroy Baldwin was on line one. Luke was pacing behind his desk before he even said hello.

"What did you find, Leroy?"

"And a good afternoon to you, too, Mr. Mansfield," Leroy retorted. "Your lady checks out one hundred percent, Luke."

Luke stopped in his tracks. His grip tightened on the receiver. "What?"

"Miami police have records on your Tess as well as dozens of other kids used by the Carswells that I should be able to hand you in a day or two. And Oxford has records of every one of the names you gave me. Oh, and here's an interesting tidbit. Four years ago, Oxford received a cashier's check from one Tess Alcott covering complete tuition and board, with interest, for a full three-year undergraduate education. Whatever game she's playing, your Tess is telling the truth in the middle of it. I like this lady more and more. Mind you, I wouldn't want to be one of her enemies because I wouldn't think much of my longevity, but she might make a helluva friend."

"Terrific," Luke muttered, slumping into his chair.

"WEB's files on her go back eight years and they confirm the career she's described. Your lady has made off with some amazing pieces of art in her time. But get this, only from private collections. There isn't a museum gig in the bunch. The jewelry she's stolen—all from private collections, too—would make the Queen of England turn green with envy. My sources at Interpol agree with WEB: Tess Alcott is the best around."

"But is she still active?"

"No one's clear on that. It's possible that she just got so good that no one can trace her heists. Or else she's telling the truth."

"Wonderful. Anything new on Weinstein?"

Leroy sighed. "The guy continues to check out good as gold. Has it ever occurred to you, Luke, that you just might be dealing with the genuine articles?"

For a moment exultation stole his breath, and then a red light began flashing: *Danger. Danger.*

He was treading perilously close to a precipice and he had to do something, anything, to save himself from plunging over the side. He had to stop being amused by the damned woman. He had to stop enjoying their verbal combat. He had to stop thinking about kissing her. He had to stop believing that her childhood could really have been as horrible as she'd described.

"Luke? Are you okay?"

Her childhood. The Carswells. *Of course!* Why hadn't he thought of them before? According to Weinstein's story, the Carswells had had Tess for six years and they might be able to prove her identity as Elizabeth Cushman. Or disprove it.

Oh, they had to disprove it! They had to rescue him from every feeling that was trying to eradicate the sober, rational road he had relied on for so long.

Luke took a deep breath. Self-preservation was his god and he called on it now.

"They are *not* the genuine articles," he grimly informed Leroy, "and I intend to prove it. Find the Carswells."

"Luke," Leroy said wearily, "Weinstein's the path to follow."

"So are the Carswells. Find them."

"I already have."

"What?"

"Luke, have you forgotten how much you're

paying me on this job? I am being very thorough on your behalf. I like the prompt way you pay your bills."

"Sorry, Leroy," Luke said, leaning back in his chair. "I must be suffering from foot-in-mouth disease."

"Apology accepted. Let me tell you about the Carswells. Both of them ended up in federal penitentiaries in Florida three years ago. Old Man Carswell got his intestines permanently sliced up in a knife fight last year. He is very dead, but Old Lady Carswell is alive and kicking. She is a pit in the fruit salad of life. You want to talk to her?"

"Oh yes," Luke said softly. "I've always wanted to see what a child buyer looks like."

The slam of the door behind Luke was hollow, jar-
ring. He stood in the small, gray interview room
and stared at the woman he had flown fourteen
hundred miles to see. Barbara Carswell, according to
her records, was fifty-two. She looked sixty-five as she
sat at the gray metal table. Her once-brown hair was
white and unkempt, her skin leathery, her face deeply
wrinkled, her body thin and shrunken in on herself.
But her brown eyes remained large and horribly alive,
cold and calculating as they watched him walk into
the room.

"Mrs. Carswell," Luke said, sitting down and
being careful not to shake the woman's hand. The
prison guards, watching them on a video monitor,
would not have been happy with such an action.
"Thank you for agreeing to see me this morning."

The woman slouched back in her chair. "It
helps pass the time, and I like French cigs. Thanks for
the carton," she said, lighting an unfiltered cigarette.

"You're welcome. I've come to talk to you
about Tess Alcott."

"Who?"

Luke handed her two photos of Tess. One had been taken by Leroy's surveillance team, one had been taken by the Miami police when Tess was ten and apprehended for shoplifting on the Carswells' orders. "Her name is Tess, the last name changes a lot. She used to work for you as a child."

"Oh, her," Barbara Carswell said with a sniff. "Who could forget her? She was a real pain in the ass."

Luke felt the bile rise in his throat. "How so?"

"Damn kid had asthma. Nearly croaked on us a couple of times. I kept telling Ernie she was more trouble than she was worth, but he always said a blond girl brings in the most dough, and he was right, I guess. She did good work when she worked."

"How long was she with you?"

Barbara Carswell stared up at the ceiling, a bit bored. "Five or six years. I don't remember exactly. We had a lot of kids coming and going."

"Do you remember how you got her?"

"Bought her, just like the others."

"Who did you buy her from?"

"I don't remember."

"Then the interview is over." Luke rose and started for the door.

"Hey!" Mrs. Carswell shouted. "Where do you think you're going?"

Luke turned back to her, his eyes as cold as hers. "I came for information. You don't seem to have it, so I'm leaving."

"Honey, that's not how the game's played. I say I don't remember, you offer me something to jar my memory, and I give you the answers you want."

"I have no intention of giving you anything, Mrs. Carswell, beyond a carton of cigarettes. You can either cooperate with me, which will go on your record and aid in your next parole hearing, or you can return to your cell and kick yourself for missing out on this opportunity."

Barbara Carswell swore, impugned Luke's family tree, then sighed and told him to sit back down, her memory had suddenly returned.

Luke sat in the chair opposite her once again. "Well? Who did you buy her from?"

"Hal Marsh," Mrs. Carswell said with another sigh. "At least, that's how we knew him. Hal went by lots of different names, which was typical in our business."

"Was he your usual supplier?"

"No, just the opposite. He used to buy kids off us when they got to be too old. You know, twelve and thirteen and the like. We'd sell the kids to him or to the kiddie porn crowd, a few white slavers, that sort of thing."

"Can you describe him?" Luke had never felt so cold, or so murderously angry, in his life. Tess had actually lived with this monster?

"Oh, sure, once you've seen Hal, you never forget him. He was tall and skinny, wiry like, with a big head of red hair, long red sideburns, a mustache he liked to keep waxed, and a laugh like a rutting moose."

"How did he get Tess?"

"It wasn't any of our business," Mrs. Carswell said, lighting another cigarette. "But we asked anyway. See, snatching kids wasn't his line of work. He said someone had palmed the kid off on him and he had seen her potential and brought her to us. We paid him plenty for her, too. Like I said, blond girls bring in the money once they start working well."

"Do you remember when you bought her?"

"Aw, c'mon!"

"At least try, Mrs. Carswell. Ten years ago? Twenty? Fifteen?"

"Ah, hell," Mrs. Carswell muttered, disgruntled.

"Ernie had his Harley then, so it was probably when I was in my redhead phase. Always liked to change the color of my hair, you know? So that was somewhere like nineteen or twenty years ago."

"Do you remember what season?"

"Late summer, early fall, something like that."

"How old was Tess when she came to you?"

Mrs. Carswell concentrated on blowing an elliptical smoke ring. "I don't know. Five, maybe four. She seemed a bit small for whatever age she was, and she could already read a bit. Maybe five."

"And how long did you keep her?"

"Like I said, five or six years."

"Who did you sell her to?"

"Some black whore calling herself Primrose or Tulip or some such thing. *Violet!* That was her name."

Luke fought hard to hide his surprise. "Did she come looking for Tess?"

"She came looking for a blond girl of around eleven or twelve and we had three of them at the time, including Tess. She took Tess. We made her pay through the nose for her, too. By then, the girl was bringing in a lot of money for us, pickpocket, shop-lifting, that sort of thing."

"Did Violet say why she wanted Tess?"

"Said she had a client with real particular tastes," Barbara Carswell said with a broad wink.

The nausea nearly overcame Luke then. It took a moment for him to regain his self-control. "Did you ever see Tess or Violet again?"

"Nah. From what I heard, Violet skipped town right after that."

"You had a lot of connections with the under-world, though," Luke persisted, almost frantic to dis-cover what new nightmare Tess had been thrown into. "Maybe you heard about what happened to Tess after she left you. She went by a lot of names: Julia Preen, Suzanne Wentworth, Jeanne-Marie St. Juste."

"*What?*" screeched Barbara Carswell, lurching up from her chair, her hands clenched in fists, her face splotched with fury. "*St. Juste?* Why, that two-timing, murderous little bitch! She's the one that set Ernie and me up! She tipped the Feds and they ran a sting operation that got us twenty years. She got my Ernie killed!"

While Barbara Carswell paced the room cursing Tess with all of the venom in her soul, Luke leaned back in his chair, nausea replaced with warm appreciation for Tess's seemingly unlimited abilities. She was *very* good at what she did.

Her nonchalant recitation of her life with the Carswells and her careless attitude about their past, present, and future had been a sham. She had repaid the Carswells for the horror of her childhood and she had done it legally. More, she had spared dozens of children the hell she had endured. She had got her revenge, just as he had with Margo.

Damn! Why, in his search for evidence to put Tess behind bars, did he keep uncovering ways that they were akin to each other?

"Mrs. Carswell," Luke said, and had to call to her once again. "Mrs. Carswell, one last question. Do you know where I might find Hal Marsh or Violet?"

"No! And I hope they're frying in Hell!"

Mrs. Carswell continued to curse as Luke rose, thanked her for her time, and left the room.

He flew back to New York, unable to do any of the client work he had brought with him, unable to do anything but think about Tess and wonder and try to puzzle it all out. Yes, he had some answers now, but he also had a lot more questions. Tess had been perfectly forthright in the presentation of her past, but she had never mentioned Violet. He could understand her reluctance, it must have been an horrific period in her life.

But still, Violet bothered him for a lot of reasons, primarily because he knew of no way that a prostitute could train Tess to become the kind of thief even WEB couldn't catch. The Carswells didn't go in for the kind of heists Leroy said Tess had pulled after she left Miami. Violet undoubtedly had kept to her trade. So who had trained Tess?

He'd have to get Leroy to start looking for Hal Marsh and Violet. If they were still alive, they had a lot of explaining to do.

He pulled out his credit card and lifted the phone from the armrest beside him, dialing the number automatically. He gave Leroy the facts in less than thirty seconds, hung up, and then called New York. It took him a minute to get through a receptionist, and secretary, to finally reach his client.

"I'm heading back," he announced.

"So what did Barbara Carswell have to say?" Jane demanded.

"A lot, not all of it complimentary. It basically boils down to this: Barbara Carswell positively identified Tess. Her age and date of purchase by the Carswells fit well with the kidnapping timeline. Carswell said she bought Tess from someone named Hal Marsh. I've got Leroy Baldwin trying to track him down. Maybe this Marsh character was one of the kidnappers, or at least knew one of the kidnappers."

"To finally capture the people who took my granddaughter . . ." Jane murmured. "This sounds very promising, Luke."

"It depends which side you're on," he muttered. "And there is something that bothers me. Barbara Carswell said that Tess had asthma as a child. Elizabeth didn't have asthma, did she?"

Jane was silent a moment. "No, she did not."

"You realize there are three possible explanations?"

"Either the asthma was psychosomatically induced by the kidnapping, or she developed asthma like so many children do, or she's not Elizabeth. But I believe more and more that she really *is* Elizabeth, Luke."

"I wish you'd tell me why," Luke said plaintively.

"Later, dear, not just now."

"Well, you know my analytical, overly suspicious mind, Mrs. Cushman. I will want proof in triplicate before I recognize the pretender to the throne."

"So will I. Thank you, Luke. For everything."

Luke slowly smiled. "No, no, Mrs. Cushman, thank *you.* I haven't been on a roller coaster since I was ten."

He hung up the phone and stared without seeing through the tiny window by his seat. He had wanted to interview Barbara Carswell to save himself from himself and instead ... The roller coaster was taking him up, up, up to the top of the highest hill. Below him lay every belief and illusion and expectation he had clung to for so many years. All would be shattered as he rocketed downhill. His heart was hammering so hard in his throat, it was an ache that wouldn't fade away.

Luke wasn't sure if he was ready to see Tess again, and when she walked into the living room that evening dressed in a long-sleeved gown of silver and green, an emerald necklace clasped at her throat and matching earrings dangling from her ears, he knew he wasn't ready ... Because all he wanted to do was kiss her again. Because he felt plunged into emotional depths. Because he was remembering Tess as an abused child, terrified, ill, hungry, alone. The contrast with the woman before him was stunning. How many people had the kind of strength and courage it took to transform themselves and their lives as she had done?

Generosity toward Tess began welling within him and Luke couldn't have been more amazed. He never cut anyone any slack. Never. But looking at Tess now . . .

His old walls were useless against her. He was thrown back on his last defense: he would have to use a blunt instrument to fend her off.

"Nice emeralds," he said as she sat beside Jane on the couch. "Belong to anyone we know?"

"Jewel thieves do not wear their ill-gotten goods, Mr. Mansfield," Tess retorted, her smile glittering, her blue eyes hard with anger. "It's an easy way to get yourself arrested. Unless," she said brightly, "you have them recut and reset."

Luke grimly held back a smile. Anger was supposed to protect him, not charm him. "And to whom did those emeralds used to belong?"

"Tiffany's. I bought them last week. Want to see the receipt?"

"That is enough, dear," Jane said firmly, patting Tess's knee. "And as for you, Luke, your bad manners will ruin my digestion. Amend them!"

"Yes, ma'am," Luke said.

Hodgkins entered to announce dinner. Luke gallantly offered his arm to Jane, she deigned to accept it, and they began to walk toward the dining room.

"The watchdog never far from her side," Tess murmured from behind them.

"I beg your pardon?" Luke said.

"Woof!"

It was a good thing his back was to her so she couldn't see his smile. "There are some, Ms. Alcott, who feel a responsibility to others."

"Jane can take care of herself. Besides, she's perfectly safe."

"No one," Luke said bitterly, "is safe in your company."

"Enough, you two," Jane said. "I want dinner, not your bickering."

Luke meekly held Jane's chair out for her and then sat down opposite Tess. Dinner was served with all of Hodgkins's usual pomp and ceremony.

"I'll have you know, Luke," Jane said after a sip of soup, "that Tess has insisted that I pull the Vermeer from next week's auction."

"Our art expert objects to selling one of the few Vermeers still available on the open market?" Luke inquired. "A painting that will bring the best price at the auction?"

"If it was real, I'd say go for it," Tess retorted. "But it's a fake and it stands a good chance of causing Cushman's an unholy amount of trouble."

"It is not a fake!" Jane insisted.

"Yes, it is."

"Ms. Alcott," Luke said with great condescension, "*The Housekeeper* has been authenticated by Ernest Hall himself."

Tess shrugged as she continued to eat her soup. "It's been authenticated before."

"Ergo," Luke said with some heat, "it is not a fake!"

"But it is."

"How do you know?" Luke exploded.

"Because I know who owns the original, illegally of course, but possession is nine-tenths of the law. I've even seen it. It's in superb condition."

Jane stared at her. "How do you know this illegal owner doesn't have the fake?"

Tess grinned and began to butter a roll. "Because the family bought it . . . well, stole it, really, before the fake was ever produced. The Napoleonic Wars saw a lot of shifting around of artwork, you know. The Vermeer got shifted into this family's private collection around 1808 and has been held secretly ever since. The heirs to the rightful owners, you see, would undoubtedly want it back."

"Undoubtedly," Jane said. "How do you know so much about this?"

"Because I know all about Anna Shively," Tess sanguinely replied.

Jane started. "Are you telling me that that Vermeer up for auction is—"

"A Shively," Tess pronounced.

"Who?" Luke demanded.

"Probably the best art forger the world has ever known," Tess replied. "Half of her work is hanging in museums the world over and called Delacroix, Chardin, Caravaggio, Rubens. The other half is hanging in private collections and called Goya, Rembrandt, Renoir. Shively was an absolute genius. She used the same canvas, the same paint, the same brushes that the masters used. She knew how to age a forgery to perfection. There are only a handful of experts in the world who can tell a Shively from an original."

"She was active in the mid- to late nineteenth century," Jane said somewhat grimly after a fortifying sip of wine. "It was, in a way, her form of protest against the male artist autocracy that kept her out of the Royal Society of Artists and every exhibition and gallery in Europe simply because she was a woman artist. Her little bit of revenge has been haunting art collectors ever since."

"A woman after my own heart," Tess said with relish. "Better pull the Vermeer until you've had Antoine Giracault take a look at it, Jane."

Jane sighed heavily. "You're right of course. A Shively. That someone would try to sell a Shively through *my* auction house."

"Oh, it's not the first time," Tess said.

Jane looked at her with the utmost horror.

Tess burst out laughing.

Luke leaned back in his chair, smiling at the ensuing argument which ignored his presence entirely. While everyone else in the art world treated Jane Cushman with slobbering deference and respect, here was Tess Alcott not merely contradicting her, but *laughing* at her. If nothing else, from the way Jane's eyes sparkled and the color stained her cheeks as she leaned toward Tess to drive home a point, the jewel thief was a wonderful tonic for the matriarch. Luke hadn't seen Jane look so alive and happy in years.

And when was the last time he had felt alive and eager to see what the next moment held? How long had he lived without anticipation? Curiosity? Joy?

It began to feel like a lifetime. He had made of his world a barren cave that habitual fourteen-hour workdays had not filled. It would have been nice to blame this on the fight he had had to wage all of his life against the assumptions others made about him because of his looks, his family, his money. It would have been nice to blame this on his parents' insistence that he fulfill his stifling duty to the family. He might at least blame this on all the women who had burned and betrayed him in the past.

But this hollow existence was his own damned fault and Luke knew it. He had been a coward, not a hero, as the various dragons of life had advanced on him. He had barricaded himself in his work and the arms of soulless women who had inspired nothing in him except boredom. He had deliberately chosen the straightest, easiest path, avoiding every bump, every turning. Avoiding life. He had turned his back on every dream, every joy, in the name of safety. He had existed, not lived.

Did he know what it felt like to be alive?

"Oh, give me a break!" Tess retorted.

Tess and Jane's argument had strayed into wildly differing opinions about artists including, Luke vaguely recalled, Jan Van Eyck, Piazzetta, Boucher, and Salvador Dalí.

He stared at Tess as she and Jane battled back and forth and it came to him that he *did* know what it felt like to be alive. He had known it the moment Tess had first walked into his life. Whatever her motives, he owed Tess Alcott a lot and it was time and past time to start treating her accordingly.

CHAPTER
7

Tess followed Jane into what she privately called the Belle Epoque salon. It was half the size of the living room and overflowing with turn-of-the-century French furniture, paintings, ceramics, and wall hangings. It was undoubtedly Eugenie's doing and she had done it very well. Tess stopped once again before the early Degas hanging over the fireplace mantel. She had wanted this painting from the moment she had first seen it during her tour with Jane.

"I don't suppose you'd consider selling—" she began.

"No," Jane said dryly, "I wouldn't."

Tess sighed and turned just as Luke walked into the room. Her wrists ached from the throbbing of her pulse. Her breath, what there was of it, came only in small, sharp bursts. He had insulted her as no other man had ever done, and yet she still felt . . . this.

She was beginning to hate Luke Mansfield with a passion of which she had hitherto been unaware. She had lived safe and secure these last twenty-five years, serene in the belief that she was frigid. Luke's kiss had demolished *that* delusion.

She hated him for that, she really did. She had kissed him in a moment of weakness and the next thing she knew, Gladys was calling to report that Luke had flown off to Miami. Tess racked her brain once again. Was there anyone or anything in Miami that could blow this job apart?

Luke sat down at the chess table. Her mouth throbbed with the memory of his kiss.

Get a grip on yourself, woman, Tess silently commanded, *or you can flush this job away.*

Jane sat in a red velvet chair near an ornate gold table. Tess would have taken the chair opposite her, but Jane shooed her away.

"Don't even think of joining me, Tess," she said. "I have a stack of reports to get through to prepare for Monday's staff meeting. I suggest that you settle your differences with Luke over a chessboard. Your little feud is beginning to bore me. You play chess, I trust?"

"A little," Tess replied, feeling mulish and not caring if it showed. "I would hardly provide entertainment for the steel-trap mind of Mr. Mansfield. I'll just see if I can find a book—"

"What? And abandon Luke to a quiet evening of boredom? Nonsense! You will play chess, Tess."

There was a frozen moment of silence in which Tess weighed her options. From what she could tell, there weren't any. With the stiffest of upper lips, she saluted Jane, spun around, and stalked to the chess table where Luke now stood meekly waiting. Jane's chuckles followed her across the room.

"Care to play?" he innocently inquired.

"*Love* to," Tess growled.

He grinned at her. It did terrible things to her brain waves. They got all tangled up.

"I tell you what," he said, "I'll make the game worth your while. Chess is always more interesting when the stakes are high enough. If I win, you tell me what you're really doing here, and if you win, you can repay me for all kisses and aspersions I have cast upon you by breaking this chess board over my miserable head."

Tess gave the proposition serious consideration—the chess board was solid marble, it had possibilities—but still ... "Not good enough. Smashing your head would only provide momentary pleasure." Inspiration struck. "Let's up the stakes. If I win, you pack your bags and leave by dawn tomorrow and you don't return until after I've checked out of the Hotel Cushman. If you win, I'll be the one checking out. Deal?"

Luke studied her a moment. "Do I frighten you so much?"

Tess gasped, outraged by his arrogance, horrified that he had spoken the truth. "Of all the egotistical—!"

"I wonder what it could be? Are you afraid Jane's watchdog will keep you from success, or are you afraid of my kissing you again?"

He is not a mind reader, he is not a mind reader, he is not a mind reader ... Tess made her expression glacial. "The sooner we begin playing, the sooner you can start packing." She sat in the chair opposite Luke.

He grinned at her—*damn* the man!—and sat down. He offered her the white pieces which she accepted with a shrug and made her opening move. For the next quarter hour there was silence in the salon except for the occasional rustle of paper as Jane turned the page of a report, a muttered "*Merde*," whenever Luke captured one of her pieces, or a soft "Hell!" from Luke whenever Tess blocked his attack and threatened his king.

That she played chess far more than "a little"

Tess did not try to hide. She was in this game to win, subterfuge could take a hike. The problem was, Luke was equally skilled and it required all of her concentration to insure that it was not she who would soon be packing her bags. Bert wouldn't like that.

A half hour slid by as Tess grimly began pushing the game to a draw. It seemed the best she could do for tonight. Her ego wanted the win, but the job required survival. She couldn't let Luke boot her out, not now. *Why* had she upped the stakes? Why had she let emotion rule her once again on this damned job?

She couldn't in the least understand the smile that flickered across Luke's mouth as she adapted her strategy to containment rather than to victory, because the smile was not smug, or superior, or even triumphant. It was more ... appreciative, and if Tess hadn't had to give the game her complete concentration, that would have worried her.

As she was contemplating her next move, Hodgkins entered the salon and approached Jane. He bowed, gravely informed her that he had locked up for the night, and then, raising his voice slightly so that it carried to the opposite end of the room, he suggested that he take charge of the jewels Jane was wearing so he could lock them up safely.

"That tears it!" Tess yelled, spiraling into a sudden, towering rage fueled by the tension of the chess game and Hodgkins's far from subtle hint. She erupted out of her chair and bore down on the stone-faced butler. "I have taken your nasty innuendos, your spying, and your veiled insults for three days now, Hodgkins, and you have just pushed me too far! If I had wanted to rip off Jane Cushman, I would have done it days ago and been so far gone from this place you never could have found me. You stay right where you are," she ordered. "All of you stay right here or I'll drag you back by your ears!"

She stormed out of the salon, up to Elizabeth's room, and jerked open a dresser drawer. She pulled out a suede packet and then stomped back downstairs.

"I have to thank you, Hodgkins," Luke was saying. "You have just saved me from a draw, at best, or defeat, at worst. I doubt if my frail male ego could have stood it."

"I rather thought chess would be Tess's game," Jane said.

"Mrs. Cushman," Hodgkins intoned, "I apologize for any upset I may have caused your guest. It was not my intent—"

"Nonsense, Hodgkins," Jane said, setting aside the stack of reports, "of course it was and now you must take your medicine. Ah, here is the doctor. What have you planned for us, Tess?"

"A small demonstration," she grimly replied.

She set the suede packet on a rosewood secretary against the far salon wall, unwrapped it, and pulled out several tools. She then proceeded to disconnect the alarm system for the room, moved aside the red-hued Degas to reveal a wall safe, and set to work in earnest.

"I've been meaning to talk to you about your security system, Jane," she said, deftly snipping wires. "It's just the pits. An out-and-out *amateur* could break into this place. You've got a valuable art collection and it needs to be protected accordingly."

"You don't think much of M and A Security?" Jane inquired.

"There were times in the past when I could have sworn M and A was working for the thieves and fences of the world," Tess retorted. "They wouldn't know a decent security system if they tripped over it."

"What about Baldwin Security?" Luke suggested.

"Leroy's one of the best in the field," Tess said,

her brow furrowed in concentration as she worked on the safe. She was totally at ease now. Work had always been her lifeline. "One of his systems nearly tossed my fanny into jail a few years back. But if you want the absolute best security available, you should go with Solitaire. The systems they come up with are nightmares. I gave up stealing many a pretty gem whenever their owners had Solitaire's Purgatory system in place."

"Just out of idle curiosity," Jane said, "how did you know I had a safe in here?"

"Old habits are hard to break," Tess said with a smile, reaching for another tool. "I spotted the security system the first day I was here, and the safe on our tour. You've got a floor safe in your study where you keep all of your legal documents. I'd have to guess, because I've never been in there, but I bet you've got another wall safe in your bedroom, slightly different system than this, of course, but still the same pitiful idea. Then there's your ballroom sideboard . . . Ah," Tess said as the safe door opened. She glanced at her watch. Seventy seconds. Not bad, but not up to her usual standards.

She calmly disconnected the fail-safe security alarm and then withdrew the leather cases from the safe. "Oh my, my, my," she said, opening one case and lifting out a large glittering necklace. "The Stromberg diamonds. I wondered who the anonymous buyer was. My hat's off to you, Jane. These are more than worth the price you paid."

"Thank you," Jane said gravely. But Tess wasn't fooled. Her face was aglow with suppressed laughter. Well, if safe-cracking amused her, Tess would play along.

"And the Greenleaf rubies!" she exclaimed with growing excitement as she opened another case. "My stars, these haven't been seen in two decades. I can die a happy woman right now just having held them."

She suddenly turned on Jane as righteous fury swelled her breast. "And you're using M and A to protect these jewels? It would serve you right if they *were* stolen!"

"I'll contact Solitaire on Monday, Tess, I swear," Jane assured her.

Somewhat mollified, Tess began to place the jewels back in the safe. "Mention my name when you do. We've done business together before. They'll come out a lot faster if they know I'm involved."

"I don't doubt it," Jane murmured.

Tess turned and grinned at her. "I'm the only thief to ever crack their Griselde system. Once I joined WEB, Solitaire had me out to their Connecticut home office to explain how I'd done it. They weren't exactly thrilled when I told them I'd stolen the Griselde plans out of their president's office. They've tightened up their own security considerably since then. So, where's the Farleigh necklace?"

"And just how do you know about that?" Luke asked.

Tess regarded him pityingly.

"It's in a bank vault," Jane said with a smile.

"Thank God for that," Tess muttered. It had been a mistake to look at Luke. He was too damned attractive.

"I trust, Hodgkins," Jane said to her icy butler, "that you will now cease and desist from your suspicions about Miss Alcott? If she were after anything in this house, she would have cleaned us out days ago. I trust that is the correct expression, Tess?"

"Perfectly correct."

"Will there be anything else, madam?" Hodgkins intoned.

"No, no, you may retire for the night."

Hodgkins did so.

"Brava, Ms. Alcott!" Luke applauded as the door closed behind the butler. "That was brilliantly done. I haven't seen Hodgkins so ruthlessly routed in all the years he's worked here."

Luke cocked his head and studied her as if suddenly seeing her for the first time, a smile playing across his sensual mouth.

Oh my.

It struck Tess that if he would promise to smile at her like that for the next fifty years, she would tell Bert to go take a flying leap and swear off safe-cracking for the rest of her life.

Tess blinked. Uh-oh. Why was it that the harder she ran from Luke, the more she was drawn to him?

She hurriedly sought sanctuary in conversation, discussing with Jane the kind of security system she would need for the estate while she bundled up her tools. Luke was silent, but his emerald gaze burned slowly down her body. It was all she could do to keep her hands from shaking.

Finally pleading exhaustion, she scurried off to bed.

Tess had never scurried in her life. She stuck her tongue out at herself when she reached Elizabeth's bedroom. Running from a pair of green eyes! How humiliating. How . . . unthinkable.

Tess crawled out of bed the next morning feeling like death warmed over. What was it about Elizabeth Cushman's bedroom that summoned all the old nightmares she had put behind her years ago? Did the child's room simply evoke too many memories of her own miserable childhood?

Every muscle aching, she stumbled into the adjoining bathroom, praying that a shower would restore her to some recognizably human form. Hot water pounded her weary body and slowly she began to revive. For someone who had gotten no more than two hours of decent sleep the night before, Tess considered this a miracle.

She left the shower in a somewhat better mood than when she had entered it. She brushed her wet hair back from her face, pulled on a blue knit halter dress over her swimsuit, and thought how happy she would be if she could only blame Luke Mansfield for last night's dreams. But since the nightmares were old childhood reruns, that particular sin could not be laid at his door. Everything else, however . . .

Distracted, lustful, running scared. She had never been these things on a job before. She was now and that she *could* blame on Luke. Somehow, he had found the key to a door she hadn't known she possessed, and he had gotten to her. Was getting to her. Was lousing her up in a major way.

She stared at the painted puffy clouds on Elizabeth's walls. *Damn* this bedroom! It had to be the source of her sleep deprivation, and sleep deprivation had to be the reason she seemed to be systematically sabotaging this job.

Why else was she letting Luke Mansfield get to her? Why else was she deliberately straying from Bert's script?

Luke's intelligence and his sly sense of humor and his code of honor and the way his emerald eyes could ignite a flame in her soul offered themselves as viable options.

"Ah, crud," she muttered. Her feelings were the real danger on this con. Luke was just the trigger.

With a sigh, she ran lightly downstairs and into the breakfast room, where her gaze collided with Luke's eyes. She hurriedly sat down and grabbed a piece of toast.

It had come to this: she could be safe, which meant avoiding Luke like the FBI, or she could do her job and get the Farleigh, which meant talking with

Luke, getting him on her side, interacting with him as if he weren't the most dangerous person on earth. *I've come too far on this job,* she reminded herself. *I can't go back now. I won't.* And that meant surviving Luke and her own traitorous feelings. There was no third option.

As soon as she could escape, Tess headed for the pool. A swimming pool had always been one of her refuges. Miami had been littered with them. She dove in, enjoying the sudden shock of the cool water and the silence as it covered her ears for a moment. Then her body moved into its usual rhythm and the pool went by in a blur. Swimming for Tess was almost meditation. The water surrounded her, buoyed her, kept her safe as her body automatically slipped through it. There was absolute peace and contentment in a swimming pool. She usually found the answer to any problem while swimming.

Tess felt more than heard the splash, felt the sudden change of vibration in the water, and she knew, without looking, that Luke had joined her. Damn the man! She reached the end of the pool a second before he did.

"Haven't you ever heard that two's a crowd?" she demanded as he stood up beside her, rivulets of water streaming down his broad, naked chest.

God, he was gorgeous.

"It's a big pool," Luke said mildly. "I thought I wouldn't disturb you."

Fat chance, Tess muttered to herself. "Do you just want to harass me," she demanded, "or can you handle some real competition?"

He stared at her in surprise. "Are you challenging me to a race?"

"I've got to get some use out of you, Mansfield, and I need a decent pacesetter."

"You don't honestly think you can win? I'm bigger and stronger, remember?"

"You'll have to prove it," Tess retorted just before diving into the water.

Luke quickly followed. For the next fifteen minutes they raced each other up and down the pool, churning the water lap after lap, until finally Tess's lungs were screaming and her arms and legs felt like lead.

She and Luke tagged the end of the pool at the same time and she grimly started to make her turn, preferring to drown rather than give in, when she felt Luke's hand grasp her arm and pull her upright.

"Uncle!" he gasped. "I give up, I give in, I surrender. Don't make me die a watery death. I look awful bloated."

If Tess hadn't been so desperate for oxygen, she would have laughed. "Do you admit you've met your match?" she demanded.

"Set, game, *and* match."

"Thank God," Tess gasped, flinging herself onto the side of the pool so that she was half in and half out of the water, her face resting on the warm concrete, her lungs heaving gratefully as she drew in desperately needed oxygen.

"Verbal duels, chess games, swimming. If we keep challenging each other like this," Luke said, "we'll both be corpses by the end of the week."

"But beating you is such fun."

"You haven't beaten me once," Luke retorted with the greatest dignity. "Every contest has ended in a draw and you know it."

"If you weren't so stubborn—"

"And if you weren't so pigheaded—"

"We might live to the end of the week."

Luke laughed, climbed out of the pool, and then lifted her fully up and out of the water as if racing for fifteen minutes straight were nothing at all. She tried not to shiver at the contact.

"Thanks," she muttered as she lay down beside the pool, drawing her knees up, letting the sun pour over her.

"Oxygen is a wonderful thing," she pronounced.

"Tell me about it," Luke said, lying beside her.

She could hear every breath he took. She could feel every inch of him, though he lay a foot away. Only a foot away.

Say something, you fool she inwardly yelled at herself. *Talk about the weather, the Yankees, anything!*

"Were you always this competitive?" she asked.

"Yes, but not always this dumb. Have you ever considered swimming the English Channel? You'd be a natural."

Tess laughed. There was a lot to be said for not fighting the man . . . fighting *with* the man. She frowned at herself. She was not used to slips of the tongue, even silent ones.

"I prefer something a bit warmer," she replied. "I thought your game was handball."

"It is. But my *exercise* is swimming."

"Remind me never to get onto a handball court with you."

"Do you play handball?"

"A little."

"*That's* what you said about chess," Luke said grimly. "What else do you play?"

Tess rolled onto her side. "Oh, I play lots of games that will get me close to whatever mark I'm working on."

"Who did swimming get you close to?"

Tess smiled with fond memory. "A very nice, dirty old man with a mouthwatering Renoir. He loved to flirt with anyone under fifty. Said it kept him young. It did."

"What's this?" Luke asked, rolling on his side to face her, propping himself up on his elbow, two fingers brushing the green-tinged bruise circling her arm.

"I bashed into the bathroom door frame my first morning here," Tess automatically replied. "I always take a while getting acclimated to new places."

"Really?"

Damn! He didn't believe her.

"It looks like a bruise left by someone's hand gripping your arm more than hard," Luke continued.

"Oh, *that* bruise!" Tess said brightly. "That's from a job I was working for WEB last week. Cyril had to haul me up over a window ledge when my climbing rope was . . . um . . . put out of commission."

"Who's Cyril?"

"One of the WEB agents I work with occasionally. Let me ask you something," she said hurriedly.

"Yes, you're very good at that, too."

"Thank you. How well did you know Elizabeth?"

The question seemed to take Luke by surprise. He studied her a moment and then replied slowly. "The Mansfields and the Cushmans go back for generations. My father was their family lawyer until he retired last year and he insisted—practically at gunpoint—that I take over the post. I was being carted over here for tea before I could even walk."

"What was Elizabeth like?"

"She was pretty, intelligent, insatiably curious, good with her hands, and an unmitigated pest. You have to remember," Luke said with a grin, "that I was ten years older than she was. Teenage boys take a dim view of female tagalongs."

"Cruel, most cruel. She undoubtedly offered you slavish devotion and you spurned her tender gift."

"Teenage boys are not known for their consideration of others."

"I wouldn't restrict that statement to adolescents, Mr. Mansfield."

Luke's eyebrows shot up. "There speaks a woman made bitter by some callous male."

"No, no," Tess said with a smile. "I am just an observer of the battle of the sexes."

"I wonder why."

Tess suppressed a shiver as Luke's eyes bored into her. "Love is alien to my nature," she retorted.

He looked nonplussed. "I wonder if you're lying to me or to yourself?"

"Look, Brother Grim," Tess said jabbing her index finger into Luke's broad chest and then hurriedly pulling it back as heat shot from her finger, up her arm, and quickly spread to the rest of her body, "don't try to second-guess me because you know nothing about me. Nothing! I am twenty-five years old and in all that time I have never had someone love me, nor have I ever loved someone. The evidence is incontrovertible. Tess Alcott and love do not mix."

"What about Elizabeth Cushman and love?"

"Elizabeth is moldering in her grave, as you very well know! Worms are on her mind, not love."

"I'm not as sure of that as I used to be," Luke said, taking her hand in his. The warmth of his touch began to melt the ice that had been clogging Tess's veins. "You're very like Elizabeth, you know. You're beautiful, intelligent, good with your hands, hence your success in your checkered career."

"Don't forget my appendix scar," Tess said, happily melting in his gaze.

"Ah, yes," he murmured, "we mustn't forget that."

Hodgkins appeared in the next moment, a

mobile telephone in his hand. "An overseas call from a Mr. Bainbridge for you, Miss Alcott," he intoned.

Tess blinked. She had nearly kissed Luke!

"Thank you, Hodgkins," she said, and it came from the very depths of her soul. Who would have thought she'd have Hodgkins to thank for pulling her back from the brink of disaster?

With a glance at Luke, she sat up and took the phone, forcing a calm mask onto her face. The last thing she needed was for her other life to blow this job wide open. "Cyril?" she said into the receiver. "I'm on vacation, why are you calling?" Mr. Bainbridge took several minutes to lay the facts before her. "Look, I pulled the heist months ago," Tess said at last, "just so you could ride into Mendoza's compound like his own personal white knight. I'm out of it now." Mr. Bainbridge took several more minutes to describe the difficulties he had encountered. "My heart bleeds for you," Tess retorted. "Look, the timeline was set nine months ago. I've done my part and now it's up to you. Think of it as honoring a contract. I have a lawyer known as the Grim Reaper sitting right here who will undoubtedly be happy to discuss with you the ramifications of breaking a contract."

"In a hot minute," Luke assured her.

Tess grinned at him and then, thoroughly distracted, turned back to the phone. "Stop complaining and just do the job, Cyril. And don't call me again unless there's a real emergency, okay? I'm working on my tan." She winced and hung up the phone. "I never knew a man to be so violently opposed to tanning."

Luke laughed. It was deep, rich laughter that warmed her soul. "Business call?" he asked.

"Mm," Tess said, thinking rapidly. "Cyril Bainbridge is doing clean-up duty on an old job and he's run into some trouble with a . . . witness. Now Cyril may look like the Devil incarnate, but he's from

Kentucky and that man could sweet-talk Queen Elizabeth into converting to Buddhism if he set his mind to it, so there really is no excuse for him calling me up to complain."

"Is this the same Cyril who bruised your arm last week?"

"He likes to keep busy and WEB obliges."

"Do you like working for WEB?" Luke asked, sitting up, his bronzed skin nearly dry, his swim trunks doing very little to disguise his masculinity.

Tess blinked. WEB. Right, WEB. "Sure. They're a great group of people on the whole," she replied. "And it's fascinating watching how the other half works. I've learned a lot. I'm a much better thief working for WEB than I used to be working on my own."

"Is that what you do? Steal?"

"Oh no, nothing so crass," Tess replied. "I just retrieve items that have gone astray or locate a piece of evidence the authorities need to incarcerate less talented operators."

Luke frowned. "It sounds dangerous."

"Not really. I usually have to work with a team and we watch out for each other. Besides, I'm good at what I do."

"You are superb at what you do. But do you like what you do?"

"It keeps me from getting rusty."

"But do you like it?"

Tess sighed as she brushed a few stray drops of water from her leg. He was persistent, she would give him that. And sweet. He'd called her superb! "Well, I guess I'm a little bored by it all. When I was working for myself, I stole beautiful things: jewelry, artwork. I wasn't interested in stocks or stamps or rare coins. It was beauty I wanted in my life. And now the things I steal are the farthest thing from beautiful. It's kind of killing my interest in the work. I've looked at other careers, but nothing has caught my fancy yet."

"I imagine it would be hard to shift gears," Luke agreed. He stopped, his eyes suddenly wide as he stared at her. "Then again, maybe not. How did you do that?"

"Do what?" Tess asked innocently.

A grin tugged at his lips. "How did you shift the entire dynamics of our combative relationship into a downright pleasant conversation about exercise, Elizabeth, and careers?"

"Oh, dear," Tess murmured, "was I being obvious?"

"You haven't got a microorganism of obvious in you, and you know it!"

Tess grinned. She couldn't help it. He'd seen right through her and, rather than getting upset because he'd blown her cover, she liked it. She liked that he was that good, that quick, that smart. She liked that she could do her job—get Luke onto her side—and enjoy doing it. Maybe she didn't have to fight her feelings so desperately. Maybe they were the key to pulling this thing off.

"Fighting's only fun for a little while," she said. "Then it gets boring. I thought I'd try something different. Like it?"

"Very much," Luke said, his emerald eyes darkening.

CHAPTER

8

Luke reached out to push a stray curl from Tess's temple. It was a mistake, of course, because his fingers brushed against her skin and now he had to kiss her. He had been aching to kiss her all morning and nothing, not even a return to sanity, was going to stop him.

"I like it almost as much as I like kissing you," he said.

"Luke, no—" she whispered as he cupped the back of her head.

"Yes," he groaned.

Her eyes—full of surprise and fear and longing—slowly drifted shut just before his lips brushed hers once, twice, the soft caress sending tremors through his veins.

Sweet, she was so sweet. His mouth met hers again with all of the tenderness he had never known dwelled in his soul and he felt her tremble. Her full lips returned the kiss as she made a sound that might have been a purr or a sigh of pain.

He hauled her into his arms then, rolled her onto her back, and kissed her, hungrily, eagerly, fiercely. Her arms went around his neck, her body arching into his as she met him with her own hunger, her own soft cries of pleasure and need.

He could feel every delicious inch of her against him, her nipples hardening against his chest, and suddenly he wanted more, needed more, had to have more. He had to have her.

It was that throbbing need that plummeted him back into reality and she came back along with him. They pulled far enough apart to stare at each other, breaths ragged.

"This is insanity," Tess whispered.

"Good word for it," Luke gasped.

There was amazement in her eyes. And terror. "Look," she said in an unconscious parody of reasonableness, "this has got to stop here and now. We're on the opposite sides of a very big fence. We shouldn't be . . . meeting in the middle. You don't trust me, you think I'm a fraud. I can't trust you, it's too dangerous. We have no common meeting ground. We shouldn't be doing . . . this."

"I absolutely agree," Luke said with a bitter laugh as he sat back up. "I hate the sweet taste of you on my mouth. I hate the way your body fits so perfectly against mine. I hate having to be suspicious of your every word, your every touch. You are every dangerous female I've ever known wrapped up in one taunting package, and I hate all of it!"

"Well, thanks a lot!" Tess shouted back at him as she surged to her feet. "Do you think I *like* this path we've stumbled on? Do you think I like the fact that you can kiss me with one breath and lambaste me as every scheming, manipulative female ever born with the next? Do you think I like the suspicion in your eyes every time you look at me?"

"Fair enough," Luke said, standing up before her, arms folded across his chest. "I'm not too happy about that, either. So go ahead, Tess, banish the suspicion from my eyes."

"How?"

"Tell me all about yourself. Who are you really?"

"I don't know!"

"Why are you here, then?"

She looked away for a moment, and then glared up at him, her expression mutinous. "The Farleigh. I want the Farleigh."

He couldn't hold back his smile. "Liar," he said softly. "You want *me*."

"Yes, dammit!" she retorted just before her arms went around his neck and she kissed him, hard.

"Tess," he moaned, kissing her again and again. That one word seemed to say everything. It filled the hollow in his soul.

"Oh, please!" Tess cried, pulling away. "*One* of us has got to be reasonable. Just because we enjoy dueling with each other is no reason to get carried away! Couldn't you draw on your puritanical Yankee upbringing and keep me from being this stupid? Bert would be *appalled* if he ever knew."

"Bert?" Luke politely inquired.

She paled. "My . . . um . . . mentor after the Carswells."

"And how did you go from Violet to Bert?"

Tess's head jerked up and she stared at him. "How did you—No, of *course* you would know about Violet," she said with a wry smile. "Doesn't everyone?"

"You don't have to tell me about her if you don't want to, Tess," he said gently.

"What's to tell? She acted as Bert's go-between with the Carswells. She drove me out of Miami in a very lurid Cadillac, dumped me in Bert's Charleston condo, and disappeared. End of story."

"You mean, Bert was the client with particular tastes?"

"You could put it like that, I suppose."

Luke grabbed her arms and shook her. "Don't treat this so damn casually!"

She stared up at him in utter confusion. "What on earth are you talking about? Bert wasn't her client, he was her pimp, among other things. And as for particular tastes . . ." Her eyes widened as understanding hit her. "No! You don't think— Luke, he didn't want me for sex. He wanted me for a con he was pulling. I did such a good job, he kept me on with him and helped to make me the thief I am today. I escaped my childhood and adolescence with virginity intact. *Nothing* happened."

Luke stared down at her a moment. Then he crushed her in his arms, almost squeezing the breath out of her. "Thank God," he said in a ragged voice. "You lived through enough horror without that abuse added to it."

"I never said a word about horror," Tess murmured against his broad chest.

"You don't have to. It shadows your eyes."

"Stop being so damned observant," she said, holding him tighter.

"Sorry. I can't seem to help noticing everything about you: the sexy way your hair tumbles around your head, the little shudder of pleasure that ripples through you whenever I pull you into my arms, those ruthless dimples of yours. It's become a habit and I like it a lot."

"You like the oddest things."

"Tell me about it," Luke groaned. "My life was a straight, steady, uneventful course and then suddenly you barrel in and I'm snooping under beds and disrupting my life and living out of a suitcase and having to fight my hormones every damn minute of the day and I hate it! I want sanity back in my world. I want peace and quiet. But more than anything, I want to kiss you and to hell with why you're here and to hell with my job!"

His mouth found hers, claiming it, claiming her. She writhed against him, pressing into him, her mouth eagerly accepting his tongue as it plunged into her, both of them moaning at the contact.

He knew then. Knew that she needed this, too. Knew that this was real and it didn't matter what con she was running, it didn't matter why she was here. It only mattered that she was in his arms, feverishly returning his kisses, because this was truth, this was honesty. Nothing else mattered.

He tore his mouth from hers to drag oxygen into his starved lungs and heard her own ragged breathing. A new smile touched his lips. He wasn't alone in this, whatever this was.

Then memories of Margo—of her kisses and her lies—threw him mercilessly back into reality. He stared at Tess with growing horror.

"I'm sorry," he said, abruptly backing away, staring down at the anguish on Tess's face, wanting to kiss it away. "I'm acting like a fool and taking you with me. You're right, this has got to stop. We have no common ground. We just need to remember that and we'll do fine." He stared at her lips swollen by his kisses. "Fine," he said raggedly, just before he turned and headed for the house and sanctuary and some form of sanity.

Instead, he found Jane going through a briefcase she had set down on a satinwood table in the Grand Hall. She looked him up and down, critically.

"I'm not sure," she said, "but I doubt if you are wearing appropriate office attire."

Luke had the most awful urge to blush. "I was swimming."

"Among other things," Jane said coolly. "If I

didn't know better, I'd swear you were courting a thief."

Luke's mouth fell open. "I would no more court a thief than I would . . . swing from a chandelier!"

"You are still suspicious of Tess, then?"

"Any sane person would be!"

"Perhaps, but then, trust is not exactly your forte, is it? That's just one of the many things you have in common with Tess. She doesn't trust anyone or anything but herself, either."

"Tess Alcott and I have nothing in common. Nothing.

"Piffle," Jane stated.

Luke cringed. She was right. But did she know how right?

"Aside from your mutual inability to trust anyone," she continued, "you are both frighteningly intelligent, you both hide a good deal of passion behind a mask of calm, you both chose difficult careers and are at the top of your fields. You have also both thrown yourselves into your work to exclude any and all human relationships because you both have been repeatedly hurt by others in the past. And you both believe, erroneously I might add, that you neither need nor want love in your lives. Shall I go on?"

Damn, she was good. "I have to change," Luke said, heading for the stairs.

"Yes, and more than your clothes," Jane called after him.

He wanted to stick his tongue out at her. It took everything he had to remember he was no longer seven years old. Jane's words, Tess's kisses, and memories of Margo were a vise twisting his brain into mush. He was in *deep* trouble.

The phone on his bedside table began to ring as he closed his bedroom door behind him.

"There's a joker in the deck," Leroy Baldwin said by way of hello.

Luke's heart clenched. "What do you mean?" he demanded.

"Have you hired another firm to watch Tess Alcott?"

"What? No, of course not! Why?"

"Because my surveillance team nearly fell on top of another surveillance team this morning. My people were very unnerved, and not just because they watched you making out with the suspect in one of the biggest fraud cases we've ever handled. Do you know what you're doing?"

"No."

"Oh, that's very reassuring. Is Tess Alcott pulling a Margo?"

"I don't know," Luke said grimly. "What about the other team?"

"My people are pros, but they didn't spot these guys until this afternoon. The thing is, this second team is working with limited equipment: binoculars, that kind of thing. No cameras, no microphones. And all they care about is Tess Alcott. They don't follow anyone else. I don't like it. Something is going on that I don't understand."

Luke's long fingers drummed on the bedside table. "Can you cover this second surveillance team?"

"It's already done. As soon as I find out what they're up to, I'll let you know."

"This whole thing is beginning to give me a migraine."

"Not me. I've just got the heebie-jeebies."

Luke's throat ached, but he had a job to do, whether he and Tess were akin to each other or not. "*Oh, hell,*" Luke muttered. "You ever come across anyone named Bert attached to Tess?"

"Not a soul."

"I think . . . you'd better dig deeper."

"You got it."

Luke hung up the phone feeling guilty and ashamed of himself. How could he kiss Tess, *need* Tess, and still try to break her story?

He stalked into the bathroom, stripped off his swim trunks, and stepped into the shower. But the water washed away none of the guilt. From early childhood, Tess had warped herself to fit others' demands and expectations, just as he had done. She walked through the world alone, as he did. They *were* akin to each other, and Luke felt as if he had just betrayed her.

CHAPTER
9

Tess watched Luke stalk back into the house and wondered if she was watching Dr. Jekyll or Mr. Hyde. Kissing her passionately one minute, pushing her roughly away the next. Why was he as messed up as she was? Why was he fighting her so hard? How could he just walk away from her as if he didn't feel everything they had just shared? Was this some kind of con of his own? Or did he really want her? And why did she want that answer to be yes? It was time and past time to get some answers.

Tess waited until Luke and Jane had left for work, then she got into a Mercedes convertible—Jane had given her carte blanche to the Cushman garage—and headed for town. In less than an hour, she pulled the Mercedes into her underground parking garage and then rode the elevator to the top floor of the restored ten-story Edwardian apartment building. She walked down the thickly carpeted hallway, pulled out her key, unlocked her door, and stepped with relief into her flat.

"Honey, I'm home!" she called out.

A tall woman with long, thick black hair,

silver-gray eyes, dressed in lavender stirrup pants and a matching sweater, padded barefoot out of the kitchen.

"Hard day at the office, dear?" the woman inquired, her Irish accent lyrical and lovely.

Tess grimaced. "It has not been pleasant. What's happening, Gladys?"

Now Gladys grimaced. "Lord, I hate that name. You're a nomenclature sadist, you know that, Tess?"

Tess grinned. "If you can't have fun on a job, what's the point?"

"Were you followed?"

"Of course I was followed. Bert's henchmen probably have orders to keep within five feet of me at all times upon pain of death. But this little visit will seem innocuous enough. Besides, my unplanned trip has a reason that will satisfy him."

"Why *are* you here?"

"I need to do some more research on the Grim Reaper."

"Luke Mansfield? Why?"

Tess's smile was grim. "He's getting in my way in a big way," she said. "I've got to find out why. How goes it with you?"

"Simply splendid, thank you," Gladys said, insinuating herself onto the gold chaise with a contented sigh. "Anytime you need a house-sitter, you can count on me."

"Thanks," Tess said with a grin as she headed for the study. "I heard from Cyril."

"So did I. He hates his code name, he hates South America, and he's not fond of Mendoza."

"Poor boy."

"Meanwhile, *you* loll in the lap of luxury."

Tess turned and grinned at Gladys. "You're not doing too bad yourself."

"We won't tell Cyril."

"Very wise. Did you find Philip Larkin?"

"At three o'clock this morning. That's why I slept in."

"Well, five down, two to go."

"Hey!" Gladys called. "Not even a thanks? Not even a 'job well done'?"

Tess poked her head back out of the study. "Job satisfaction is not enough?"

Gladys threw a pillow at her and missed her head by a scant half second. Tess ducked back into the plant-filled study—it resembled more of a jungle than a work area—and, chuckling, headed for her computer. She began to hack in earnest, eager to find answers to some very disturbing questions. Yes, she needed to know everything about Luke so she could handle him properly on this job. But there was so much more. Who was he really? Why did he affect her so? How had he made her long for his touch, his kiss, the sound of his voice, in spite of Dennis Foucher?

She shuddered. She had thought of Dennis Foucher every day since meeting Luke. She could still feel the too-small school uniform that Bert had ordered her to wear. It had made her look thirteen instead of sixteen. Dennis Foucher had liked them young. She could still hear Foucher's harsh breathing, feel his rough hands tearing at her clothes, her throat tightening with her screams of nine years ago as Bert had ransacked Foucher's library safe for certain incriminating documents.

Tess shuddered again. How could she want Luke when Foucher still haunted her?

It took almost an hour of hard hacking before she got beneath the surface gloss to find some answers. She almost shut the computer off. There was misery here, similar to her own, and she didn't think she could stand it. But she needed some answers.

First on the hit parade was Jennifer Eire. The

story Tess pasted together from newspapers and magazine stories and a plethora of gossip columns raised the bile in her throat. "You bitch," she whispered.

Luke and Jennifer had been law students together. He fell in love with her and got engaged at twenty-three. Tess scanned the newspaper announcements. It was startling to see this younger version of Luke. The hardness of his mouth, the cynicism in his eyes, were gone. He looked like exactly what he was twelve years ago: an intelligent, handsome, rich young man giddy with love. Jennifer Eire, at his side, was certainly a beauty, but her eyes had a hard look to them, and her adoring smile up at Luke didn't quite ring true.

If only Luke had been so discerning, Tess thought. Jennifer had been using him, or rather his wealth and family and connections, to get a head start on her own legal career. With the Mansfields behind her, she could have skyrocketed into the legal stratosphere. But somehow Luke had discovered the truth about old Jennifer. Tess found a report that Luke had left Harvard just before Christmas break, driving up to Canada for some reason, basically nonstop. He hadn't returned to school until the fall semester. Jennifer had transferred to Stanford. From what Tess could find, the two had never seen each other again.

She sat back in her chair, staring at the computer screen. She knew what it was to be young and violated, and Jennifer had violated Luke. Tess knew the pain and horror of being used for someone else's strictly mercenary purposes. From everything she knew and had found thus far, Luke had not deserved such treatment. He had led an honorable and honest life. He had betrayed no one, stepped on no one, deliberately hurt no one. And then Jennifer Eire had hurtled into his perfect life like a wrecking ball.

The social columns in the newspapers for the next few years told the story. Cynicism had started to harden his mouth and invade his eyes. There was no giddiness in his smile for the camera. According to the columns, he didn't date anyone for almost a year after Jennifer. And then it was a new girl every few weeks. The gossip columnists said he was playing the field. Tess suspected he had been doing his best to dodge any bullets or knives aimed at his back. Luke had always been intelligent. Jennifer had made him shrewd.

That posed a problem for number two on the hit parade: Ellen Monroe. By every account Tess could dig up, it was Ellen who began pursuing Luke when he was twenty-seven and well launched on his career. After a while, Luke had begun to like being pursued. According to the society columns, Ellen lasted for more than a few weeks. There she was with Luke at a Halloween costume ball for charity dressed as Titania to his Oberon. Tess shivered. Luke made a very sexy Oberon. His costume consisted almost entirely of nudity with a few strategically placed forest leaves. It had caused quite a stir. Ellen too had not been averse to displaying nature's wealth. She was almost as scantily clad as Luke, a wreath of flowers crowning her short brown hair.

There was Ellen with Luke at a Thanksgiving bash at Rockefeller Center. There she was with Luke at a Mansfield Christmas party of about five hundred people, looking adorable in her little elf costume. She and Luke were smiling at each other in the picture with obvious affection, but again there was no giddiness in Luke's smile and Tess, to her horror, was glad of it.

She searched the files but could only come up with one more picture of Ellen and Luke together. They had gone on a ski holiday to Taos. There was Ellen on the slopes, the quintessential ski bunny in her designer skiwear, Luke's arm around her shoulders as they smiled for the cameras. And then nothing. The next picture of Luke showed him dining in New York with some elegant blonde who dabbled in fashion design. What had happened to Ellen? Had Luke gotten smart? Or had Ellen screwed up?

Tess ransacked the New York gossip columns. An appreciative whistle broke from her lips. Witnesses reported a rumor swirling through the Taos Ski Valley to the effect that the Mansfields had lost all their millions. A completely false report, of course, started—it was whispered—by Luke Mansfield himself. Witnesses also reported a one-way screaming match from the Mansfield-Monroe suite. Ellen had done all the screaming, demanding to know if the rumor was true, shrieking that Luke was not such an innocent as to believe that losing tens of millions of dollars meant *nothing* when their combined income was only a hundred and eighty thousand dollars a year. She had flown back to New York that night. Luke had stayed in Taos for the rest of the week, seemingly enjoying himself to the hilt.

"You set her up," Tess whispered in admiration as she once again leaned back in her chair. "You ran your own little sting operation to get the truth . . . and you got it." Tess paused, a frown crinkling her brow. "But I think, Mr. Mansfield, that you also got stung."

The first woman he had begun to trust since Jennifer had also tried to use him for his money and his connections. Luke had a real knack for meeting duplicitous women.

"Nice of me not to break the pattern," Tess muttered.

She grimaced when she remembered telling Luke how easy he had had it. Jennifer and Ellen had been hard lessons to survive for anyone, let alone someone as innately good as Luke. She had survived her own hard lessons. She had learned distrust at the hands of others. Maybe this was why she was so drawn to Luke: their similar histories had forged cords that kept pulling them closer to each other. Where was the knife to help her cut that cord?

After two more hours of steady digging through Luke's stellar legal career and strictly casual personal life, Tess found Margo Holloway. She had been accused of electrocuting her rich and ruthless father. Luke, with the help of Baldwin Security, had gotten her acquitted. The computer was beeping at her. Why were there more entries? Tess paged down and suddenly stopped.

"Oh, my God," she whispered.

Eight months after her acquittal, Margo had been arrested and convicted of engineering the deaths of her half brother and half sister in a car accident.

Heart pounding, Tess began to scroll through the many articles on the case. Luke was only mentioned in reference to the first case. But still . . . Something nagged at Tess. Then she saw the headline from the second day of the second trial: Baldwin Testimony Key to Prosecution's Case.

Wait a minute! It couldn't just be a coincidence that Leroy Baldwin had worked on both of Margo Holloway's cases.

Tess spent an hour vainly trying to access Baldwin Security's files.

"Damn!" she said, slugging the top of her monitor. "Cough it up or face a major upgrade." Still nothing. "Gladys, I need you!"

Gladys leaned against the doorjamb. "Yo."

"Yo?"

"I'm learning American," Gladys said with a grin as she walked up to Tess. "What's the problem?"

"Can you access Baldwin Security's files?"

"Baldwin? The same blokes who have you under surveillance?"

"The very same."

"Piece of cake," Gladys said, nudging Tess out of her chair.

"I need the Luke Mansfield and Margo Holloway files beginning five years ago."

"Coming up."

It was almost dusk when Tess finally shut off her computer. She felt ugly, dirty. She had made herself those things and Luke had sensed it from the start. No wonder he distrusted her with Jennifer and Ellen and Margo having honed his intuition to a keen edge.

Well, now she knew the real enemy, the real wall keeping Luke from believing the con. It was the truth. The truth of who and what she was and why she was here—lost for brief moments in their kisses—reared its ugly head whenever they weren't kissing.

How was she going to get around that?

And how was she going to get around the increasingly glaring fact that the more she learned about Luke, the more she felt as if she were betraying him, and the more inclined she felt to just chuck this job and head for the hills?

"Find what you were after?" Gladys asked, looking up from the blueprints she was studying as Tess stomped into the living room.

"Yeah," Tess said.

"You don't look thrilled."

"I'm not. The man is a walking time bomb. I've got a bad feeling I might end up getting caught in the explosion."

"No one said this job would be skittles and beer. Come give me your advice. I'm pulling the Kincaid heist tonight."

"Solo?"

Gladys smiled. "I'm a big girl and I trained with the best."

Tess spent an hour going over the Kincaid job with Gladys. She wanted to push it to two hours because, truth to tell, she was more than reluctant to return to the Cushman mansion . . . and Jane . . . and Luke. Still, if Gladys could concentrate on work, so could she.

She drove back to the New York countryside, the top down on the convertible so she could get some oxygen in her lungs and the wind could wreak havoc with her hair. Fortunately, Jane and Luke hadn't gotten back from work yet. She could swim some laps and hopefully work off this tension and this small knot of fear forming in her belly. She changed quickly and dove into the cool water. But it didn't work.

Everything she had learned about Luke today crowded into her brain and with it the feeling of being unclean grew. She was using Luke just as every woman in his adult life had used him—for her own ends, with no consideration of his feelings, his needs, his own hopes and desires. Only it was worse. She had trespassed twice, once with Luke and once with Jane.

Tess slapped her hand on the edge of the pool and turned for another lap. She didn't like the woman she had become on this job. She was a user and—having been used by everyone in her life—she knew just how loathsome such a creature was. She was selfish and deceitful and a coward, for though she was coming to hate using and hurting Luke and Jane, she wearily accepted the truth: she would not give up the job. Everything she had ever wanted depended on it.

She couldn't bring herself to meet Luke's eyes across the dinner table that night. It was the first time they had been together since that morning's kisses, the first time they had been together since she had fully learned how badly she was betraying him. With a sadness that was shocking, she knew without looking that Luke had sealed himself off from her. He did not watch or study her. He didn't even glance at her. Not only had she grown used to his gaze on her, she had grown to like it. Its absence made the meal even more difficult to get through.

And the weekend. Luke apparently didn't like taking a day off from work. He went to his office Saturday and Sunday. And at night, when he came back to the estate, he avoided her.

"Tess, dear," Jane said over breakfast Monday morning, "I was wondering if you would mind my doctor running you through a short physical examination."

Tess carefully lowered her spoonful of granola and stared at her. "Don't I look well?"

"You're looking better and better. That is why I want the examination performed."

Her heart hammering against her breast, Tess managed a nonchalant shrug. "Suits me. Just as long as it isn't gynecological in nature. Speculums and I have never gotten along."

"No, no, nothing like that," Jane said with an amused smile.

Tess, having felt, at best, bleary when she had entered the breakfast room, was now wide awake. Maybe the nightmares were omens which she had foolishly disregarded. Maybe this was her punishment for liking Jane, for kissing Luke, for enjoying herself, for enjoying them.

For wanting them both. For betraying them both.

She was a fool. *Nothing and no one is safe.*

Jane was proof of that. She had just thrown a tiger pit in her path.

CHAPTER

10

"Luke, dear!" Jane said. "I have the most marvelous news. Tess passed her physical examination with flying colors!"

Luke stared at his phone without really seeing it. "There's no mistake?"

"No, none, you overcautious lump of skepticism."

Luke loosened his tie. "Have you told Tess?"

Jane laughed with what sounded like pure delight. "Yes. She was just as surprised as you. It was one of the few times I've ever seen her break character. Not only does she have the appendix scar, Dr. Weston says she has a three-inch-long scar near the crown of her head, caused either by a blow or a fall, that might be directly linked to her amnesia. Which also checks out, by the way."

It took Luke a moment to marshal his thoughts. Tess had passed the exam?

"There's still a lot we don't know," he said cautiously.

"But a good deal more that we *do* know than we did before," Jane retorted.

"I don't recommend putting Tess in your will just yet."

"There are times, Luke, when you irritate me. Of course I'm going to play this close to the chest! I have a good deal at stake here and no intention of making an error in judgment this late in the game. I know what I know, and I also want cold, hard evidence in my hands. I won't make a move until Mr. Baldwin comes up with definitive proof, one way or the other. But I'm feeling hopeful, Luke, and I haven't felt that in twenty years."

Luke hung up the phone and stared without seeing at the view of skyscrapers outside his window.

She had passed the physical!

Every piece of the puzzle—her appearance, her character, her flashes of "memory," her amnesia, the chronology she had given for her life—all pointed to Tess being Elizabeth . . . or else, Tess had arranged that every piece fit that pattern. Lord knew she was talented enough to pull off something even that fantastic. He would have to decide if he believed her or not.

He didn't want to decide. Damn the job! It was playing havoc with his happiness, his peace of mind, his heart.

His heart?

His heart.

He had been so unused to listening to his heart all these years that he had failed to hear some of its more important messages, including the fact that he liked Tess Alcott. He liked her a lot. He liked her intelligence, and her wit, and her multitudinous abilities, and her temper, and her pride, and the way she gave him everything that she was in her kisses, and . . . Well, he just plain liked everything about the woman. He particularly liked kissing her and not for the first time damned himself for running away from her Friday morning and avoiding her ever since. The problem was, if Tess's eyes met his even once, he would drag her into his arms and damn the consequences.

When was the last time he had been this stupid? He didn't have to think twice: Margo. *Is Tess pulling a Margo?* He didn't know. He might not know until it was too late. Or was it already too late?

Tess had passed the physical exam. Every secret thought and feeling he had refused to acknowledge within himself were jumping up and down and cheering.

He searched desperately within himself for a bucket of cold water. She had to have manipulated the test results. She had to! She couldn't be Elizabeth. There wasn't a fantasy world going that could touch that one. And yet, when she was in his arm she felt so real, so right. In those moments, every secret thought and feeling within him insisted that he was holding the truth.

Luke groaned. Why, when he looked at her, did he see a strong, loving, haunted woman instead of the thief and con she claimed to be and he knew she was? Why, when he looked within himself, did he see thirteen years of suspicion and pain shattering like the glass bars of a jail cell? Why was the world looking so different? Why was he so different?

And he *was* different. A hunger to love and be loved was growing in his soul. He was enjoying each moment, relishing each day. He was reclaiming his own truths.

Because of Tess.

He was different because of Tess, better because of Tess, happier.

And knowing this now, did it really matter if Tess was Elizabeth or not?

"My God!" Who was this man?

Luke wasn't scared anymore. He wasn't scared of Tess or of these new whisperings of his heart or even of this longing to get off the narrow train track his family had laid out for him. He *wanted* to jump onto a broader path of twists and curves, its end hidden from sight.

He wanted to live every dream he had put into cold storage when he had overheard Jennifer telling her best friend thirteen years ago how she had manipulated him into their engagement and how she intended to use him for her own benefit after they were married.

He wanted to change his life *now*, take it out of cold storage, feel the sunlight in his soul once again. He was doing things he hadn't done in years. Just before Jane's call, he had actually been scanning the newspaper ads for a storefront office somewhere in downtown Brooklyn where the people who needed and could not afford good legal help lived.

It had been his secret dream, the dream that appalled his parents, horrified Jennifer, made Ellen erupt into laughter, and enabled Margo to play him for all he was worth.

But still, it was *his* dream. Was he going to let other people keep him forever from what he really wanted in his life?

"Luke? Luke?"

"Hm?" Luke looked up to find his paralegal standing in his office doorway. "Sorry, Carol. What is it?"

"Newest duplicate files from the district attorney on the Wallingham case," she replied, setting a banker's box on his desk. "I've gone through and sorted it for you."

"You're an angel."

"You pay me well."

Luke smiled, and jumped off the train track. "So, tell me, Carol, how much more would I have to pay you to get you to work for me in downtown Brooklyn?"

Her hazel eyes widened. "Are you serious?"

"Very."

"Wow. Which side of downtown Brooklyn?"

"The wrong side."

"Figures," Carol said with a grimace. But she couldn't hide her growing excitement. "I'd have to acquire a whole new level of expertise: grand-theft auto, robbery—"

"The whole gamut," Luke agreed.

"Would Roger come along, too?"

"And Harriet, if I can convince her."

"What about Mr. Roper and his staff?"

Luke smiled gently. "It would be a new office, Carol. Just l'il ol' me spreading my wings and relying on the best legal staff in New York."

"Okay," Carol said decisively. At twenty-nine, Carol was the most assured person Luke had ever met. She must have put her parents through hell as a kid. "I'll want to be reimbursed for cab fare home every night because only a woman with a death wish would take the subway. I'll want a strong security system *and* a security guard to handle any client or defendant who gets a little out of hand, *and* I'll want ten thousand more a year."

"Six."

"Eight."

"Done."

Carol looked at him in the utmost astonishment, and then grinned. "You've lost your mind, boss, but I intend to take full advantage of it. I'll go type up the new employment contract while you've still taken leave of your senses."

"Send Roger in before you start and don't say a word about this to Harriet."

"My lips are sealed. How on earth are you going to support me on pro bono cases? That's mostly what you'll be working on, you know."

Luke leaned back in his chair, hands clasped behind his head, nearly giddy now that he had begun this new adventure. "I know. I've got a dandy little trust fund that should support you in style for the next hundred years, Carol. And Harriet and Roger, too."

"Geez, I feel like salaaming or something. Can I break the story to the papers? *Please?* This is practically headline stuff: Scion of Old New York Family Goes Bonkers."

"Once I've made all the arrangements, I'll give you the go-ahead."

"You're a prince."

"I'm psychotic."

"Yeah," Carol said with a crooked grin, "but it gets the old heart pumping again, I've got to tell you, Luke."

He stared at the door after she left. Oh yes, indeed, his scarred heart was pumping at full blast. His blood was so oxygenated he felt light-headed. A thief—a sexy, talented, haunted thief—had derailed him from the straight and narrow with an ease that would have been shocking a month ago, and now seemed inevitable and right. The desire to thank her welled within him. Whatever game she was playing, Tess Alcott had rescued him from himself in the middle of it. There weren't words to express this surge of gratitude within him. Which god had he pleased that Tess should enter his life? What good had he done that so much good should come to him?

He left the office at five, his staff staring at him in openmouthed astonishment. He wanted to see Tess again, had to, now. He needed her soft scent to inundate him, her sassy voice to energize him, her blue eyes to blaze with a passion that matched his own.

But when he reached the Cushman mansion and his gaze collided with Tess seated across from him at the dinner table, he found a wall, not passion. Tess was closed in on herself, almost depressed. She had passed the physical, why would she be anxious *now*?

For all their similarities, Tess remained an enigma hidden in a puzzle wrapped in a mystery. She did her best to avoid his gaze, his conversation, him. He wasn't hurt by this—thank God he wasn't that far gone. But still, he was curious. So he allowed himself the pleasure of studying her until she finally finished eating and escaped to her room.

Tess slowly dressed for bed, feeling edgy, ill at ease.

How had she passed the physical? The question had been a litany that had haunted her all day, and she still had no answer. How could she have a scar on the back of her right knee identical to a scar that Elizabeth had? Nothing in the voluminous materials Bert had gathered for her to study had mentioned that particular scar, and the reports Bert had gathered had been very thorough about every physical mark and ailment Elizabeth had ever had. Had he known about the scar? Oh, he must have! So, why hadn't he discussed it with her? What game was he playing?

Or was this Jane's game? Or Luke's? He had studied her so relentlessly tonight. Or was Elizabeth's supposed scar a phony? Had the doctor used one of Tess's own marks as a sham tie to Elizabeth to set her up . . . for what? The biggest fall of her career?

"Oh *God*, why do I feel like I'm the only one who doesn't know what's going on?" Tess muttered. Wearily she slid into bed and curled into a tight ball under the covers.

Nothing was going as she had expected! She had planned to be on top of everything from her first meeting with Bert, and instead she felt as if she were drowning in a combination of confusion, guilt, fear . . . and happiness.

"What the hell?" Tess said, sitting upright.

How could she be happy? Why should she be happy? She was a con and a thief. She didn't *deserve* happiness!

But there it was.

"Well, I'll be damned," Tess murmured as she slowly stretched out under the covers. She had always wanted to belong to a place, to a person, anything. Rationally, of course, a mongrel jewel thief and con artist did *not* belong in this house in Luke and Jane's company. A grin curled across her mouth.

But somehow she did belong and she *was* glad she had taken this job because she was tasting, however briefly, what it was like to have a sense of place and time and belonging. She was glad she had taken this awful job because now she knew what she wanted to be when she grew old: she wanted to be Jane.

And she was glad she had taken this job because of all the things Luke had taught her about herself. She liked this woman she was discovering with his help. Yes, she loathed conning Jane and Luke. But this other self that was being rediscovered and reclaimed, this woman who loved the challenge of Luke's conversation and company, this woman who delighted in making Jane charge into battle, this woman who burned with the most delicious fever in Luke's arms, this woman she liked quite a lot.

"Well, what do you know about that?" Tess said, grinning into the darkness.

She had never really liked herself before. Somehow Luke had changed all that. He had changed everything, really. She was a different woman because of him. Newborn, in some ways. The emptiness that had been her soul for so many years, that her work could not banish, that she had refused to feed with friends, had been filled. Luke had derailed her from her intended path the first moment his eyes had met hers, switching her onto a new road, a rougher road she hadn't even acknowledged until now.

She had no idea where it would end or how it would end. But it seemed to be important to follow it, whether she won the Farleigh or not, whether she landed in jail or not, whether Luke and Jane damned her in their prayers every night or not.

This rough, scary, devious road was where she belonged.

"I'd rather be in Philadelphia," Tess stated as she rolled over. But a faint smile touched her lips.

She was not at all surprised when sleep didn't come. For two hours she tossed and turned, alternately happy whenever she thought of Luke and Jane, and miserable whenever she thought about her job. She hadn't known until now that happiness and guilt could live side by side within her.

With a groan, Tess rolled onto her side and allowed exhaustion to finally lead her to sleep.

And the nightmare came.

It was always the same. Some details might be hazy, but the plot never varied. She was a princess in a medieval world of bright sunshine, knights galloping about on horses, maidens laughing and dancing upon the grass, her parents seated together, royal heads touching as they shared confidences and joined in the laughter all around them.

Suddenly storm clouds blotted out the sun. As everyone looked everywhere but at Tess, a large hand clamped itself over her mouth while an arm encircled her waist and lifted her off her feet.

She couldn't breathe, she couldn't scream, but she could see. A faceless giant lifted her high into the air, high above the trees, high above the castle. She was in the black clouds, the giant's hand still over her mouth.

She couldn't breathe!

Looking down at her world, she saw that no one knew of her abduction. Everyone was scurrying inside the castle to warm themselves. She was abandoned to the mercy of this monstrous, faceless giant.

Suddenly he threw her from him and she was falling down and down and down. She knew when she reached the ground she would die and there was nothing, absolutely nothing, she could do to prevent it. The ground came closer, and closer, hurtling at her.

Tess's strangled scream jerked her awake. She sat up in bed, her skin cold, her breath ragged in the dark room. "Damn Elizabeth!" Tess swore through clenched teeth, her fist hitting the mattress again and again. "Damn her, damn her, damn her!"

The nightmare had been a constant in Tess's childhood. It had plagued her until, at the age of fifteen, she had forcibly put it away from her through a combination of self-hypnosis and pure blind rage at such weakness. Now, in Elizabeth Cushman's bedroom, the nightmare had returned. Every night it had returned.

The dream was at least twenty years old and in all the nights she had endured it, never had there been anyone to hold her, to comfort her, to tell her it would be all right.

Her heart finally slowing, her lungs filling easily with oxygen once more, Tess pushed herself from her bed and started downstairs for a book, not even bothering with slippers or a robe. It was after two in the morning, the house was still, and Tess intended to get a firmer grip on reality. *Crime and Punishment* seemed in order.

And then she entered the library.

Luke was standing at the fireplace, one hand on the mantel as he gazed down into the empty grate. He turned suddenly and stared at her, his welcoming smile fading as worry shadowed his eyes. "What's wrong, Tess?" he asked gently.

Oh, how she longed to throw herself into his arms and weep away every fear.

"I just . . . woke up and couldn't get back to sleep."

"Is that all?"

"Sure," Tess blithely replied, turning so he wouldn't see the longing in her eyes. "What are you doing up so late?"

"I think"—and then Luke smiled—"I've been conducting an experiment to see if mental telepathy really works." His smile grew. "It does."

"Sorry to interrupt—" Tess began nervously. She had never seen him use quite that smile before. "I just wanted—" She ground to a halt as he walked to within a foot of her, his green gaze raking her from head to toe.

"Those pajamas are the sexiest things I've ever seen," he said, his voice ragged.

He pulled Tess into his arms before she could form a coherent protest, or even think that she *ought* to form a coherent protest.

"Dr. Jekyll, I presume?" Tess said, staring up at him, her heart shuddering in her breast as she luxuriated in his strength and warmth.

"Aha. You've met my evil twin, I take it?" His hand glided through her hair and cupped the back of her neck.

"He—" Tess gasped. It was becoming harder to breathe. "He actually made a good deal of sense."

"He acted like a fool," he said as he pulled her closer. "I'm sorry, Tess. I won't be that scared or that stupid again."

She moved easily, naturally against him, her body eagerly absorbing his heat. Oh yes, this was what she wanted. "But Luke, this isn't safe, this isn't sane, this isn't even smart!"

"I know," he said, his hand gently sifting through her hair. "But I can't stop it. Can you?"

She looked up at him and trembled as the truth found its voice. "No."

"Good," he said, lowering his head to hers, "I don't want to be in this alone."

His arms enfolded her and she went joyfully. She needed to feel him, all of him. Needed to feel branded and claimed and wanted. This was real, this was honest, this was true. His kisses burned everything away, until there was only this spiraling joy that made everything seem right.

"Tess," Luke murmured, his lips pressing a scorching trail across her cheek, her throat. "Tess."

And everything that was in her cried *Yes* to his touch, to his hunger, to his unvoiced need.

As if in a dream, she watched him reach out and shut the door behind her. Then he pulled her roughly back into his arms, his mouth devouring hers as Tess arched mindlessly against him, all confusion and nightmare swept away by the ferocity of her need for him and by the joy his need released.

"Luke," she murmured, her voice heavy with passion and unfamiliar to her. She cried out as Luke's teeth grazed one sensitive earlobe before sampling her arched throat. Need burned away everything else.

Desperately Tess's fingers tore at the buttons of his dress shirt. Her fingers glided across his smooth, broad chest, absorbing the ripple of muscles hidden beneath the clothed sheen of civilization. Her lips feasted on his skin as Luke gasped, his hands at her hips dragging her hard between his legs, to feel his own uncontrolled need.

With a driving urgency, her mouth closed around one of his hard male nipples and she sucked, glorying at the groan this caress tore from his throat.

His hands swept up to cup her face and he

pulled her mouth to his greedily, his tongue sinking into her again and again with an erotic rhythm that her hips unconsciously matched. His mouth left hers to trail hot, fevered kisses down her throat as one hand swept up under her cotton pajama top. Long male fingers glided across the underside of one breast that swelled eagerly in his hand, her nipple tightening as his thumb brushed against it.

"Tess, Tess, beautiful Tess," Luke murmured as his hands molded her eager breasts. "I want you so much. I need you. *Need me.*"

"I do," Tess cried. "I need all of you." Her breath became a sob as Luke's fingers quickly unbuttoned her top and pushed it off her shoulders.

"Want me, Tess," Luke murmured, his tongue sampling the silky skin of her breasts.

"I do," she moaned, her head sinking back as she arched toward his mouth. "I want . . . I can't—Oh Luke!" she cried out as his lips captured the pink bud of one nipple and drew it into his mouth, sucking to an ancient rhythm that reverberated into the very core of her being. Her hands swept around to his back, her fingers digging in, holding on to him.

"My golden woman," Luke murmured against her skin, his tongue hot and wet, gliding across the nipple of her other breast. His mouth captured it, drawing it in, sucking as his hand swept down over her belly and within the waistband of her pajama bottoms, moving slowly, deliberately.

"Luke!" Tess gasped as his fingers brushed against the swollen locus of her desire. Her knees buckled.

His strong arms held her as he gently lowered her to the floor. "I want to make love with you, Tess," he whispered, his lips pressed to her sensitive ear. "I've wanted you from the first moment our eyes met."

"Is that what I felt?" Tess demanded, almost

frantically. "Is that why the world dropped away from my feet?"

"That's why," Luke groaned just before his mouth closed on hers, hard and demanding.

"Oh yes," Tess cried and they both knew she was agreeing to more than the kiss.

It was a breathless, vital race to see who could strip the clothes off the other first. Luke won, but just barely, and in the end it didn't matter for they were sitting on the floor, legs crossed over each other, breast to breast, skin to skin. Where they wanted to be.

This first embrace of her flesh against his was, for Tess, a revelation. Luke was heat and hard muscles and velvet skin against her and perfect. The other half of her soul sliding into place. For the first time in her life she felt wholly within her body and alive, gloriously alive. His fingers returned to that hot, tender core of her passion, his mouth once again suckled her breast as Tess, her head arched back, her fingers clenched in his thick chestnut hair to hold him tight against her breast, rocked with the flaming waves his fingers sent pouring through her veins. Tension coiled in her belly.

She had never known anything like this. She felt as if she were being torn apart inside and she longed for it, hungered for that shattering end to this heated torment because she couldn't bear this pleasure a moment longer.

And couldn't give it up.

"Luke!" she implored.

His lips left her breast, his mouth claiming hers with a hard, savage need. "Come to me, Tess," he urged, his fingers tightening the coil of tension within her until Tess thought she would scream, or shatter, or both. "I want you so much. Give yourself to me. All of you. I want all of you *now*."

Her sharp cry was stark in the silent room.

Luke's strong arms and gentle kisses tenderly

pulled her boneless body back together again as she shuddered against him, rocked by a release that left everything clear.

That clarity staggered her. There was no longer darkness or doubt or hardness or turmoil within her, only a brilliant clarity that pulled her head up so she could gaze into Luke' eyes. Oh, those green eyes. They looked down into hers with a tenderness that made her tremble and with a heat that wasn't just physical passion, but something else, something she had never known before and couldn't quite recognize.

"Luke," she murmured, her mouth seeking his, joining it in a gentle embrace that seemed to Tess to say so much.

He held her tightly in his arms, her head resting against his chest. She heard the fast, hard beat of his heart and didn't understand it at first until sensation fully returned and she felt the tension of his body against hers. She felt the hard heat of his desire, and still he held her, his arms wrapped around her as if he would never let her go.

The world felt different somehow. It took a moment for Tess to find the word.

Safe.

She was safe for the first time in her life.

And so she went a little mad. She pushed Luke onto his back, her mouth finding his as her hands explored his taut skin, desperate to learn every inch of him.

"Tess—"

"You don't know," she said, talking quickly, "you can't know how much I need to touch you, how much I need you. You don't know."

Her fingers traced every inch of his skin, her mouth following in heated kisses, her tongue occasionally lapping out, tasting, savoring, as Luke began to writhe beneath her. She knew the utmost satisfaction, that she could please him, make him want her, strip away his own defenses as he had stripped away hers. Never had she known such pure joy.

"I want you in me now," she gasped.

With a groan, he rolled her onto her back, kissing her as if he meant to devour her. She returned each hot caress, arching against him, her hands feverish against his back, pulling him closer, imploring, cradling him between her legs.

"There's never been anything . . ." he gasped. "I've never . . . Oh *God*!"

He thrust into her then, fully, deeply, both of them crying out. Tess's head was thrown back, her cry a mingling of pain and the stunning newness of this bonding.

"Tess," Luke said, gazing down at her, his face taut with worry.

"*Don't*," Tess gasped. "I don't want your concern. I don't want tenderness. I want *this*," she said, arching up into him, pulling him even deeper into this fevered joining.

The world shattered all around Tess as Luke began to move within her. Nothing existed except this heat and this wrenching pleasure and this passionate man in her arms who was guiding her on a journey she had never anticipated. All she could do was wrap her arms and legs around him and ride out the storm they had created, listen to their ragged gasps of breath, feel everything, feel every millimeter of herself and Luke, and this roiling storm.

One hand clenched in his chestnut hair, she dragged his mouth back to hers, her tongue slipping into him to plunder and join, mirroring his own urgent thrusts. There was a pressure within her, a tension she had never known. She was afraid to let it claim her. Afraid to let it go.

"Luke!" she cried out, asking for something she couldn't name.

He cupped her head in his hands, his emerald eyes burning into her, burning away the fear.

"Take me now," he said hoarsely.

Their sharp cries blended in the gentle silence of the library.

Tess slowly drifted back into consciousness, feeling warm and utterly content and safe . . . until she opened her eyes and saw Luke resting on his elbow and smiling down at her.

Oh God, what had she done?

With a recklessness Tess could not comprehend, she had opened herself, heart and soul, to this man who meant to see her ruined. In that moment, Tess knew the ultimate definition of vulnerability. It was this feeling curling through her body, making her aware of every inch of the man beside her.

"Oh crud, what do we do *now?*" she burst out without thinking.

Luke began to laugh even as a blush crept into her cheeks.

"I meant—" she began.

"I know," Luke said, shaking with laughter.

Tess couldn't help but smile. She *was* being ridiculous. After what they had just shared, she couldn't go back to hiding her feelings, let alone denying the truth within her. She had known glory in Luke's arms and a joy that still shimmered in her blood. She smiled because there was just so much that drew her to this man who a few minutes ago had been as open and vulnerable to her as she was to him. There was no ruse, no hidden agenda. What they had just shared was real and right and true and Tess couldn't have been more amazed.

Amazed not only because a lifetime of her self-built walls lay crumbled to dust, but amazed that a man who had endured so much betrayal and pain in his life would still leap off that harrowing cliff into . . . what? Tess had no name for what they had just shared. But she knew what they were sharing now: comradeship.

"Are you quite finished?" she politely inquired as Luke finally got himself under control.

He flashed her a decidedly wicked grin. "For now."

Tess blushed again. "My question still stands. What *do* we do now, and no lewd suggestions, please. We are sitting naked in the Cushman library, our skin is flushed, the scent of sex is in the air. Even Hodgkins could figure out what's been going on and *he* would be horrified."

"Are you?" Luke asked, brushing a wisp of hair from her forehead.

"Appalled, perhaps," Tess conceded, "but not horrified, at least not now."

"Good," Luke said, leaning across and kissing her lightly on her mouth, "because I refuse to retract one second of what just happened between us."

Tess grimaced. "It is the oddest sensation to be sitting naked with a man discussing *sex*."

Luke chuckled. "Which raises an interesting point: what do you mean by being a virgin?"

Tess blushed again. "It used to be an acceptable state for the unmarried female."

"Are you telling me that not one of those princes or millionaires or talented jewel thieves was able to lure you into bed?"

"There he goes," Tess said with a sigh, "getting a swelled head."

"That's not the only thing that's swollen."

"*Luke!*"

He erupted once more into laughter.

"I'm glad at least one of us is having a good time," Tess said grimly.

"I haven't felt this good in years," Luke assured her. "So what *do* we do now?"

"I suppose," Tess said, biting her lower lip, "that we'll have to stop spitting and hissing at each other."

"That sounds reasonable. I am personally in favor of a truce."

"Truce?"

"I think we've accomplished a cessation of all hostilities, don't you?"

"I wondered what that was."

"What else should we do now?" Luke innocently inquired.

But Tess wasn't fooled. Her blush deepened. "Maybe," she said casting him an anxious glance, "we should both agree that why I'm in this house isn't as important as it used to be."

"Oh, that's a given," Luke said, his eyes dark with passion.

It was hard to catch her breath. "And I guess, at least in private, that we should probably start acting like . . . like . . ."

"Lovers?"

Tess paled. She drew her knees up to her chest and buried her face in her hand. "I *am* losing my mind."

"I noticed. I like it . . . a lot."

Tess raised her head. "You like the oddest things."

Luke smiled at her. "You've reminded me of them ever since I met you. I had forgotten how much I like adventure. You've brought adventure into my life with a vengeance and I love it. I love the anticipation, the excitement. I love that no day, no hour, is the same as the last. Oh, I hate it, too. I hate floundering around in the dark. But I haven't felt this alive since I was a kid. I owe you more than I can say, Tess Alcott."

And what would he say a week or two from now when the con was over? Tess wondered. The thought chilled her.

"Getting cold?" Luke asked and, when she nodded, he scooped up her pajamas and handed them to her. "Here, you'd better get dressed."

Tess was more than happy to oblige. She pulled on the pajama bottoms and then the top. Luke's long fingers suddenly closed over her hands and pushed them away. Then he methodically began to button her cotton top one button after the other. Tess trembled inwardly. What she really wanted was for Luke to undress her and make love to her all over again.

Instead, they stood together in the library, she dressed, he still gloriously naked.

"Um," she said, not quite able to meet his gaze, "how exactly have we agreed to act with each other?"

"As lovers."

"Yes, but what does that *mean*? I've never been . . . I mean . . ."

"I know. I'm a bit rusty myself," Luke said gently, one hand sifting through her hair. "We'd probably better move slowly. Our conflicts of interest haven't evaporated, they've just been put on the back burner." His green eyes grew darker. "The far back burner," he groaned as he pulled her into his arms and kissed her as if he would never let her go.

"Oh," Tess gasped when he finally let her catch her breath, "we'd probably better agree to do that at least once a day to start."

"Twice."

"Three times."

"Sold." Luke bundled her tightly against him.

Tess had never known such happiness. Luke's heart was beating against her cheek, his arms holding her safe.

Why had she ever been afraid of this?

CHAPTER

11

It took several minutes for Tess to make the return trip upstairs, because Luke—wearing only his slacks—was her escort and every few steps he—or she—would lunge for the other and the clinch tended to be both long and dizzying. Finally, however, Tess found herself back in her bed—alone—and feeling very odd.

Did lovemaking always create this awe that welled within her now? New—or reclaimed—emotions were surging to the surface. It was hard, in many ways, for Tess to recognize herself. Where was the frigid, passionless, calm, methodical woman she had known all of her adult life?

"Lovers," she said softly into the room. She trembled slightly. "We are lovers." She believed it.

She felt like Dorothy walking out the front door into a Technicolor Munchkinland. She considered herself with a sense of wonder. The shadows of her soul had not yet returned. She felt almost newborn, innocent in a way her life had never let her be, because she trusted and believed in someone other than herself.

She was still Tess Alcott, but a Tess she had never met before. Would this new Tess stay? Or would the cold realities of her job and the ever-present threat from Bert catapult her back into her old self?

Tess grimaced. She liked where she was, who she was, just now. To return to that other Tess would be stultifying, claustrophobic imprisonment.

She rolled onto her stomach. She was new now and she liked it. Her body reminded her of every moment in Luke's arms. *That* had been freedom. With a smile, she slowly drifted asleep.

Tess dreamt that she stood only two feet away staring at the most beautiful woman she had ever seen. Margo Holloway's long, dark brown hair was pulled back into a chignon, emphasizing the sculpted planes of her face. Her eyes were large, dark brown, luminous. Her mouth was lush, ripe, intoxicating. The prison gown she wore did nothing to hide a figure that would drive any sane man to lust.

Suddenly Margo reached out and grabbed the front of Tess's shirt, jerking her forward until they were standing almost nose to nose. "Be very careful around Luke Mansfield, kid. He's a cobra whenever he thinks he's been betrayed. Sleeping with him, however much he claims to have enjoyed it, is just another way to put the noose around your neck. Trust me," Margo said, stepping back into her jail cell, "I know."

The slam of the cell door jerked Tess awake. She sat up, shivering in the gray predawn.

"Making love was not a trap," Tess said aloud over and over again, like a mantra. "He meant every kiss, every caress, every word. He did!"

Still, she couldn't shake the dream. With a sigh, she lay back down and pulled the comforter to her chin. Maybe the best way to banish Margo from her thoughts and her dreams was to see her, talk to her, make her real. Find out if Luke really had used sex to get back at her.

But no, that wasn't like Luke! He would never use someone like that.

Except, according to Baldwin Security's files, he *had* fallen in love with Margo, he *had* made love to her, they had lived together and, once Leroy Baldwin had proved to him, after her acquittal, that she *had* murdered her father, Luke had been the moving force behind the firm's around-the-clock surveillance of Ms. Holloway that had finally landed her in jail for life.

"All right, all right," Tess muttered. "He's a dangerous man *and* everything in the library was real. I've just got to hold on to that, and my sanity, and everything will be fine."

There were no more nightmares. Still, Tess woke into the bright morning sunlight feeling a little disgruntled that last night's happiness had been dimmed by Margo Holloway. She definitely had to banish the murderess from her dreams. What she and Luke were creating was too lovely to be lessened by an old ghost.

She showered and dressed quickly, placed a call to Gladys to ask her to arrange a meeting with Margo, and then headed downstairs, uncertain what the day would bring, uncertain how to act with Luke, uncertain about what she even wanted.

Until she came to a screeching halt on the third to the last step of the stairs.

Luke stood in the Grand Hall staring hungrily up at her with his clear green eyes. Tess's heart rate became erratic; her brain function ceased.

"Luke," she said, unaware she had spoken.

"Tess," he growled, dragging her down into his arms.

Her breasts were crushed against his broad chest as his mouth slanted across hers, hungry, insatiable, demanding . . . everything.

She felt like dry paper held near a roaring fire, setting her ablaze.

She arched up to merge her fire with his. He demanded entrance and she parted her lips eagerly, a moan welling up from her throat as he began an intimate exploration that left her trembling in his arms, arms that pulled her closer so that she felt the full, hard length of the man and it was glorious.

With a gasp, she pulled from his arms and backed up a few steps, her breast heaving with the effort to draw oxygen into her lungs.

"That's one out of three," she managed.

Luke grinned at her. Every dark suspicion that had ever lurked in his eyes had melted away. "No rapid back-pedaling? No frozen pronouncements that we've got to return to a saner path?" he inquired.

"Are you nuts?" Tess demanded, arms akimbo.

"Certifiably," Luke said, kissing her gently once, twice, and then stepping back. "I've got to go to work."

"I'll bet you say that to all the girls."

He smiled down at her in utter delight. "You're really getting the hang of this."

"I was always a fast learner," Tess said modestly.

Chuckling, Luke kissed her once more and then headed for the front door.

With a happy sigh, Tess journeyed to the breakfast room to be met by the frozen gaze of Hodgkins who brittlely informed her that Jane had breakfasted in bed and would be down shortly.

"Your usual hot chocolate, miss?"

Tess considered this. "Not today, thanks. I feel like having a glass of lemonade with breakfast."

"I beg your pardon?"

"Lemonade. It's a drink. You use lemons. I'd also like some toast and scrambled eggs."

Hodgkins slid out of the room as Tess took her seat at the table.

A moment later, Hodgkins stolidly reentered the breakfast room, portable phone in hand. "Dr. Weinstein is calling for you, Miss Alcott," he announced with no trace of emotion.

Really, the man's manners were improving every day.

Tess took the phone and watched the butler leave the room. "Hello, Max," she said when she was sure she was alone. "What's up?"

"We need to talk, you little fool. Now!"

Tess's happy bubble exploded. Fear replaced all thoughts and feelings. She knew that tone of voice. It had preceded some horrible beatings in her childhood. "Um, no can do, Doc. Jane wants to take me to the office with her."

"You will meet with me now or I will come there and personally tear you limb from limb! Your choice."

"Well, gee, Max, if my mental health is in such grave danger, I'll be right over," Tess replied. She hung up the phone, her fingers drumming for a moment on the receiver.

So much for her rose-colored world. She could feel the hardness sliding back into place to reinforce the mask she habitually wore.

Hodgkins placed a breakfast tray before her and Tess stared at the food. She had no appetite. The thought of eating made her stomach churn. But still, if she was going to be meeting with Bert, she would need all the strength she could get. She forced herself to choke down the eggs and half of the toast. The lemonade was a cool, tart blessing that steadied her stomach and her nerves.

Pushing back her chair, Tess started for Jane's suite of rooms on the second floor and met her only halfway up the stairs.

"Ah, there you are, my dear," Jane said. "Hodgkins said you had a call from Dr. Weinstein?"

"Yes," Tess said, the lie already fully formed in her mind. "One of his patients went into crisis on a business trip to Seattle and he has to fly out tonight. He wants to see me for a few minutes this morning to make sure I'm doing all right before leaving me in the lurch."

"What a considerate man," Jane said. "Shall we rendezvous at my office in two hours and then go to lunch?"

"That would be perfect, Jane. Sorry for the change in plans."

"Don't give it a thought," Jane replied with a kiss on her forehead. Tess nearly jumped. "Shall we?" Jane said, offering her arm.

Tess looped her arm through Jane's when she wanted to run instead. Jane had used physical affection on her constantly and it was constantly throwing her off balance. Was this some sort of weird manipulation, like the physical examination, to catch her unawares and get her to make a mistake? She wouldn't put it past the matriarch. Jane Cushman was nobody's fool and everybody's nightmare when she was on the attack.

Was Tess a target? *Nothing and no one is safe.*

Everything that was in Tess wanted to wail. All the old patterns were once more solidly entrenched within her. It was as if the miracle that had been last night had never happened.

She and Jane walked out to the garage and climbed into their cars: Jane's a Mercedes 500E and Tess's a more circumspect Mercedes 190E. She made herself wave gaily to Jane and then drove the sixty-minute trip to Weinstein's apartment in forty minutes.

Two hours later she and Jane and Monsieur Antoine Giracault were walking into Elaine's for lunch, the unpleasant interview with Bert banished from Tess's eyes and thoughts, her whole being concentrated on her chosen role. She was not Luke's lover, she was a con pulling a job and nothing more. Bert had made it clear: it was either him or Luke. Bert could do the most physical damage, Luke the most internal harm. Neither choice was safe. Still, she knew what one of Bert's beatings was like. She had no idea if she could survive whatever Luke threw at her. In a choice between the known and the unknown, Tess thought it safest to choose Bert and this con and who she had been before Luke. The shadows were once again lodged in her soul.

This noisy, packed restaurant was just what she needed to help entrench sanity back in her brain. She gave all of her attention to Jane and to the man who sat between them: Antoine Giracault, although only in his early forties, was one of the world's great art experts. He had spent five minutes with the supposed Vermeer and, before Jane's appalled staff, pronounced it to be a Shively. He had insisted on coming to lunch to grill Tess further on her astounding knowledge of art. Jane too seemed in an interrogatory mood.

Tess knew there was a reason Jane had wanted to give her a tour of the Cushman empire and to introduce her to her senior staff that afternoon. This was yet another test: how did Tess fit into Elizabeth's natural milieu? How did she interact with other people? *Was* she capable of taking over the empire if she really was Elizabeth? Tess thought the inference was clear: Jane was close to giving Bert and her everything they had worked for: ascension into Elizabethdom. She was not Luke's lover. She was a con close to pulling off the biggest job of her life.

During their first course, she and Monsieur Giracault shook their heads together over a fanatical

European collector of Rubens who, only last year, had ignored all of Giracault's warnings and bought in a private sale a very large, and very expensive, Shively. As Tess cut into her lasagna, Jane led them into a discussion of faux-bamboo Regency furniture, American Impressionists, and French illuminated manuscripts. Occasionally Tess felt herself in almost over her head, but she had long been adept at treading water.

"But how," Monsieur Giracault inquired, gazing deeply into her eyes as he habitually did, "can so knowledgeable an art devotee dismiss Picasso's Cubist works out of hand?"

"I don't!" Tess protested. "I like *Guernica* very much *and* I loathe *The Accordionist*. Unless there's an intense message behind the painting, I just tend to be drawn more to beauty than to technical wizardry."

"Technical wizardry?" Jane sputtered and was soon in full cry. Tess was more than content to sit back and let her expound on one of her favorite artists and art styles.

It occurred to her, halfway through lunch and Jane's diatribe, that Antoine—as he insisted she call him—was flirting with her quite expertly. She had been so involved in the conversation that she hadn't really noticed it before. She considered this man whom she had openly admired from the moment they had met for his knowledge and love of art. He was a little shorter than Luke, a bit thinner, his blond hair beginning to recede from his forehead. He also had beautiful hands, a brilliant mind, and a self-deprecating smile Tess couldn't resist. He was not handsome, but he had a Gallic attractiveness that many other women in the restaurant had noticed.

Tess had noticed. But that was all. Here was a man who in so many ways fit into her world, a man who seemed ideally suited to her interests and her temperament, and Tess was not in the least drawn to him except as a partner in conversation. She thought this very odd. There was Luke, who set the blood pounding in her veins even as he tried to have her thrown in jail, and *he* was the man she wanted, instead of the far more sane and accessible choice of Antoine Giracault.

Fortunately, Antoine and Jane distracted her from these treacherous thoughts by challenging her opinions on Poussin, Flaubert, and Maria Callas.

None of this was a hardship for she was helped along in her role by her growing fascination with Jane's world. After lunch and Antoine Giracault's reluctant departure, Jane once again ushered Tess into her dominion and Tess was enthralled. She wanted to explore every nook and cranny at Cushman's. As far as she was concerned, it was a candy store and she was six years old again. Everything that was beautiful was here. She couldn't ask enough questions, couldn't stop enjoying every minute of the afternoon.

Even the paperwork was fascinating, because behind every memo and spreadsheet and analysis was a beautiful vase, sumptuous carpet, or delicious Delacroix. For the second time in two days, Tess had found a place where she belonged.

Driving back to the Cushman estate that evening, she thought it incredibly ironic that she had finally found a career that would challenge her and give her pleasure—and that career was strictly forbidden to her. When this job was finished, when Jane knew the truth, she would undoubtedly blackball Tess in every auction house in the country, and probably Europe, too. She wouldn't be able to get a job sharpening pencils.

She pulled into the garage behind Jane, parked, and then followed her into the house.

"You had better hurry and dress for dinner, dear," Jane said as they walked into the Grand Hall. "Luke should be here soon."

"Right," Tess said, trying to hold her blush at bay, and failing. She ran up the stairs, well aware that Jane's eyes were still on her.

In her room, she stared into her closet in despair. There was nothing to wear.

She stopped at the thought. Every conceivable item of clothing was in this closet and she had nothing to wear? Bemused, Tess shook her head. There were plenty of clothes, but none of them were attractive enough for Luke's eyes or bullet-proof enough to protect her from those eyes. With a sigh, she finally just reached into her closet and grabbed the first evening dress that came to hand. She grimaced.

But she refused to give in to the stereotypical female fluttering over dressing for a man. *He is not my lover, he is a mark,* she reminded herself. She relentlessly pulled off her clothes, pulled on the chocolate-brown dress, found a matching pair of shoes, and then went to her dresser to brush her hair. She stayed an extra minute or two before the mirror, her brush attempting to smooth her anarchic curls into some semblance of order. Realizing what she was doing, she stuck her tongue out at herself in disgust.

"Fool," she muttered. She walked out of her room, down the stairs, and into the dining room where the first thing she met was Luke's hot gaze. Paralyzed, she watched Luke advance on her, like a lion stalking his prey. All brain function ceased when she saw the hunger in his eyes. It matched her own heat, the ache deep within her, the rapid-fire leap of every one of her nerve endings.

"Come here," he said just before he pulled her into his arms, his mouth closing on hers, demanding everything. With a groan, Tess realized how much she had needed this all day, how much she had wanted to feel his hunger meeting her own, how much she had wanted him. She eagerly chucked out all rational thought and returned his kiss with equal heat. Bert could take a hike. If danger felt this good, she'd welcome it and gladly.

Finally, when the need for oxygen became too great, they pulled slightly apart, foreheads resting against each other.

"Hard day at the office?" Tess asked with her first lungful of air.

"Long," Luke muttered. "It was very, very long."

Hearing Jane talking to Hodgkins in the outer hallway, they quickly separated and took their seats opposite each other at the table.

Tess evinced great interest in removing her napkin from the porcelain napkin ring as Jane walked into the room, but she had the most awful feeling that Jane wasn't fooled in the least. Did she approve or disapprove? Condemn or applaud? Was she suspicious of Tess's intentions, or could she not care less?

All through dinner Tess did a creditable job of joining in the innocuous conversation, her face giving nothing away as she wrestled with the greatest challenge of her career. However much she tried to deny it, however much Bert scared her, she was Luke's lover, and that put her life in jeopardy.

Bert's nerves were already stretched to the breaking point by the casual pace Jane had set in making her decision about Tess. This morning's little chat with him had proven that. If he saw Tess make some foolish Luke-inspired mistake now when they were in the homestretch, he would not hesitate to direct his fury at her. Tess had seen the destruction Bert could wreak on a human being with his bare hands and she shuddered inwardly. He would, she knew, take particular delight in doing the same to her if he thought she had ruined this honey of a deal.

Luke's low rumble of laughter roved up and

down her spine and she looked at him, really looked at him, for the first time that night.

He was leaning back in his chair, wholly at ease, a glass of wine balanced in one hand, laughing at some barbed witticism of Jane's, and it struck Tess that he looked different, he *felt* different. Something had changed, but what? Then he glanced across at her, inviting her to join in the laughter, and she had her answer. His face, even his eyes, had lost every hard edge. He was open, happy—not defenseless, for Luke Mansfield was the most alert creature on two feet—but certainly more . . . accepting, trusting, gentle.

The guard he had always seemed to keep up around her had apparently crumbled away for good last night. Had her own?

She felt a smile tug at her mouth as Luke and Jane continued their verbal duel.

Oh yes. If he could affect her so easily, draw her out with just a glance, warm her with his laughter, her own shield was mortally wounded. No matter what Bert threatened, Luke and she were lovers and she would not give that up. She had to take the biggest leap of her life. She had to trust that a man would not deliberately hurt her. She had to trust that Luke's words and his lovemaking were the truth. She had to trust that somehow she could avoid Bert's wrath.

"How about an after-dinner stroll through the rose gardens?"

Luke was standing at her side, his smile warm and enticing.

"I'd love to," she said happily, ignoring Jane's curious gaze as she gave him her hand.

CHAPTER

12

The summer heat of the day had finally burned itself out. The night air was slightly cool and rich with the scent of roses and a chorus of crickets. Tess walked at Luke's side, her arm looped through his. Life, he thought, couldn't get much better than this.

He shook his head at himself. He had definitely fallen off the straight and narrow. Into what, he did not know. But he was different today—the world was different today—and all because of the con artist and thief strolling contentedly by his side.

It wasn't smart, it wasn't reasonable, it wasn't even justifiable, but Luke was happy, truly happy, for the first time in years and he didn't want to give it up, couldn't give it up, absolutely refused to give it up.

"So, how was it meeting the Great Giracault?" he asked into the peaceful silence between them.

"Educational, pleasurable," Tess readily replied. "He makes the most marvelously subtle passes."

"I have never liked the French," Luke said with a scowl.

Tess laughed. "What do you like?"

"You."

He felt her hand spasm on his arm.

"Not very wise, Mansfield. The odds are stacked against you. With my history, I'm bound to disappoint you sooner than later."

"You're talking through your hat," Luke stated. "You're the one who has confessed to having no family, no friends, no lovers. What do you know about intimacy?"

"Nothing at all," Tess agreed. "But then, neither do you."

"*Au contraire, ma chère.* I have been engaged. I have both family and friends. I've even had lovers."

"Then where are they?" Tess shot back. "You dumped Jennifer twelve years ago, you bamboozled Ellen Monroe nine years ago, and you got the stuffing kicked out of you by Margo Holloway five years ago. Not another female has held your long-term interest."

"My, my, you *have* been researching me," Luke said, more than impressed. He was intrigued. Why had she dug so deeply into his past? And why had she let it slip?

"Friends have not called you at Hotel Cushman," Tess continued, "family has not visited. Admit it, Luke, you're an outsider just like me."

"Jane did once say we have a lot in common."

"Jane is off her rocker."

"Oh, I don't know," Luke said, stopping to trail a finger down her satin cheek, delighting at her slight shiver which mirrored his own, "we're both good at our jobs, we're both passionate, we love to argue, we enjoy making love together, and we both have avoided intimacy."

"Okay," Tess said with a grimace. "I guess we have a few things in common. I can understand your aversion to romance after getting trampled into the dust by the Terrible Three, but why avoid intimacy with your own family?"

"We have a conflict of interest," Luke said, a touch of grimness in his expression. His family was as much of a sore spot for him as Tess's amnesia was for her.

"That hasn't seemed to stop *us*," Tess observed.

Luke grinned down at her and then pulled her along the main gravel path in the rose garden. "Maybe our conflict isn't as big as we've both assumed."

"Maybe your conflict with your family isn't, either."

"*Tess—*"

"*Luke—*"

He couldn't help but chuckle. "Okay, okay. My parents are the type of Old Money New Yorkers who believe in wearing the right clothes, having the right friends, vacationing in the right places, and marrying the right people. They insisted on corsets for themselves and their children."

"Made you toe the line, hm?"

"Every damn moment of the day. It didn't matter that I liked hot dogs and drive-ins and making out with the head of the cheerleading squad. That was beyond the pale for a Mansfield and off they shipped me to a private all-male boarding school to better myself and avoid polluting my brother and sisters. You see, I was different from the eldest son they expected me to be and they found that difference . . . distressing."

"And yet, they loved you."

"Yeah," Luke said, staring up at the stars. "In their own narrow, suffocating way they did and do love me."

"Sometimes," Tess said quietly, "families aren't all they're cracked up to be."

"The Cleavers we weren't," Luke wryly agreed. "We were the Mansfields and from the moment of my birth it was hammered into me what was expected of me, who I was supposed to be, what I was supposed to do. My life was a straight line that they had drawn. I rebelled every chance I got, but I always ended up doing what was demanded of me. There's just something about Yankee guilt ... I didn't even want to be a lawyer, as is expected of the eldest son. I kicked and screamed all the way to Harvard. Funny thing is, once I got there, I discovered that I actually love the law. I dreamt of becoming Clarence Darrow, defending the poor, the weak, the indigent. Championing truth and justice. I damn near made a cape for myself."

"And instead, you ended up at Mansfield and Roper."

"The eldest son always carries on the family practice," Luke said with a sigh.

"Bleah."

"Exactly."

"Let's see," Tess said, "your folks sent you to the Mansfield family alma maters, then they shoved you into the family business, and now they've got you dating their friends' daughters. Sounds like you've played the dutiful son more than long enough. Luke, you're thirty-five. You can do whatever the hell you want."

A very satisfied chuckle welled up from his chest. "I am."

"But you're at Mansfield and Roper!"

"Not for long."

Tess jerked him to a stop. "You're plotting something. I can tell by that self-satisfied smirk. What are you up to, Grim Reaper?"

"You'll laugh."

"No I won't."

"You'll accuse me of being a bleeding heart."

"I have *never* associated you with that phrase."

Luke chuckled. There wasn't a male ego going that Tess couldn't deflate with both hands tied behind her back and hopping on one foot. "All right. I'm planning to open a storefront law office in downtown Brooklyn on the wrong side of downtown, of course, near Borough Hall and the cluster of courthouses there. I'd like those people to know that the law can occasionally be on their side."

Tess stared up at him. "You've seen *The Adventures of Robin Hood* one too many times . . . and I think it's the best possible thing you could do for yourself."

"One of the best," Luke said, surprised at how happy she had just made him.

"Gaslight to grunge in a two-block radius," Tess murmured. "You'll have more cases and more kinds of cases than Harvard even knows about!"

"Exactly," Luke said with the utmost satisfaction.

"When do you move?"

"Two months."

"How did your family react?"

"Well . . ."

"You haven't told them?"

Luke flushed. "Hey, you're the one who pointed out that they haven't even bothered to call or visit me here. Besides, it takes weeks to get a reservation at the Twilight Room."

"You're scheming, Mansfield."

It was lovely that she could read him so well. "Appalled, horrified, enraged my parents may be at my announcement, but no Mansfield would ever consider throwing a public scene, particularly in one of their favorite restaurants."

"*Very* crafty," Tess said approvingly.

"Thank you," Luke said, grinning down at her. "And what are your plans? Do you think you'll like running the auction house?"

"If I'm Elizabeth Cushman, I'll love it. If I'm

just plain old mongrel Tess Alcott after all, I don't know," Tess said with a shrug. "I guess I'll find a new psychiatrist—because if I'm not Elizabeth, then Max really blew it. I'll probably keep working for WEB until something better comes along."

"And what about us?"

"Us?" Tess faltered. "Are we an . . . us?"

"The term 'lovers' tends to imply some form of coupleship," Luke informed her.

"Ah."

His fingers caressed her soft cheek. "Having second thoughts?"

"A *hundred* and second thoughts," Tess retorted.

"That beats me by about seventeen."

Tess guffawed. "Oh my, we are royally tangled up together, aren't we?"

"Royally," Luke agreed. "So what about us?"

She looked up at him, blue eyes solemn. "Luke, I have no idea what tomorrow will bring, let alone the next day. Things are going very fast, the world is spinning around on a new axis, and I'm a little . . . befuddled."

"That makes two of us.

Tess shocked Luke by impulsively hugging him. "Good," she said, her arms wrapped around him, her cheek resting against his chest. "I don't want to be in this alone."

She was such a miracle! He kissed the top of her head, and then one sensitive ear, her cheek . . .

"Um, Luke?"

"Hm?"

"We are being watched."

"By whom?"

"By your Baldwin surveillance team, of course."

Luke stared down at her for a moment and

then grinned. "You are *very* good at what you do. As it happens, though, I know of a certain arbor that not even the strongest lens can pierce."

"Oh my," Tess sighed as his mouth caressed the creamy skin of her arched throat.

"Have you ever fantasized about making love in a rose garden?"

"We are definitely out of our minds," Tess moaned as she melted into him.

Luke had meant to be sensible the next morning. Making love with Tess was one thing, but trusting her wholeheartedly?

Then she walked into the breakfast room, the shadows under her blue eyes making them seem huge, the fragility lurking in their depths clearer today than ever before, and he didn't have a chance.

He grabbed her, hauling her into his arms, and kissing her with all the fire their night passion had inspired. He didn't stop kissing her until his wristwatch alarm went off. Even then, it was hard to let her go.

"One of us," she gasped, "has got to come up with some self-control."

"I *am* beginning to feel like a lemming rushing to the sea," Luke confessed.

She laughed then and Luke realized just how much he relished her laughter, how much he loved making her laugh, how much he loved drinking her laughter into every hollow cranny in his soul. It was real, like her kisses, and wonderfully addictive.

An hour later he walked into his office with the sweet taste of Tess still on his mouth and a song in his heart that did not skip a beat when he met Carol, a pencil behind each ear, her arms loaded with law books as she staggered into her office, nor when he encountered Harriet, his grim fifty-eight-year-old secretary, waving dozens of phone messages in his face. He took the pink slips with a smile and a compliment about the new plant she had added to her already overburdened desk. Then he walked into his office, sat down in his office chair, and released a sigh of utter contentment.

He opened a desk drawer and pulled out the two eight-by-ten photographs he had shown Barbara Carswell. The first was an enlargement of a mug shot taken of Tess when she had been ten and arrested for shoplifting. Her face was hard, sullen, her eyes terrified. Those eyes were real, not her face. Then, as now. Her face could mask anything, but occasionally her eyes could not, as when he kissed her. Everything was revealed there, at least for him.

He looked at the second picture that Leroy's surveillance team had taken. She stood at Elizabeth's bedroom window, supposedly staring out at the grounds of the Cushman estate, but in truth her eyes saw nothing of the lush lawn or woods. They saw something darker, something haunting, within her heart or within her memory, it was hard to say. She seemed utterly transfixed and absolutely . . . lost.

Luke knew that feeling well. He had been lost from himself for so many years that it was a shock to finally reclaim the man he had been, or should have been, it was hard to tell which at this late date. Whatever con Tess was running, however carefully she conducted herself every minute of the day, she couldn't hide these brief moments of truth, not staring out Elizabeth's bedroom window, not when she kissed him, not when they made love.

Luke shivered with delicious memory. Oh no, when Tess was in his arms there was absolute honesty between them. Only now when he had shared in such honesty could he fully admit to himself the extent of the wound he had carried in his soul these last twelve years. He had even enlarged it, increasing the pain tenfold by blaming himself for Jennifer, and then Ellen, and finally Margo.

He had internalized more of his parents' teachings than he had feared. A Mansfield never shows weakness. A Mansfield never acts inappropriately. A Mansfield never lives.

But he had been living. Ever since he had met Tess, he had been vibrantly alive and as that life swirled within him, he found an unexpected compassion for himself, and for the man he had been. He should have gotten help for all the pain and guilt and fear and rage he had carried for too many years. But he hadn't. So apparently the universe had sent Tess Alcott to take care of things properly.

Luke stared down at the pictures of what most people would consider a hardened criminal. But he knew better. Tess Alcott had a very hard exterior, it was true, but inside she was all luscious whipped cream. A wry smile touched his mouth. Despite every appearance, the man absolutely devoted to self-preservation might just have found the right woman at last.

He blinked.

Good God. For the first time in five years his heart had overruled his very obstinate head. *He loved Tess.*

"Well, of all the stupid—" he began.

Leroy had called late yesterday afternoon to announce that he was on the point of proving Weinstein a fraud and if Weinstein was a fraud then Tess was a fraud, no matter what Jane said.

And he loved Tess. With all of the reasons not to staring him in the face, he loved her! What would happen when he and Leroy finally dug out all the truths of her past? Would he still want her kisses then? Would he still love her? Would his heart still be intact?

"Dammit," Luke muttered. How on earth had he gotten himself into this mess?

He remembered Tess's rich laughter, a mind that would concede to no man, however superior he thought himself, her haunted blue eyes, her blazing anger, her heated kisses.

"She is the other half of your soul," his heart whispered.

"Oh well, that explains it," he muttered. Then he suddenly grinned. "Oh, what the hell." He was in love and this time was the right time. In spite of themselves, they were right together, they were good together, a perfect fit, yin and yang. One.

Luke leaned back in his chair. Having finally admitted that he loved Tess, that he had loved her from the start, his heart cracked open and he could see clearly now, see the man he truly was. He could actually feel compassion for his parents, for the difficult, narrow lives they had chosen. He could even acknowledge that he loved them. Her lack of a family had taught him how blessed and grateful he was for his own imperfect clan. For all their differences, they *were* a family, something Tess had never known.

He could feel the fondness he had long carried for Harriet and Carol and even Roger, his habitually gloomy office manager. He could even feel the pride he took in his work, a pride he had held at bay because he wasn't doing the "right" work. He could feel laughter in his soul. After so many years, he once again knew what joy looked like, felt like, tasted like.

At thirty-five, Luke Mansfield finally knew who he was and what he wanted.

And Tess was first on the list.

Before he could reclaim any semblance of sanity and begin going through his phone messages, as his conscience insisted he do, Harriet buzzed him on the intercom to announce that a Mr. Leroy Baldwin wished to see him, despite his lack of an appointment.

A moment later Leroy strode into the office. He

was a tall, heavily muscled African-American in his late thirties, casually dressed in gray slacks, polo shirt, and sports jacket. He held a VCR tape and briefcase in one hand as he held the other out to Luke.

"Leroy, it's a pleasure to see you again," Luke said with a smile. "Have a seat and tell me what brings you from bucolic Boston to my humble abode."

Leroy groaned as he sat in the chair before Luke's desk. "Oh man, I wish you weren't so happy because I don't like raining on someone's parade, particularly when that someone pays my exorbitant bills so promptly."

Luke sat back down behind his desk and studied the security man, his heart beginning to freeze in his chest. He had the most awful feeling that history was about to repeat itself.

"What's up?" he managed.

"You want this undiluted?"

"If there's good news and bad news, I'll take the good news first."

Leroy sighed. "I'm afraid it's mostly all bad. We haven't found your Hal Marsh yet, but we did trace Violet. Real name Anna Mae Smith. She is very dead."

"How?"

"Murdered fourteen years ago. Police suspected her pimp, but they could never get anything on im. Physically he was more than capable. She was rangled by someone's bare hands."

"My God," Luke breathed. *She drove me out of Miami in a very lurid Cadillac, dumped me in his Charleston condo, and disappeared. End of story.* Disappeared. Bert the pimp had seen to that. Definitely the end of Anna Mae Smith's story. And Tess had lived with and been trained by that monster? "What else?" he managed.

"I've been able to break Weinstein's story."

Luke sat up in his chair. "How?"

Leroy's smile was weary. "The wonders of modern technology. I faxed some of the pictures my team has taken of him, along with a full set of fingerprints we lifted from the car he drives, to a variety of federal and international police agencies. We got a positive ID from three of them. As it happens, there really *is* a Dr. Maxwell Weinstein, he's just not *your* Max Weinstein. They look alike. Or at least enough alike to fool most of the people most of the time."

Leroy opened his briefcase and tossed a couple of pictures onto Luke's desk.

"The real doctor was flown into the Antarctic a few weeks ago on a very hush-hush secret government mission. It seems some of the scientists on a three-year assignment at the base down there are going crackers and Weinstein is quietly trying to put all the crumbs back together. No one is supposed to know he's down there, not even his wife. While she's vacationing with her son and daughter-in-law in Minnesota, she thinks he's in Europe attending some sort of secret conference with the Russians. That's how your guy has been able to use Weinstein's apartment and office."

"My God," Luke said. "Whoever *my* Weinstein is, he's got to have some pretty amazing connections to find that out."

"Oh, he does, he does," Leroy said, pulling several eight-by-ten color photos from his briefcase and handing them to Luke. "Your man is one Arnold Clifton. He goes by lots and lots of aliases and he's a very bad boy. He has been involved in his long and far-from-illustrious career in everything from major con games to prostitution rings to cocaine smuggling. There have even been hints of a murder or two. The man is so good at what he does, that he has never been arrested for those deeds. Never. He's big league, Luke. Very big league."

Ice covered Luke. "What is he doing with Tess?"

"I was afraid you'd bring that up," Leroy said, glancing around the office. "Can I use your VCR?"

"Sure. What have you got?"

"I've had my people tailing Mr. Big this last week, keeping him under surveillance, that sort of thing," Leroy said, inserting the tape cassette into the VCR. "He's been very circumspect in his actions, very innocuous. Yesterday morning he had a visitor and for the first time he didn't close the blinds. My people were able to get everything on tape." Leroy looked at Luke. "You aren't going to like it."

"Tess?"

Leroy nodded. "I'm sorry, man. She's pulling a Margo."

Pain sliced through Luke's heart like shrapnel. His mind emptied of everything except fear. "Let's see it."

Leroy turned the VCR on and returned to his chair. Luke remained behind his desk, nausea beginning to roil in his stomach as he watched on the monitor Arnold Clifton, alias Max Weinstein, pacing a very expensively furnished apartment. There was a triple knock on the door, a pause, and then a double knock. Clifton stalked to the door, his face tight with anger as he opened it.

There was Tess.

Clifton grasped her arm and jerked her into the apartment, slamming the door shut behind them.

"You stupid, blundering bitch!" Clifton shouted at her.

Luke winced.

But Tess stood calmly. "What's wrong, Bert?" she said.

Bert? Arnold Clifton was Bert? Her mentor?

Violet's pimp and probable murderer? Tess was still working with that monster?

"Wrong?" Bert screamed. "I'll tell you what's wrong! I leave town for a few days to attend to some business and you deliberately try to ruin this job, *that's* what's wrong!"

"I thought things were going well," Tess replied, not flinching in the face of so much fury.

"You are not in this job to think!" Bert bellowed as he raged up and down the living room. "Every time you *think* we get in deeper and deeper. What the *hell* do you mean by trying to seduce Luke Mansfield?"

"What?" Tess said.

Five years in jail had dimmed none of Margo Holloway's beauty, Tess glumly noted as she sat down opposite the woman. No wonder Luke had wanted her. No wonder he hadn't been able to see behind the façade. She was all feline grace and sensuality, from the way she styled her hair, to the way she crossed her legs beneath her. But her eyes . . . those big brown eyes that had looked so innocent and vulnerable in the newspaper photos were now hard and cold. Deception was not necessary here.

"You don't look like a writer," Margo said.

"You don't look like a murderess," Tess calmly replied.

Margo smiled, a very unpleasant, self-satisfied smile. "You should be devoting your entire book to me, not one measly chapter."

"I may," Tess said. "Or rather, I may devote the sequel to you, if this interview goes well. You fascinate me, Miss Holloway. You were acquitted of your father's murder, and then you turned around and got yourself convicted for the double murder of your half brother and sister. What went wrong?"

"Luke   Mansfield,"   Margo   venomously
ground out.

"Don't play games with me, little girl," Bert
growled, his hand knotting in Tess's golden hair and
jerking her head back, "or so help me I will kill you
here and now."

"You've got it all wrong, Bert."

"The hell I do, you stupid little slut!" Bert
raised one large hand and Luke flinched, anticipating
the coming blow.

"Don't," Tess said, her voice cold and sure as
she punctuated each word. "Don't damage the mer-
chandise, Bert."

Miraculously that stopped him. He glared at
her a moment and then, his hand still tangled in her
hair, he threw her across the room as if she were no
more than a rag doll.

Luke's hands went white gripping the arms of
his leather chair.

Tess fell to the living room floor in a heap. For
a moment there was silence. Then she shook her head,
stood up, straightened her clothes, and looked directly
at Bert.

"My seduction of Luke Mansfield," she said,
her voice hard with carefully restrained anger, "is simply
the most expedient means of keeping him off balance
until the old lady comes through with the necklace!"

Luke died in that moment. This woman on the
television screen—her blue eyes cold and vicious—was
a stranger.

"There are safer ways!" Bert roared.

"He showed an interest," Tess said flatly. "I
decided to use it. You always taught me to use every
angle that presented itself on a job, Bert. You want
me to forget all those valuable lessons you passed on
to me?"

•   •   •

"What happened?" Tess asked.

Margo shrugged. "He didn't like being used."

"And how did you use him, Miss Holloway?" Tess said, feeling cold inside.

Margo's smile was decidedly catlike. "How do you think?"

"You seduced him," Tess said flatly. "You made him fall in love with you so he would defend you and get you acquitted."

"Very good. You should be a detective."

"But did you have to make him your lover?"

Margo regarded Tess with amusement. "I like to live well. And Daddy's twenty million dollars said I was going to live very well, indeed. That meant getting acquitted and *that* meant getting Luke to believe I was as innocent as a newborn babe. I figured he couldn't make love to me *and* doubt me at the same time. Besides, seducing him was no hardship. One thing I'll give the Boy Scout, he's a great lay. I was kind of sorry to cut him loose after the first trial."

"Then why did you?"

Margo laughed. "Honey, I'll take twenty million dollars over Mr. Mansfield's performance in bed any day of the week."

Bert ripped the leonine wig from his head and threw it across the room. "Sex can blow up in your face, you *know* that!"

"Yes, of course I do," Tess said impatiently. "That's why I kept him dangling for so long. Didn't your surveillance team mention that, too?"

That startled the behemoth. "How did you—"

"Give me some credit, Bert. You trained me, remember? Of course you don't trust me. Of course you're having me watched. But you can relax now. The old lady is almost ready to call me Granddaughter and clasp me to her aged bosom. We'll have this honey of a deal all sewn up in another week or so."

Bert's massive fist pounded the wall. "What the hell is taking her so long? This job should have been finished by last weekend!"

Now it was Tess who was surprised. "What? Come on, Bert, we never had that timeline! Look, the old lady is tough, she's smart, she's cautious, but she *is* coming around. Just like Mansfield. You always said he was the biggest hurdle. He's still in the ring, but he's lost his punch. I'll have him neutralized soon enough. I tell you what: I'll push a bit harder and see if we can't wrap things up sometime next week. Okay?"

"I've read all the newspaper stories of course, but they don't have the inside dope. How *did* you end up in here?" Tess asked.

"Greed," Margo grimly replied. "I wanted all of the twenty million, not just my third. And then I went and misjudged Mansfield."

"How?"

"I thought I'd neutralized him. I thought he spent his days mourning my loss." Margo shook her beautiful head in self-disgust. "Instead, he had some private investigator watching every move I made. The PI began working on me when Luke took my first case. In fact, he uncovered the evidence I had planted and needed to get acquitted. But he didn't stop there. I guess he somehow found out the truth about Dad and told Luke. Since I couldn't be charged with the same crime twice, Luke had to wait and watch until I made a mistake. The only mistake I made was not knowing I was being followed. When Cindy and Rob were killed in the car accident I'd manufactured, the PI was all over that car and all over the police until they found enough evidence to put me away."

"The evidence was pretty convincing," Tess agreed. "But Luke didn't testify, did he?"

"No, he didn't need to," Margo said bitterly. "The cops had enough on me. Mansfield contented himself by sitting in the back of the courtroom every day of the damn trial and watching every move I made. He wanted his revenge, and he got it."

There was a pause. "Okay," Bert said at last. "But don't make any more tactical decisions until you talk to me first, do you hear?"

"I hear you, Bert."

"If I see even a hint that Mansfield is causing trouble or using *you*, I'll remove him. I can even work it to eliminate the old lady and still have you claim the necklace and inheritance. There are options, babe, there are always options."

"Hey, come on, Bert, there's no need for extremes! I'll get the necklace just like we planned. Why are you freaking out like this?"

Bert's massive hands gripped Tess's arms in a painful vise. "I want the Farleigh now, babe. One of my former associates is in federal custody and making this country a little too hot for me. It's time to leave, in style. No more rewriting the script, little girl. I want this deal signed, sealed, and delivered by midnight Sunday, or you will wish you were never born. You think on that, Tess baby, and get your tail out of here."

He stalked to the front door, threw it open, and Tess walked nonchalantly out of the apartment.

Leroy rose and turned off the VCR.

There was only silence in the office.

Tess walked slowly back to her car, the gray chill of the prison seeping into her soul. Margo had used Luke for her own terrible con. He had been betrayed. And he had betrayed his own deep love of justice by getting her acquitted at the first trial.

He would have felt compelled to atone, Tess knew. And Margo was right, Luke would have wanted his revenge, too. No one—particularly a man with Luke's honor—could tolerate Margo getting away with deception and murder. He had set Margo up brilliantly. If she was a writer, Tess could have had a best-seller on her hands with the Mansfield-Holloway story.

Instead, she had a very dangerous and very devious Luke Mansfield on her hands. Tess shivered beneath the sun. She was using Luke as Margo had used Luke. Did he know? And was he, in turn, setting her up as he had set up Margo?

"At least we know who's directing the other surveillance team," Leroy said at last. "Tess's Bert is Albert Carne, another of Clifton's aliases. I figured seeing it was the only way you'd believe me."

"Thanks," Luke said, his mouth dry. "Leave me the tape, will you? I'll have to show it to Jane."

"This copy is yours to keep. I've got the master in my New York office. You going to be okay, Luke?"

Luke looked up at Leroy and saw compassion in his dark eyes, and concern. "No," he said wearily, "but I will survive. Thanks for stopping by."

"You want me to talk to the police about this?"

"No. I want to sit on it a little while."

"It's your call," Leroy said as he walked toward the door. "But be careful. Like I said, these people play in the big leagues. I'd take Clifton's threats very, very seriously."

"I'll be careful," Luke replied.

He sat in his chair for the next hour staring out the windows of his corner office at the magnificent New York skyline—and seeing none of it.

• • •

Jane sat grimly in her Edwardian office chair as the VCR ejected the Baldwin video.

"It will give me great pleasure to put that monster in the deepest, darkest jail cell we can find," Jane said at last, her blue eyes fierce. "Do you think he hurt Tess?"

"I don't think so," Luke said slowly. "Tess looked as if . . . she knew how to fall."

"She's playing a very dangerous game."

"Yes, and I'd like to know what's at the bottom of it. Wouldn't you?"

"Very much so. What do you recommend?"

Luke smiled. "Let's give Tess what Bert wants."

Jane stared at him a moment and then began to chuckle. "I have always admired your mind, Luke."

He bowed. "I think the best way to pull this off is to do it in a big way."

"With a big carrot."

"Exactly. It's time to take the Farleigh out of its bank vault. I'll have my office contact every news and media agency in the book. I want the return of your long-lost granddaughter to play every newspaper, magazine, television, and radio station in the country. Think that will convince Bert that we're convinced?"

"Oh yes, but it needs one adjustment."

"What do you mean?"

"Why, a party, of course! A very big party to welcome Elizabeth home."

"I have always admired your mind, Jane."

CHAPTER

13

Something was wrong, Tess thought. Terribly wrong.
Luke was chatting with Jane at dinner, cheerful and
affectionate as always, and yet something was eating
at him. His green eyes, usually so forthright, were shuttered whenever he looked at her. There was something
different in his voice whenever he said her name. Something had happened to him, changed him from the man
she had kissed this morning to the man with secrets in
his green eyes tonight.

Something was about to blow up in her face.

Tess was overwhelmed by the urge to run,
to hide.

"Don't you agree, Tess?"

"Hm?" she said, looking blankly at Jane.

"Do you or do you not agree with me?"
Jane said.

"Oh, I always make it a point to agree with
anyone who provides dinner."

"So you think Catherine O'Connor should win
the Tony for best actress in a musical this year?"

"Um ... Isn't she in the revival of *Finian's
Rainbow*?"

"My dear Tess," Jane said, "she is the star of *Finian's Rainbow* and you haven't been listening to a word we've said. Are you feeling all right?"

"Actually, I think I'm a little under the weather tonight. Would you mind if I called it quits and went to bed early? Sleep usually chases away any illness trying to ambush me."

Jane was instantly solicitous, asking if she wanted Hodgkins to bring her some hot chocolate, and ordering Tess to do what Tess wanted to do: escape. Luke mildly expressed a hope that she would feel better in the morning. She forced herself to smile apologetically at him, thank Jane for her understanding, and then she fled.

She closed and locked Elizabeth's bedroom door behind her and then leaned wearily against it. Tears welled up in her eyes. It was all she could do to force them back.

What was wrong with her? What was wrong with Luke? Not once had his emerald gaze raked over her, searing her with his desire. Not once had he laughed or teased her. Not once had he tried to kiss her.

Not once had he done anything she had begun to rely on.

That she had begun to need.

It was the lack of everything he had given her that told Tess the truth.

She loved the man. She loved Luke Mansfield and that was why her heart was aching and the tears were filling her eyes. That was why she couldn't think straight and why her very being throbbed with pain, because he had denied her tonight all that he had given her this morning, and yesterday, and every day since they had met.

She loved him!

Legs wobbling, she made it over to the bed and sat down with a thump.

She had loved Luke almost from the start and that was why she had been afraid of him from the start, and afraid of herself. He held the mirror of truth before her and made her truly see herself for the first time.

Only a week ago she had believed that love was alien to everything she had ever known and ever been.

Instead, it was a vital part of her being. It filled her with great waves of light. Unfortunately, the man she loved, far from returning that regard, was about to detonate something along the lines of a nuclear device. She felt it in her bones. Tess had not survived as a thief for so many years by ignoring her instincts. And her instincts were telling her to quietly fold up her tent and get out of the Cushman con now.

On one side stood all of her hard work, all of her plans and dreams, and all she had hoped to win with his job.

On another side loomed her guilt at using Jane and Luke for her own ends. Guilt had been gnawing at her every minute of every day for the last week and a half, slowly ripping her apart as her feelings for both of them had grown.

On the final side of this awful triangle stood Bert, desperate to finish this job. He was dangerous when desperate. *There are options, babe, there are always options.* Incredibly dangerous.

"This is wrong," she said as she began pacing the room. "It's all wrong. Are Luke's and Jane's lives worth finishing this con?"

The answer was obvious.

"I've got to get out of here," Tess muttered, her hands raking through her hair.

She should have pulled out yesterday after her little chat with Bert, Tess thought angrily as she dragged her suitcase from the closet. What a fool she was! Jane and Luke had been in danger for twenty-four hours and she'd done nothing. Nothing! Bile rose in her throat as she stared down into the empty suitcase. She should never have taken this job in the first place. It went against all of her ethics. When had she become so ruthless? So driven by greed?

How could she have used Jane so brutally? How could she have lied to Luke day after day when she loved him?

The *job*, the damned job had been all that she'd seen, all that she had wanted until Jane's strong-minded kindness had got under her skin and Luke's gaze had heated her blood to the boiling point. She had betrayed herself by agreeing to this con. She had betrayed them by running it.

All she could do now was act and hope she was in time.

She began to pack methodically, her mind racing.

She'd have to wait until Luke and Jane were asleep before she left the estate, and she'd have to make sure none of the Baldwin Security people or Bert's henchmen saw her leave. The first thing to do once she was clear of the estate was to contact Amanda McCormick at Solitaire to arrange protection for Jane and Luke. Then she'd have to call Gladys and Cyril and fill them in on her plans. They'd been a big help in the past. Maybe they could help her find a way to neutralize Bert. If he could be neutralized.

Tess shivered, staring down into the full suitcase.

"I should never have agreed to this con," she whispered, closing and locking the suitcase. "Never, never, never."

She placed her gowns in her garment bag, did a quick check of the room and bathroom to make sure she had left nothing, and then she sat on the small bed and stared at the clock. Luke usually went to bed around ten-thirty and Jane somewhere between eleven and midnight.

It wouldn't be safe to leave for another two hours.

Which meant she had two hours in which to sit and think about what it meant to pull out of the con now.

To leave Jane now.

To leave Luke.

She was about to lose everything she had ever secretly wanted.

Pain sliced into her and Tess wrapped her arms around herself. "Oh God," she whispered, "never to see Luke again." Never to kiss him, or touch him, or feel the blaze of his green eyes raking over her. Never to hear his low rumbling laughter.

Nothing lasts forever. It was another one of her mantras. It had been the truth of her life. It was the truth now.

Tears slipped down her cheeks. Only now did she openly admit to herself that all she had ever wanted in life was a family, to love someone and be loved. Jane and Luke had given her a glimpse of that Shangri-la and it had been sweeter and more joyous than anything she had ever imagined. They had given her an incredible gift, and she had repaid them with betrayal. She, Tess Alcott, had deliberately placed their lives in danger.

She wasn't fit to sit in this room, let alone enjoy their regard.

Everything that she truly was, all that she had ever wanted, everything that she was now losing, flooded her brain until she curled up on her bed and wept for the next hour.

It took all of her concentration to finally accept the searing pain, to stop the relentless tears, to get her nerves calmed, and her mind focused on getting away from the estate unseen. No distractions now. She couldn't afford them. Jane and Luke couldn't survive them. Bert would see to that. She could become a basket case after she had insured their safety.

She demolished a box of tissues and then shuffled into the bathroom to wash her face. She stared bleakly at herself in the mirror. She looked as awful as she felt.

Feeling like a pygmy holding the door closed against the ravening hordes of her emotions, she wrote a note to Jane and one to Luke. They were essentially identical, explaining that she was a fraud, explaining that it was best she leave before things went too far. Saying nothing of her heart. She sealed the envelopes, began to reach for her box of chocolates, then stopped.

Chocolates wouldn't help. Nothing could help.

The pain would be with her always. And the guilt.

At twelve-fifteen, Tess gathered her things together, opened her door, listened carefully for several minutes, and then moved stealthily down the back stairs. She walked past the library and across the black and white tiles of the Grand Hall, setting her suitcase down to open the front door.

"Isn't it a bit late to be going for a stroll?" Jane said behind her.

Still facing the door, Tess knew utter despair. There was a punishment for every sin. This was hers. She took a resolute breath and turned around.

Jane and Luke were staring at her with friendly interest.

"Going somewhere?" Luke asked.

"Sorry," she said, relieved that her voice was clear and firm. "I'm not very good at good-byes."

"So it would seem," Jane said.

Tess forced herself not to weep. "You've been very kind to me, Jane. The best way I can repay you is to leave. Thank you for your hospitality. It's been an honor knowing you. I would have liked stepping into

Elizabeth's shoes, but they'd never fit. I'm not Elizabeth, Jane. Never have been, never will be. I'm a fraud. Always have been, always will be."

"I think not," Jane calmly replied, holding out her hand.

The Farleigh dripped from her fingers, staggering chunks of dark green emeralds and gold glittering in the hall light.

Cold perspiration broke out on Tess's skin. "What are you doing?" she whispered.

"Giving you what you said you wanted: your past," Jane replied.

"I've arranged for a huge press conference to be held this Saturday," Luke said, his eyes boring into her, "to announce Jane's discovery of her long-lost granddaughter Elizabeth. We intend to make this the biggest news story since Armstrong walked on the moon."

Tess stared at him, unable to see clearly, her vision blurred with unshed tears, her heart shuddering in her breast. What was going on?

"And I have arranged a major weekend bash to celebrate," Jane said with a smile as she walked up to Tess and settled the Farleigh around her neck. It was heavy and cold against her skin. Tess's breath caught on a little gasp. "A dinner party on Friday night for sixty of my nearest and dearest, and then a ball on Saturday night. *Everyone* will be here. Oh, the music that will fill this house again! I can't wait to dance in that old ballroom."

Tears slowly slipped unheeded down Tess's face. "Don't do this," she pleaded. "I *can't* do this. I may not know who I am, or where I come from, or who my people are, but I do know that I am not Elizabeth. You've got to listen to me!"

"My dear," Jane said with a fond smile as she brushed the tears away, "I understand that you do not yet believe yourself to be my granddaughter. But I am convinced that you are Elizabeth and so is Luke. We plan to act on that conviction. Be a dear and humor us, won't you? It would make me so very happy."

Appalled, Tess stared blindly at Jane and then turned to Luke. He was watching her, as if studying every tear, every breath. And he was smiling.

No, she inwardly wept, *no*. They were doing exactly what Bert wanted. If she went along with it, she would get what she had originally wanted and Jane and Luke would be safe. But, oh, the pain and betrayal they would feel when the truth was forced on them.

She couldn't do this.

Her breath suddenly became short, as if the Farleigh were choking her.

"Don't!" she gasped. "Please don't do this!"

"My dear," Jane said fondly as she pulled Tess into her arms, "we must. Welcome home, Elizabeth. Welcome home."

CHAPTER

14

If she had spent a more miserable night, Tess had blocked it from her memory. After calling Bert with the news of her ascension to Elizabethdom, nightmares old and new had tormented her hour after hour. Guilt had seen her asleep, guilt had awakened her in the morning. A shower brought no relief.

She hadn't drawn a full breath of oxygen since last night.

Feeling tattered and fragile and confused past bearing, she left her room and walked downstairs. How was she to act with Jane and Luke now that the pretense of Elizabeth had become entrenched? How was she to devote all of her thoughts and energy to finishing Bert's con when all she could think about was how despicable she was?

Tell them the truth. But they wouldn't listen. They hadn't listened last night and Tess knew with despairing finality that they wouldn't listen to her today.

No, that was a lie. The truth was she was a craven coward. She could make Luke and Jane believe her if she really wanted to. But she didn't have the courage to lose them just yet. And she wasn't brave enough to give up the Farleigh when she had worked so hard to win it.

Loving Jane and Luke. Wanting the Farleigh. They were mutually exclusive and she was despicable. She was a fraud pretending to be an heiress who insisted on being a fraud, all for a few more days of ephemeral happiness.

A headache pounded at her temples.

At least Luke and Jane were safe now. She wouldn't have to worry about them. The con only had to run for four more days and then she'd be out of this mess for good. She wouldn't stay in this house with Jane, that charade would be ended. She'd insist on it. Tears again started to her eyes and Tess ruthlessly forced them back. She would not become some weepy woman boring everyone to death. She wouldn't! She would leave the Cushman mansion and that would be an end of it.

She would leave Luke.

A sob caught in her throat. Oh, damn the man! He had stolen her heart the first time she had looked into his emerald eyes. "Who's the thief in this house anyway?" she muttered.

The thought of facing him over the breakfast table clawed at her nerves. She didn't want to, she had to, she hated all of it. She walked downstairs, heart pounding painfully in her breast, and walked into the breakfast room to find only Jane sipping her morning coffee.

"Luke sleep in?" Tess managed as she sat down, ordering her hand not to tremble as she poured herself a cup of hot chocolate.

"On the contrary," Jane replied, "he was up and gone before I even came downstairs."

"Gone?" Tess said, trying to keep her voice neutral.

"He left a message that he had a thirty-six-hour

day at the office. We won't see him until late tonight, if at all."

"Oh," Tess said, feeling small.

As the day trudged slowly onward, she began to be afraid. Last night Luke had openly declared that she was Elizabeth Cushman, but he couldn't wait to get away from her this morning. Was he trying to avoid her?

She went shopping to distract herself, convinced that when she got back to the estate, Luke would be there. But he wasn't. When he didn't return in time for dinner, fear began to gnaw at her. What would she see when he finally did appear and she looked in his eyes?

She stayed up as late as she could, ostensibly to read a book in the Belle Epoque salon, but really trying to wait, without seeming to, for Luke. By eleven o'clock she couldn't fake it any longer. She said good night to Jane and went to bed, lying awake as one hour passed, and another, before finally drifting disconsolately to sleep.

He had already left for his office by the time she came down to breakfast the next morning. She wanted to scream with frustration. Why was he doing this? Why was he avoiding her? Why didn't he even want to speak to her? Why, when she needed them so badly, couldn't she come up with even one answer to one question? Was something about to blow up in her face?

Would it be Luke?

Friday night crept slowly across the Cushman estate. Tess took an hour-long bath, trying and failing to luxuriate in the hot water as she rehearsed in her mind once again the interpretation she planned to give to her role as the long-lost granddaughter. But all she

could think about was Luke and loving him and fearing him.

Tess shivered and pushed herself up and out of
the bathtub. She used the huge bath towel vigorously
on herself, rubbing her skin pink. She stepped into the
gold gown she had bought for the dinner party. It had a
full skirt that fell to her feet from a V-necked halter
bodice. Then she slipped a gold and blue sapphire necklace around her throat, clipped on the matching set of
earrings, slipped into her shoes, and surveyed herself in
the mirror.

Not bad, she thought, studying herself from
every angle. There was definitely a hint of Cinderella at
the ball, but this Cinderella seemed to know what time
it was. Tess grinned at herself in the mirror. She looked
good enough to give herself some confidence and she
needed all the confidence she could get now that she
would finally be facing Luke again.

In the Grand Hall, Jane, dressed in a silver and
black full-length gown, was already greeting the first of
her guests when she saw Tess coming down the stairs.
She caught her arm and drew her to her side with a
fond smile. From then on, she introduced to Tess each
person who came through the front door, and introduced her to them simply as "Tess." They received several curious glances, but no one asked about the
privileged position of a stranger in the Cushman mansion. Tess, recalling the duchess she was modeling herself on—an English country woman addicted to dogs,
gardening, and the jolliest parties—remained cool,
calm, and collected throughout these introductions
and measured glances . . . until Luke walked through
the door.

He was dressed in an Armani tuxedo that
draped itself across his lean, muscular body. His eyes
swept to hers and held her gaze, the emerald darkening
as he studied every inch of her. Tess felt as if she were

being devoured and she loved it! Then he was standing before her and she stopped breathing.

"You are stunning," he murmured. For one wild moment she thought he was going to kiss her, despite Jane, despite all the people around them, but then he blinked and began to introduce the five tall people who had entered with him.

His family.

Tess felt the color drain from her face, but she managed to keep her smile firmly entrenched as she shook hands with his two sisters, Hannah and Miriam, and his brother, Joshua. The smile only faltered when Luke introduced his parents.

Luke's mother, Regina, was a good ten inches taller than Tess, her skin ivory, her gown Yves Saint Laurent, her hair and makeup by Elizabeth Arden, her green eyes shuttered as she took Tess's hand.

"I am so glad to meet you," she said coolly to Tess. "Luke has told us nothing about you. But then, he was always fond of a secret. You are lovely, my dear. You seem very familiar. Haven't I seen you somewhere before? Cannes? Rome, perhaps?"

"Mother," Luke said.

"She has a very cosmopolitan air, Luke, and I was only asking."

Luke shook his head in amusement. "I'll give you her pedigree later. Now move along."

"That's right, give the rest of us a chance," said Mr. Daniel Mansfield as he shook Tess's limp hand. He had Luke's height and lean build, but his hair was salt-and-pepper gray, his eyes black, his face remarkably free of the lines that would indicate his true age. "You *are* lovely, my dear. Divorced?"

"Dad!"

"Single," Tess replied.

"University?"

"Dad!"

"Oxford."

"Excellent. Do you like to foxhunt?"

"Not even on a bicycle," Tess retorted.

"Pity. We're getting up a bit of a party next weekend, thought you might be interested."

"That is enough snooping for now, Dad," Luke said firmly.

"I wasn't snooping! No Mansfield would be so vulgar. I was merely soliciting common interests."

"Uh-huh," Luke said. "Come along, parents mine. We're holding up the receiving line."

"You've survived this first onslaught very well, my dear," Regina Mansfield said, her eyes drilling into Tess. "I daresay you could take on the entire Mansfield clan with one hand tied behind your back."

"Only if you give me lots and lots of drugs first," Tess retorted.

Regina Mansfield allowed herself an amused smile and then walked into the living room with Luke, the rest of her family trailing behind.

Tess sagged against Jane. "If she's an example of your friends, I'd hate to meet your enemies."

"Regina was always a very . . . determined sort of woman," Jane replied.

When sixty of Jane's nearest and dearest had assembled, she led them in to the dining room and took her place at the head of the table with Luke on her left and Luke's father on her right. Tess was assigned the chair at the foot of the table opposite Jane. No sooner had her guests taken their seats than Jane rose and called for silence.

"My dear friends," she said, "I have asked you all here to witness the most important announcement I have ever made. The dinner tonight and the party tomorrow are a poor means of celebration, but with you around me I am sure this announcement will be given its proper due. Ladies and gentlemen, after twenty years of searching, I am finally able to state with all certainty and happiness that I have at last found my granddaughter Elizabeth. She calls herself Tess now and is seated at the foot of the table."

There was a collective gasp from everyone in the room, including the servants. Every gaze swept to Tess, who was feeling somewhat like Cinderella making her entrance at the ball dressed in a slip. A half-slip.

"But this is impossible!" a young woman in sequins cried out, and then immediately blushed at her faux pas.

"On the contrary," Luke stated in a clear voice that carried the length of the room as his entire family stared at Tess with an intensity that seemed to be genetic, "every detail has been checked and rechecked, every test possible has been run. Tess," he said, his green eyes locked on hers, holding her spellbound, "is Elizabeth Cushman."

It took twenty minutes for the roar of congratulations, stupefied questions, and eager declarations that they had always known Elizabeth would be found, before Jane could bring the room back under control and offer a toast to her granddaughter. The guests rose and turned to Tess, their glasses raised.

She couldn't keep the blush from creeping into her cheeks, but Tess could hold at bay the tears hovering on her eyelids. She thought if only Elizabeth had lived what a homecoming she would have had, and envied her the love and happiness these people were so eager to bestow on the Cushman granddaughter. Sadness welled within her, for she would never in her life know the kind of family Elizabeth had had. But she smiled at these people, her charade intact, and then rose to offer a toast to Jane.

"To my grandmother," she said, her voice quavering only slightly, "for her generosity, kindness, and love. It's good to be home again."

The night went by in a blur. All she clearly saw was Luke . . . and that he was never nearer to her than twenty feet throughout the evening. She was surrounded by well-wishers and curiosity seekers every minute of the night. Whenever she had a moment to catch her breath and try to get to Luke, she was waylaid by yet another old family friend who couldn't exclaim enough over the joy at her return.

It took only an hour of this frustration to create a roaring headache that pounded on her brain. Her breath had been coming only in short little puffs since she had first sat down to dinner. She wanted to weep. She wanted to rage.

Never had she been this close to cracking. She wanted to just chuck the job and hide herself away. New Zealand came to mind. Instead, she smiled nonstop at Jane's friends and watched every move Luke made.

She knew a moment of hope at around two in the morning when Jane announced in her clear, authoritative voice that if they wanted to party in earnest on the morrow, they had best go to bed tonight. The thirty guests who still remained, including the Mansfields, were all spending the night at the Cushman mansion. Tomorrow was Saturday. Luke's office was closed, the press were coming. Luke *had* to stay as well. He no longer had an excuse to escape the house, to avoid her. There was even a chance she could still speak with him tonight.

But Tess had reckoned without his family. A very determined bunch, the Mansfields, she noted sourly. His parents collared their eldest son and dragged him off to the library just as Jane looped her arm around Tess's waist and insisted on escorting her to her room personally.

It was the first time since they had met that Tess had actively disliked Jane.

But she went upstairs to Elizabeth's room, bid a fond good night to Elizabeth's grandmother, and then ruthlessly stripped off all of Elizabeth's trappings; the gown, the jewels, the sexy hairdo. She pulled on her cotton pajamas and stared at herself in the mirror with relief. She was herself again. She was Tess Alcott, mongrel thief, without a drop of blue blood in her veins.

Without Luke Mansfield in her arms. "Oh *damn*!" she said as she threw herself onto her bed.

CHAPTER

15

Tess moved among the two hundred guests who had gathered for Saturday lunch and would be dancing the night away at the ball later that evening. She wore an Oxford shirt, tweed skirt, and sensible walking shoes, laughing and chatting with whoever approached her or whoever she sought out. But Luke did not approach her, and she was afraid to seek him out.

As she uttered cheery banalities to whoever wanted to talk to her, she could feel Luke's hot gaze on her. *Why* was he watching her every move? *Why* didn't he come to her, speak to her, kiss her? Oh, this was agony wanting what she could not have, fearing what the next minute would bring. What type of bomb would it be? When would it detonate? How would it detonate?

Just get it over with, she wanted to yell at Luke. He was setting her up. He had to be setting her up. It was the only explanation. She had never imagined he and Jane could be so cruel, luring her into supposed safety by declaring her to be Elizabeth, and then snapping the steel trap shut around her at their leisure. What were they waiting for? Why the party and the ball and the reporters? Was this some sort of monumental revenge? Had she trespassed so badly?

Tess allowed herself a grim smile. *That* was a foolish question. Of course she had trespassed that badly. She had laid waste to every moral precept, every ethical consideration, she had ever held. She had betrayed Jane, she had betrayed Luke. This torturous waiting and wondering was the perfect punishment.

At two o'clock, the reporters began gathering in the Cushman ballroom, chairs set up in rows for their comfort. At three o'clock, Jane marched to the front of the room, followed by Tess and Luke. He said nothing to her though they were only two feet apart. Facing the reporters, Jane calmly made her announcement. A collective gasp filled the room, quickly followed by a barrage of questions that Jane and Tess easily fielded, Luke speaking up only when necessary to substantiate their story.

Knowing what she had to do, Tess played the reporters for all they were worth to create the image she wanted of the prodigal granddaughter returned home at last. The reporters loved her, either not knowing or not caring that she was manipulating them. Her newest role was quotable, photogenic, funny, brave. She was the sort of story their readers and viewers would be talking about for weeks to come. She was the sort of story editors and producers loved.

Tess thought Bert would be pleased with her media coverage. But it was a double-edged sword for her. She was kissing the career she had loved good-bye. With her picture in every newspaper and magazine, and on every television set around the world, she would now be recognized wherever she went. She would never be able to pull another heist in safety. She would never be able to work with Cyril and Gladys again.

At the same time, she was glad. That old Tess

had been washed away with her tears. She didn't want to be a thief anymore. She didn't want to con one more person. Unfortunately, what she did want was Luke, and Jane, and she could never have them. She'd need a new job, *something* to occupy her brain instead of this constant guilt and pain. At the moment, all she could hope for was to work as an advisor, a consultant sitting safely behind a desk. Tess grimaced. Maybe Cyril could turn her onto something. Word was, he was well connected.

At the end of two hours, she walked out of the ballroom and was once again surrounded by eager well-wishers and unregenerate snoops. Everyone wanted to know about every minute of the last twenty years of her life. This, at least, was safe ground. Tess gave them the spin on her life she had given the reporters, the same spin she had given Luke and Jane when she had first come to the Cushman mansion.

She could practically recite it in her sleep, which meant she was free to feel Luke's eyes on her every minute, her own gaze following him unerringly as he moved through the crowd. Finally, just after five o'clock, when she could stand it no longer, she let her feet do the walking. She wasn't feeling brave enough to openly accost Luke. But she could eavesdrop and maybe insinuate herself into a conversation, maybe get him to speak to her, touch her. She edged around the huge oak tree, three feet from where Luke was standing as he surveyed the crowd with a decidedly grim expression on his handsome face.

"Probably thinking about me," Tess muttered to herself.

"Stop frowning, boy," Daniel Mansfield commanded as he reached Luke's side. "We Mansfields have a reputation of pleasant civility to uphold."

Luke grinned. "Sorry, Dad. I wasn't thinking."

"No, you were simply thinking of something grim. The press conference go well?"

"Perfectly. Tess should have gone on the stage."

Tess's mouth went dry.

Daniel raised one eyebrow. "I gather there is more here than we are being told?"

Luke's eyes met his father's steady gaze. "Much more."

"Jane isn't going to be hurt, is she?"

"Not if I have anything to say about it, and I do."

Daniel Mansfield let out a sigh of relief. "Good boy. I always knew blood would tell. So what's up?"

Luke's grimness returned. "Mayhem."

His father looked him up and down, as if seeing him for the first time. "Sounds interesting," Daniel said. "You will keep me posted on all this?"

"Absolutely."

"There's a rumor going around that you're breaking out. Running mad in the streets. Something like that. Any truth to the rumor?"

"Some."

Daniel sighed heavily. "You were always a problem child. Well, if the Mansfields could survive blue jean haute couture, we can survive anything. So out with it, boy. What are you up to?"

"I've made a dinner reservation at the Twilight Room for next week."

Daniel Mansfield blanched. "Is it that bad?"

"Yep."

"You're not marrying Maria Franklin?"

"No."

"Thank God," Daniel said with a shudder. "I need a drink. Want one?"

"No, thanks."

"I'm off, then," Daniel Mansfield retorted, wandering away in search of scotch and soda.

"There you are, Elizabeth!" burbled a stout matron with blue hair.

Tess jumped guiltily and hurriedly turned from her contemplation of the grim Luke Mansfield to the beaming Amelia Franklin, grandmother to Maria.

Mrs. Franklin began to chatter her delight at Tess's return to the family fold, to hint at a possible future family connection through her grandson Marshall, and to discuss her own most recent sojourn at Cannes. It was one of the most tiresome conversations, monologues really, in an already wearying day and Tess began to desperately plot her escape when rescue came from a wholly unexpected quarter.

"Mrs. Franklin, I hope you don't mind, but I must steal Tess away for just a few minutes."

Tess stared up at Luke, dumbfounded.

"Oh, of course, my boy, of course!" Mrs. Franklin cried and spent five minutes saying good-bye before Luke tucked Tess's arm firmly through his and led her away.

At last. "I can't tell you how grateful I am."

"There's no need," Luke said with a smile. "I've met the entire family. They're all like that."

"God," Tess said with a shudder. "However did you stand the Giantess?"

"Daily shots of Novocain over several years can do wonders." Luke suddenly stopped, his free hand reaching up to brush her cheek. "How are you?"

There were so many meanings Tess could impute to those three words that for a moment she could say nothing. "Tired of smiling all the time," she finally replied.

"These parties are a monumental bore, I know, but Jane likes them and this one is necessary, if frustrating. I've been wanting to get you alone all day today, but you've been too popular."

Tess's heart began to thump against her ribs.

"You haven't looked forlorn. You and your father seemed to be sharing one of those male-bonding fests."

"I suppose, for the two of us, that that *would* be an apt description." Luke's smile was replaced with a frown of concern. His fingers brushed the dark shadows under Tess's eyes. "You won't be able to beam at Jane's guests if you go batty from lack of sleep," he said gently.

"I'll try to get a nap in tomorrow," Tess said, shivering a little as his fingers brushed against her skin. She was flooded with the physical memory of how she had shuddered in his arms Tuesday night. She nearly threw herself at the man to beg for a replay then and there.

"You haven't been sleeping well for some time, I think," he said.

"Since I got here," Tess said.

Luke's hands cupped her face, his warmth penetrating her cool skin, as he forced her eyes to meet his. "What's wrong?"

"I've been having nightmares," Tess replied, surprised to find herself answering him. Who would have thought a man's hands could do so much? "I . . . um . . . I used to have them when I was a kid. I guess the stress of all this is getting to me. It's hard . . . being Elizabeth."

"Poor Tess," Luke murmured.

His lips were tender on hers for a moment before he put an arm around her shoulders and they walked into the park.

"Finding your past can be scary," Luke said.

"I've had easier jobs."

"Such as putting the Carswells behind bars?"

Tess stumbled to a stop and stared up at him. "W-what? But . . . I didn't!"

"That, my dear Tess, is sheer perjury."

"But ... but how do you know about the Carswells?"

Luke seemed particularly smug. "I paid a call on Mrs. Carswell last week. Apparently I let the cat out of the bag about you setting her up to get nabbed by the Feds. She was not a happy woman. The name Jeanne-Marie St. Juste was particularly irksome to her."

Tess blinked. She felt off balance and unable to correct the problem. "You mean I'm no longer her favorite child?"

Luke laughed. "That was the impression I got."

"Alas."

"What did you say no to at sixteen?" he asked, brushing the crescent scar at her right temple.

Tess couldn't suppress a shiver, or the truth. "Distracting Dennis Foucher."

"What happened?" Luke demanded.

"I was convinced to go forward with the job as planned."

"And did you distract Dennis Foucher?"

"A little too well," Tess said with a grimace. "He wanted to rape me. I managed to change his mind."

"Did he hurt you?"

"It was a long time ago."

"He hurt you badly, then."

"I didn't say so!"

"No, but your eyes did."

"Stop being so damned observant," Tess muttered, grabbing his arm and continuing their walk.

"Someday, Elizabeth Aurora Cushman, you're going to tell me all about your horrific past."

"I'm not that stupid."

"But I am that persistent."

She was afraid to look for the true meaning in that statement. He had certainly been persistent in getting his revenge with Margo Holloway. Was his persistence now on the same track toward vengeance? But how could he want revenge when he didn't know she had betrayed him? Or did he? *There are times,* Tess thought, *when I hate my life.*

Sooner than she wanted, Luke led her back to the house. It was time to find a pumpkin and get ready for the ball. She walked into her room and stared at the now-familiar and oddly soothing mural on the walls. This would be her last night in this room. What was she going to do with it? She had vowed to go along with the con so she could have a few more days of happiness with Luke and Jane. She could worry herself into an ulcer tonight, or she could choose to plunge whole-heartedly into that happiness and commit every moment to memory, for it would never come again.

A snatch of a song wafted through her head. " 'Taking a chance on love . . .' " She smiled and headed for her shower.

Two hours later, Tess walked down the grand staircase to join the other guests for dinner. She had piled her blond hair on top of her head, a few loose tendrils curling around her ears. She wore a strapless black velvet sheath that slithered to her toes and molded itself to her body like spray paint.

"You're staring, Luke," she said with a smile as she joined him at the bottom of the stairs.

"Are you deliberately trying to send me into cardiac arrest?" he growled.

Tess's smile was blinding. Whatever was going on, he still wanted her. That was real. That was something she could hold on to tonight. "I'm glad you like the gown. I was thinking of you when I bought it."

Luke stared down at her a moment and then pulled her arm through his, leading her to the dining room. "You are not leaving my side this entire evening, is that clear?"

Tess laughed. "Yes, sahib."

CHAPTER

16

Apparently, Luke had arranged Jane's place-cards to his advantage. Tess was again seated at the foot of the mammoth dining table, but Luke was on her right and neither could ever say with any certainty who was on her left. They talked about countries each had visited, artwork each had coveted (although Tess had coveted far more actively than Luke), and animal movies they always cried through. Tess had never known a lovelier time.

They rose with the other guests and adjourned to the ballroom. The eight-piece band began with Jerome Kern. Luke pulled Tess into his arms and onto the dance floor. It felt so good to be enfolded in his arms again! She was duty bound during the evening to dance with any man who asked her. But Luke never let more than half a dance go by before he cut in. By midnight, the other male guests had given up and he was able to dance with her undisturbed.

"I never knew lawyers were such good dancers," she murmured, her fingers caressing the nape of his neck.

"Comes from tap-dancing around judges in

court," Luke replied, one hand gliding across her bare back.

She had felt barren every time another man had led her onto the dance floor; whole and alive only when she was back in Luke's arms. They danced as if they had always danced together, their bodies moving intuitively within the small circle they had claimed on the ballroom floor. His body was warm against hers, molding perfectly to her softness, his subtle scent intoxicating her.

If this was a trap, she didn't care. She knew absolute joy, because she felt his desire, fully, deeply. It burned through into her very soul, igniting her own desire, until she was clinging to him, out of her mind with love and longing, their bodies slowly swaying to the music.

Lost in a delicious haze of love and desire, Tess was yet sufficiently conscious enough to notice when Luke steered them onto an outer balcony, crickets singing in harmony with the orchestra, a warm breeze brushing her cheeks. She and Luke were alone beneath the white stars. Tess had never known such bliss.

While one hand skated across her back, Luke raised her hand to his mouth, his tongue darting out to caress the center of her palm, her gasp driving him to deepen the kiss. She trembled, both from the sensual caress and from his emerald gaze turned smoky with passion. She murmured his name, her voice heavy with desire and somehow not her own and yet wholly hers. But rather than meet the unspoken request, his lips brushed one bare shoulder.

"You feel so right in my arms," he said, his voice ragged. "So right." His lips brushed against the sensitive skin of her throat and Tess arched into him.

With a cry that seemed wrenched from his heart, Luke pulled her into his arms, his mouth finding hers in the next moment, claiming her as she locked her fingers in his thick hair, her tongue dueling with his. Liquid fire melted her bones, shattering the last of the walls she had erected so long ago to protect herself.

It took a moment for her dazed senses to realize that Luke had lifted her into his arms. She stared at him, his face taut, his eyes burning into her.

"I know the perfect way," he said, his voice ragged, "to banish those nightmares of yours."

She breathed a sigh of utter contentment, her head resting on his broad shoulder.

"Yes, please," she said.

Without another word, Luke started for the ballroom door, but Tess, chuckling, stopped him.

"No, no, no," she said with a loving smile. "People will talk and think very scandalous things if they see us like this."

"I don't give a damn."

"Neither do I, actually, but perhaps Jane will. We could always use the back stairs."

Luke's smile was decidedly wicked. "Only once," he said, heading for a parlor door at the far end of the balcony.

"I can walk."

"But not fast enough for me."

In a moment, Luke had found the back stairs to the second floor and was taking them two at a time.

Conceding the point, Tess spent the trip happily nibbling on his ear, which she discovered was as sensitive as her own.

"Need any help?" she asked as Luke stopped in front of his bedroom door.

"No, thanks," he said, tossing her over his shoulder. As she giggled, he opened the door, walked into his room, kicked the door shut, locked it, and then set her down on the floor. He leaned his back against the door, his smile sensual and sure as he held her in his arms. "Marry me, Elizabeth."

Whoever would have thought three words could set the world to heaving under her feet?

"Marry you? *Marry you?* You've been trying to toss me into jail ever since we met and you want me to *marry you?*"

"Yes," Luke calmly replied.

Shock replaced the surprise. He meant it. Tess nervously shook her head. "Don't, Luke. Not now. No."

Rather than looking hurt, Luke smiled. "Wrong answer. Try again. I told Jane my intentions toward you are strictly honorable, but that look in your eyes is chasing away all my good intentions. Marry me, Tess."

"I can't," she whispered, unable to move from his arms.

"Of course you can marry me," Luke said. He kissed her molasses slow and sweet, stirring the hunger in her. As his mouth moved over hers, she forgot the answer to the question. She forgot the question and everything else except the need to take everything this glorious man offered and return it tenfold.

Luke's hand found the zipper at the back of her black gown. "I've been wanting to take this dress off you all night," he said, his fingers slowly tugging the zipper down.

"Why else do you think I bought it?" Tess murmured as her trembling fingers unbuttoned his jacket.

"You bought it to drive me insane," Luke said, his mouth tasting the warm flesh of her throat.

Tess was finding it difficult to talk. "I . . . didn't realize I was so transparent."

"Not transparent," Luke said, his hands sliding the black gown down until it pooled at her feet. "A maze, a delectable maze. But I've found the path to the heart of you." He gazed down at her as she stood naked except for a very brief pair of black satin panties. "My God, you're beautiful," he breathed.

His hands swept up, as if compelled, to cup her breasts, his thumbs brushing across her nipples. They hardened instantly at his touch, reaching out as if begging for more, her breasts swelling in his hands. Slowly he dipped his head and drew one taut nipple into his mouth, tugging at it. Tess's moan came from deep within her.

"Luke, please! I want to see you, touch you, love you."

"I'll try not to be selfish," Luke murmured, his gaze traveling the length of her once more. "But I think you're going to have trouble getting equal time."

Tess smiled as she methodically removed his bow tie and began to unbutton his silk shirt. "Such a generous lover," she said, pushing his shirt and jacket off his shoulders, heedless of where they fell on the floor.

With only the tips of her fingers, she explored the muscled planes of his chest, hypnotized by taut flesh and his sharp intake of breath as her hands swept over him. She had never thought she could want a man like this.

"I feel," she said shakily, "like I could devour you."

"I want you in my bed *now*!" he rasped just before he picked her up, lifting her out of her shoes, and carried her to the massive mahogany bed.

"As if I would complain," Tess murmured. She slid to the middle of the large bed, resting on her knees as she watched Luke quickly discard the rest of his clothes.

There was a roaring in her ears. She forgot to breathe as she stared at him.

Oh, beautiful! Why hadn't anyone told her that

a man could be so beautiful? They had made love twice before and his impact seemed only to grow. He was sharply defined planes of muscle, broad chest, narrow hips, long, muscular legs, his hunger for her stark, compelling. She looked up, meeting his gaze, and trembled at his need for her. It was as raw and primitive as her need for him. It filled her, consumed her, ruled her.

"Come here," she said, her voice husky.

With a growl, Luke pushed her back onto the bed, his hands sliding down to their only remaining barrier. Tess eagerly arched her hips and he brushed the black satin away. Then he reached for her, breathing a ragged sigh as her arms wrapped around him and held him fast.

"Hey!" he said when she suddenly rolled him on to his back. She grinned lasciviously and began to feast on him.

Her mouth teased his already hard male nipples as a leg stroked one of his hair-roughened legs, loving the harshness against her smooth skin as she loved the groan that welled up from within him. Then her fingers discovered the hard heat that told of Luke's own need. She stroked him as she gazed down into his eyes.

"Tonight you are mine," she whispered.

Luke's hands cupped her face and pulled her mouth down to his. "Yes," he said, shuddering at her continued caress, "more than I can ever show you."

"Try," Tess urged.

With a wrenching moan, Luke rolled her onto her back, his teeth grazing her shoulder, her throat, as his hands made love to her breasts, her gently rounded stomach, her thighs. Her soft whimpers grew louder as his fingers brushed against the engorged core of her desire, one of his legs thrown across her restless ones, holding them still.

"Luke, please!" she gasped, arching against the feather-light touch of his fingers.

"Marry me," he commanded.

Her eyes widened with shock as she stared up at him, a cry torn from her throat as his fingers brushed harder against her spiraling need. "I can't!" she said. "You don't know—"

"Marry me," Luke repeated before drawing an eager nipple into his mouth, his fingers moving rhythmically against her now.

And Tess, her body remembering the delicious pleasure Luke had taught her twice already, could only shake her head in helpless denial as the heat of his touch burned away everything but the desperate need to have him fill the dark, hungry void within her. He was stretching the painful tension within her, drawing it out, teasing her with what might be until she was pleading with him to take her, to fill her, to release her from this torment.

And all that Luke said was "Marry me."

"I can't!"

"Yes you can," Luke murmured as he pressed feather-light kisses to her mouth, her cheeks, her eyes.

His fingers kept pushing Tess closer and closer to the edge as they explored her wet heat, his own body taut beneath her hands, the length of him pressed against her telling her how much this denial of what they both wanted was costing him.

"Marry me," he said, his fingers sliding partially into her. Tess's hips surged up, striving for more and meeting only denial of what she now needed more than oxygen, more than her own sanity, more than her own fear. "Marry me, Tess," Luke whispered.

"Yes, oh God, yes!" she cried. "Only take me, Luke. Take me now!"

He thrust into her then, both of them crying

out at this union that was unlike anything Tess had ever known. Her heart was singing in her breast to the rhythm of the pounding of Luke's heart. Something new was being born.

Her arms clutched Luke's back, her legs wrapped around his hips so she could feel all of him within her as he held himself still, his muscles rigid, letting them both fully feel this exquisite connection.

Light shimmered through Tess. She trembled as it chased the darkness from her soul. "Oh Luke, I love you so much!"

Groaning, he slowly began to move, Tess holding him tightly, her fingers digging into his back as her body eagerly matched the rhythm he had set, moving with him as he moved in her.

"Mine. You are mine," she whispered again and again, as her body fused with his.

Her hands swept to the back of his head, pulling him down until her mouth claimed his, ravenous, demanding, her tongue thrusting into him as he thrust into her. A primitive force held her in thrall. It burned away the last threads of her control, stripped away any remnants of civilization. It seemed to go on forever, and for just a moment. It was like nothing she had ever known. It was everything she had ever wanted.

Ruthlessly she rolled Luke onto his back so that she was on top of him, riding this incredible wave of tension and pleasure that only grew as she pulled him deeper into her, moaning as his hands cupped her breasts, his thumbs stroking her engorged nipples over and over again.

She was burning up. She was dying. She was flying past the moon.

"*Come with me,*" Tess demanded, arching, pulling Luke into the very core of her being.

Time stopped. Then a tidal wave slammed into them. They both cried out, gasping, shuddering in each other's arms as they were tumbled over and over in the waves, clinging to each other, their hearts pounding as one. Their ragged cries grew softer. The waves pushed them gently together, lapping against them.

Luke's heart was a steady, life-giving drum beneath her cheek.

CHAPTER

17

Tess woke with the morning sunlight trying to push its way through the curtains. The first thing she realized was that, although she had slept, there had been no nightmares. She gazed down lovingly at the man sleeping beside her. He had definitely found a way to banish bad dreams.

They were lying on their sides, facing each other, Luke's arm thrown possessively over her hip. If she shifted even fractionally, his arm would automatically tighten, holding her close. Tess smiled. She liked Luke being so possessive. She liked this feeling of trust that had warmed her all night long as they had slept together for the first time.

What had she told Jane Wednesday night? That she didn't know who she was? Well, she did now. She was a lover of art, emeralds, and Luke Mansfield. She was, it turned out, hopelessly romantic and amazingly old-fashioned when it came to love and marriage. And she liked it that way.

Tess could not remember ever feeling so good. It was impossible that anything that had come before could make her this happy, this secure, this downright ecstatic. This man—this gorgeous, loving, intelligent, funny, sexy man—wanted to marry her, in fact *intended* to marry her no matter how often she got cold feet.

And she had agreed. She had actually said yes!

Marry Luke Mansfield. What a crazy, dangerous, imperative thing to do. It couldn't be a trap. Not even Luke would go this far. No, this was real and true and she was feeling downright giddy.

Her world had been turned upside down. It was amazing to Tess how much her life had changed in only two weeks. From con artist to married lady . . . well, engaged lady, but she'd be a married lady soon if she had anything to say about it. She liked waking up in Luke's arms in the morning. She'd brave every fear within her to continue such pleasure.

And yet . . . And yet and yet and yet, the truth of why she was in this house would come out. It had to. And Luke would hate her then. As Tess had been hating herself from the moment she had first walked through the Cushman front door. She had deceived and used the people she loved for her own ends. How could they forgive her that?

She had to protect them from the truth. She had to protect her own heart. But how?

She searched desperately for something, anything, that would help her now. Luke's arm tightened around her and her heart opened like a blooming flower. She had her answer.

Maybe . . . Maybe she *could* become Elizabeth! They already believed her to be Elizabeth. They had said so. Jane needed an heir, Luke wanted a wife, Tess longed for a family. Maybe . . . Tess began to tremble. Maybe it would work. Maybe her love could create a new life for herself.

Her mind exploded with the future she could claim. Jane would not be hurt, Luke would never know the shameful truth, and she would have their love. They would have hers. A hundredfold. She could do it! She could turn fantasy into reality. She could have the family she had always longed for.

The idea left her dizzy, exhilarated, terrified.

Then she realized that Luke's eyes were open and gazing woozily at her. Oh yes. She would do whatever it took to wake up every morning for the rest of her life in this man's arms.

"Good morning," she said, her lips warm on his for a moment and then she pulled away. "Would Monsieur like one or two bowls of Wheaties this morning?"

Chuckling, Luke rolled them over so that he was on his back, Tess lying on top of him. "I would rather have you for breakfast," he said, his teeth grazing her shoulder.

"No, no, no!" Tess said in her French accent. "The affianced bride is not on the menu this morning, monsieur. You had her for a midnight snack, if you will recall."

"Oh, I do," Luke blithely assured her, "intimately. But not only am I still hungry, I'm addicted. I have to have all of you, always."

Tess felt her happiness explode into a one-million-kilowatt glow. "I think," she murmured in her own voice, "that that can be arranged." She slowly slid down the length of his body, kissing, biting, licking her way down, pushing the comforter back as she went. "As it happens, I've become a raving addict myself."

"Glad to hear it," Luke gasped.

"Today," Tess said solemnly, looking up at him, "is the first day of the rest of our lives."

Luke groaned. "Platitudes at dawn! What have I done?"

Tess smiled a very wicked smile. "I'm about to show you."

Then she saw the clock on the bedside table.

"Oh no!" she cried, pushing herself off both Luke and the bed.

"Hey!" Luke lunged for her, but missed. "What do you think you're doing?" he demanded as Tess hurriedly gathered up her dress.

"It's nearly seven. People will be out and about soon." It was a good excuse. Mostly, she was worried about Bert's henchmen being out and about. She wanted them reporting none of her extracurricular activities to Bert. He had already made his disapproval clear.

"So?"

"So, I can't very well creep back to my room in this state with people watching me from every doorway, can I?"

"I like your state."

"Thank you. Where did you toss my . . . um . . . panties?"

Luke clasped his hands behind his head and failed to look innocent. "Hm?"

"Luke Mansfield, where are my panties?"

He leaned over the bed, snagged a black scrap with his index finger and lifted it into the air. "You mean these?"

"Yes, thank you. Luke!"

He had placed the black satin under his pillow, which he plumped. He then resumed his former position. "Hm?"

"Luke, hand them over. Now!"

Luke smiled a very friendly smile. "You'll have to come get them yourself."

"Oh, sure," Tess scoffed, arms akimbo, "and end up in bed for the next fifty years. I am not that gullible. Hand them over. I cannot saunter down the hallway without my panties."

"Why not? Your very delectable derriere will

be covered by that scandalous dress. Who's to know of the absence or presence of undergarments?"

"*I'll* know. Hand them over."

"Uh-uh."

"Knowing a little of my history, Luke Mansfield, you should not be toying with my tendency for revenge."

Luke took his time considering this threat, then sighed and tossed her the scrap of black satin.

"Thank you," Tess said, beginning to dress.

"There must be better ways to thank me."

"Undoubtedly. But none of them would get me out of this room before noon, and I do not want the thirty people who spent the night in this house to know that we're . . . um . . . involved. I have enough questions to answer as it is."

"All right," Luke said, sitting up and running a hand through his rumpled hair. "The engagement is hush-hush until Jane's guests leave. But that doesn't mean—"

"Yes, it does," Tess said, stepping into her shoes. "No reports of lust from this quarter, if you please."

"Hell," Luke muttered.

Tess blew him a kiss, opened the door, checked left and right, and then scurried to her room, only breathing when she had closed her bedroom door behind her.

Standing in the middle of her bedroom, she stared at nothing, just feeling the glow that had been ignited last night. It warmed her skin and her heart. With a happy sigh, she began to strip off the clothes she had so recently put on. She would have to see to it that she never again had to leave Luke in the lurch, because it left her in the lurch as well and, although they had made love for hours and hours the night before, Tess found that she wanted more. Needed more. She could have happily spent the day in bed with him, and the night, and the next day . . .

"Hell," she muttered, striding into her bathroom.

She turned the shower on scalding and then stood under the water, letting it pour over her body which recalled in every nerve, every muscle, every inch of skin the love she had received and expressed the night before.

Then the shower door opened and Tess was no longer alone.

"Excuse me," she said with the greatest dignity, holding her soaked hair away from her eyes, "what are you doing here?"

"Finishing what you began, and fulfilling a little fantasy of my own," Luke replied as he pulled her against his naked, aroused body.

Tess gasped at the contact, her body flooding with heat. "M-m-most household accidents occur in the bath, you know."

"Really?" Luke said, his hands sliding over her slippery skin. "How interesting." His mouth covered the pulse at the base of her throat and sucked gently.

"W-w-we shouldn't," Tess said, although her hands were already stroking him.

Luke's fingers slid against the slippery center of her own need. "You're in no state to protest," he murmured.

"I—I—I know! Luke, please, I can't wait. I can't—"

"So ready for me," Luke marveled, his fingers intimately caressing her as he pressed her back against the shower wall. Both arms supporting her trembling body, he suddenly thrust up into her, Tess muffling her cry as her teeth sank into his shoulder, Luke's ragged moan mingling with the pounding hot water.

An hour later, they were showered, shampooed, dried, dressed in appropriate attire, and grinning at each other.

"You go first," Luke said. "It will look less suspicious that way."

"Me go first?" Tess said. "Anyone with half an eye would see that I can barely stand. You go first and let me have a minute to get my strength back."

"We could go down together."

"Brilliant," Tess said. "Our hair is damp, our skin is flushed, our eyes are glowing. Even a nun could figure out what was going on."

"All right, all right," Luke said. "I'll go first."

"Get that self-satisfied smirk off your face first."

Luke sighed heavily. "A night and morning of rapture and I have to act like I haven't enjoyed anything more exciting than a game of Scrabble. This is not the way I planned to spend our engagement."

"I *know* how you planned to spend our engagement and we'll discuss it later," Tess said firmly. "Now out!"

Luke salaamed his way to the bedroom door, opened it, looked left and right, threw her a lazy salute, and then sauntered into the hallway. Tess, whose legs felt like half-melted gelatin, collapsed onto her bed and concentrated on removing the flush from her skin and the glow from her eyes.

Ten minutes later she walked downstairs, outwardly calm, inwardly glowing, and into the main dining room to find a huge breakfast buffet set up on tables that lined all four walls. Discovering that she was famished, she piled a plate with enough food to feed two lumberjacks—and their progeny—and then went in search of the glow maker.

There weren't many people out and about yet, but Luke wasn't among those loitering on the back terrace. She checked two parlors and the living room before she found him all alone in the Belle Epoque salon, seated at the chess table, his breakfast before him.

"Eating for two?" he asked with a leer as he waved a fork at her overburdened plate. "We never managed to find a means of protection last night, or this morning, you know."

"I am refueling my badly depleted stores of energy," Tess loftily retorted as she walked to his side, "and I don't need to protect myself from anything you and I might create. Luke!" she screeched as her affianced husband pulled her down onto his lap. "Be careful, my breakfast!"

"Damn your breakfast," Luke muttered just before his mouth captured hers in a long kiss that turned Tess's legs to gelatin once again.

"Should I be shocked?" Jane politely inquired from the doorway.

Tess cringed.

"Morning, Jane," Luke called, one arm holding Tess firmly on his lap when she surreptitiously tried to escape. "How are you feeling after last night's revels?"

"Oh, I'm in fine fettle," Jane replied, her pale blue eyes gleaming as she gazed at Tess and Luke. "You two disappeared rather early, I thought."

"Tess and I spent hours wrestling with our . . . future," Luke gravely replied, a grin tugging at the corners of his mouth as Tess's blush deepened. "I am happy to report, Jane, that I have been able to make good on my promise to you. Truth, justice, and the American way won out. Tess and I are getting married."

"Well, that's marvelous!" Jane exclaimed to Tess's utter surprise. "And about time, too. When is the happy day?"

"We haven't really talked about it yet," Luke said. "I figure three days for the blood test or three hours for the flight to Vegas if my patience can't hold out."

"Very sound thinking," Jane said, beaming at Tess. "I couldn't be happier for you, dear."

"Thank you, Jane," Tess said, her eyes filling with tears as she realized in that moment just how much she loved the older woman. "That means a lot to me."

"If you can stand to wait three days," Jane said, "I'd very much like it if you could be married here. This old house needs a good dose of love and gaiety."

"Oh Jane . . ." Tess said.

"My dear, I insist," Jane said, cupping her face and smiling down at her. "Now you two eat your breakfast and we'll talk some more after I return from church."

"Jane!" Tess called. "The engagement is a secret until tomorrow."

"Yes, dear," Jane said with a smile, and then she was gone.

Tess glared at Luke. "Just when, exactly, did you promise Jane you'd marry me?"

"Wednesday. I'd have promised her sooner than that, but she never asked."

Tess sighed, slid off Luke's lap, and took the chair opposite him, setting her plate down on the marble chess board. "Are lawyers always so sure of themselves?"

"Not at all. I was just sure of you."

"Just because I'm putty in your hands is no reason to get cocky."

"You want to rephrase that?"

Tess groaned and buried her face in her hands. "It wouldn't help."

As they turned to the breakfasts before them, other guests entered the salon, cheerfully greeting them as they took the other chairs in the room to eat their breakfasts, occasionally calling out a comment to the pair, but generally leaving them alone. Luke watched as Tess slowly, and methodically, cleaned her plate.

"That was impossible," he said as she finally leaned back in her chair with a satisfied sigh.

"I told you I was rebuilding my strength."

"No woman can eat that amount of food and live."

"My energy reserves were depleted. *You're* the one with the high testosterone level, so don't go chastising *my* appetite."

Luke's eyebrows shot up. "My, the double entendres are flying fast and thick this morning."

"Don't be mean," Tess said, sinking lower into her chair as her blush climbed higher into her cheeks. "I've never been engaged before. *Everything's* coming out wrong."

"I wouldn't say that," Luke said with a grin.

"Sadist."

Laughing, Luke rose, caught her hand in his, pulled her to her feet, and together they walked outside to take in the fresh air and sunshine.

Tess had only just recovered her equilibrium, when Hodgkins approached with chilly formality to announce that Dr. Weinstein had come to call. Hodgkins had placed the doctor in the morning parlor, he hoped Miss Cushman approved.

"I'll come with you," Luke said.

"No, it's not necessary."

Luke held her hand firmly in his. "It's necessary to me. I can't bear having you out of my sight."

Tess was too dazed by this declaration to think of any sort of argument.

They entered the morning parlor arm in arm to find Bert, dressed as Max Weinstein, glasses and leonine wig firmly in place, standing beside a window that looked out over the front drive.

"Hello, Max," Tess said cheerfully. "Welcome back from Seattle."

Bert turned and beamed at Tess, his face betraying no surprise at seeing Luke by her side. "Tess, I saw the morning papers. I couldn't believe it! Why didn't you call and tell me?"

"Jane sprang the whole thing on me Wednesday night, Max, and you were out of town."

"I am so very pleased for you, Tess," Bert said, taking her hand in his. "Certainly I am happy that Mrs. Cushman has found her granddaughter again. But you, Tess, do you truly believe now that you are Elizabeth?"

"I haven't got much choice, Max. The proof is kind of overwhelming."

"She put up a good fight," Luke said, "but we were able to convince her in the end. Jane and I . . . owe you a great deal, Dr. Weinstein."

"Ah, Mr. Mansfield," Bert said. "If *you* are convinced of my patient's true identity, then I know I need not worry."

"Good of you," Luke said.

"It's all been so crazy, Max," Tess said quickly to cover Luke's tension. What on earth was wrong with the man? "I feel like I've met half the state of New York this weekend. Jane . . . I mean my grandmother, is introducing me to *everyone*. Oh, and she wants me to sign some legal papers tomorrow that Luke's office is drawing up. She's making a new will for herself and she's transferring some of Eliz . . . I mean *my* inheritance over to me immediately. Do you think you could drop by afterward, say around two, to help me celebrate? I was thinking along the lines of magnums of champagne."

Bert smiled a pleased, silky smile. "I would be honored, Tess, although I'm not much of a one for drinking. I'd be happy to raise a glass of champagne in your honor."

"It would make everything complete for me," Tess said. "After all, if it weren't for you, I never would have found my family again."

"And your memory?" Bert inquired with professional concern.

"A few snatches of things have come back, mostly about my parents. I can see their faces more clearly in my mind. But nothing really concrete yet."

"Well, now that you are back home to stay, I'm sure your memory will return soon."

"Speaking of which," Tess said and then turned to Luke. "Luke, would you mind if I had a minute alone with Max? Patient-client privilege? You understand."

If he could have glared at her, he would have, Tess knew. Instead, all Luke could do was smile, say "Of course," and leave the room.

The minute the door was closed, Bert burst out laughing. "Tess, baby, you were great! How the hell did you pull it off?"

"I told you patience was a virtue, Bert. The accumulation of evidence overwhelmed the old lady to the point that she was begging me to wear the Farleigh."

"I knew you were the one to pull this off. I knew it!"

"Ah now, Bert, don't make me blush. Look," Tess said, taking his arm and pulling him away from the window, her voice low, "I'm serious about you turning up tomorrow afternoon. These papers I'll be signing will bring me into *beaucoup* bucks right off the bat, with more to follow when the old lady finally kicks the bucket. I figure tomorrow afternoon you and I can go off by ourselves for a minute. I'll be wearing the necklace, we make the switch with the paste job, and you walk out into early retirement."

"Sounds good, babe. I need to make a few plans myself. I'll meet you here at two. Just one thing: this Mansfield goon seemed a bit tense. Is he going to mess things up?"

Tess laughed. "Bert, I've got that poor guy so tied up in knots, he doesn't know whether he's coming or going. He was tense because you interrupted us in the middle of a . . . private conversation."

Bert guffawed.

"The guy's neutralized, Bert. There's no need to worry."

"That's my girl, every angle covered." Bert walked to the door and then turned to beam at Tess once again. "You did good, babe. You came through like a pro."

"What can I say? You taught me well."

Bert laughed and walked from the parlor.

Jane, Luke, and Tess stood on the flagstone front steps of the Cushman mansion waving good-bye to the last of Jane's guests a little after five on Sunday afternoon.

"My, that was fun!" Jane said.

"You're not the one who smiled nonstop for seventy-two hours," Tess said with a groan. "My jaws will never be the same again."

Jane chuckled and put an arm around Tess's waist, leading her back into the house, Luke trailing behind. "You were marvelous, my dear. Everyone was billing and cooing over you. I was very proud."

"You know a good bunch of people, Jane," Tess said. "The weekend was no hardship . . . except for the incessant smiling."

Jane patted her hand. "Now that you are officially my granddaughter, I think it's time to let you in on a family secret. Come along, Tess, there's something in my bedroom you ought to see."

"Jane, are you sure this is the right time?" Luke said.

"It is time and past time," Jane retorted. "Come along."

"What's going on?" Tess asked as they walked upstairs.

"It is time you knew the truth about yourself, Elizabeth," Jane said.

Puzzled by a secret that had Luke looking worried, Tess entered Jane's inner sanctum. It was a large room with an Art Deco design. Books lined one wall, a pale green carpet covered the floor.

"Have you ever seen a picture of my great-grandmother?" Jane asked. "No? She was very beautiful, even in her seventies and eighties. The women in my family have always been long-lived, you know. I inherited her portrait from my mother and I have always treasured it. My great-grandmother, you see, had the drollest sense of humor, and she never coddled me as the rest of my family did. I always went into her company with a sense of relief and freedom. She was a priceless treasure. As are you, my dear. That's her portrait, over the bureau."

Wondering what in the world Jane was up to, Tess obligingly looked up at the portrait.

It was a picture of a woman in a sea-green antebellum ball gown, a woman who was Tess's twin.

She felt as if someone had just punched the air from her lungs.

"I don't understand," she managed to say.

"You see, Tess," Jane said gently, "while I have always suspected that your Dr. Weinstein was a fraud, I have known that you are Elizabeth from the moment you first entered this house."

"We know you came here to work a con,

Tess," Luke said quietly. "We know all about that monster you call Bert. We know about the threats he made against our lives. We know he wants the Farleigh."

The world was crashing around Tess, lacerating her heart with jagged chunks of glass. *Nothing lasts forever.*

"How . . . do you know?" she said raggedly.

"Baldwin Security has been taping his every move," Luke replied. "Bert got careless on Wednesday. We got your entire meeting on video."

Tess swayed with sudden vertigo. So Luke knew she had betrayed him and he'd been using her ever since to get a little of his own back. She was Margo Holloway all over again.

Every moment in his arms had been a lie and she hadn't known!

"So that's why you avoided me Thursday and Friday," she said, feeling dead inside.

"Avoided you?" Luke said with a frown. "I was working, Tess. I wasn't avoiding you. I thought about you every minute of those two days. I've been so distracted by you that my work went to hell and my staff broke out in open rebellion. I had to work so I could have this weekend free. So I could be with you."

"Very pretty. But if you knew about the con," Tess said in a low voice, trying not to let them see the trembling that threatened to overwhelm her, "why did you let me make a fool of myself this weekend? Why didn't you throw me out or call the cops? Why did you . . . Last night . . . I don't understand."

"The con never mattered to either of us, Tess," Luke said gently. "You stole our hearts the moment you first entered this house. We love you. That is all that matters."

"You are my granddaughter," Jane said firmly,

"whatever your purpose in coming to me. That is all *I* care about."

For one brief moment the world spun wildly around her, and then Tess got a firm grip on herself. Despite the harsh pounding of her heart, she shook her head again.

"No. If you know about Bert, then the jig is up. Take the wish out of your hearts and accept that I am a fraud. Bert probably knew about this portrait and that's why he chose me—because of the physical resemblance. I've told you and told you and told you: I'm not Elizabeth. I'm not!"

"It isn't only the physical resemblance to my great-grandmother, Tess," Jane said. "You have the appendix scar from an acute appendicitis attack that Dr. Weston tells me probably occurred when you were four. That is when Elizabeth had her appendix removed. You have the scar behind your right knee that not even your Bert could have known about. You were two and you accidentally dropped a glass of juice in the kitchen. It shattered, you slipped and fell, and a shard of glass punctured the skin behind your knee."

The dizziness returned. For one horrific moment, Tess felt glass cutting into her leg. Pain stabbed into her knee and thrust up into her head like a sword. Slowly she rubbed her temples.

"Stop it," she said. "I don't want to be cruel, but you're deluding yourself, Jane. I know every inch of this house because I memorized the blueprints Bert copped. Everything I said about Elizabeth was lines Bert fed me."

"Yes, of course," Jane said soothingly. "But there are times when you are reading a book or eating a meal, when you look exactly like John. You even have Eugenie's mannerisms."

"And you have Elizabeth's laugh," Luke said.

"No!" Tess said. It was harder for her lungs to pull in oxygen.

"Tess, Bert probably knew that you are Elizabeth," Luke said, his hands on her shoulders. But she couldn't feel them. The heat of his skin didn't penetrate the arctic chill that was suffocating her. "That's why he used you. He was probably a partner of Hal Marsh's, or maybe he had something on Marsh, who knows? But it gave him a line on you and—"

"Hal Marsh?" Tess whispered. She couldn't feel her lips. Her breath came in gasps.

"Barbara Carswell told me that she bought you from someone named Hal Marsh," Luke said. "I've got Leroy Baldwin trying to track him down now. Once we get a line on him—"

"The Carswells bought me from Hal Marsh?" Tess said. She couldn't see Luke. She was in a black vortex sucking the air from her lungs.

Dimly, she was aware that Luke's grip on her shoulders had tightened. "Tess, what is it? What's wrong?"

"I . . . I can't breathe! I can't—"

The vortex pulled her under and she plunged into darkness.

CHAPTER

18

Luke stood in a corner of Elizabeth's shadowed bedroom, the faint light of a bedside table lamp illuminating Jane's pale skin as she sat on the bed beside Tess, who was still unconscious. Dr. Weston had left two hours ago, telling them that Tess was merely suffering from shock and to keep her warm and let her rest. Luke had stood in this corner since then, and Jane had sat at Tess's side holding her hand or brushing a wisp of hair from her forehead.

"I should never have told her in that manner," Jane said for the tenth time that hour.

"I think Tess would have had the same reaction no matter how you told her," Luke said gently. "Her mind was used to hiding the truth, not facing it. Don't punish yourself."

Tess began to stir, her head restless on the pillow, a frown tightening her face.

"What is it? What's wrong with her?" Jane said.

Luke walked to the bed and knelt beside her. "Tess told me she has nightmares. She'll be all right."

"Nightmares," Jane said dully, staring down at

Tess. "Her life has been a nightmare and there was nothing I could do to protect her."

"But she inherited your strength, Jane, and that helped her to survive. She's here now and she cares for you very much. Hold on to that and not the pain."

Tess suddenly screamed. Terror and despair poured into the room before Jane enfolded her in her arms, slowly rocking her.

"It's all right, my dear," she crooned. "Grandmother is here. You're not alone. I won't leave you, I promise."

With a sigh as if a great weight had been lifted from her, Tess slumped in her arms and Jane laid her gently back on the bed. A moment later, Tess was deeply asleep as Jane continued to hold her hand, staring down at her, motionless.

Luke, however, couldn't stand still a moment longer. He stalked to the window overlooking the back gardens.

"Luke?"

"Yes, Jane?"

"I am not a violent woman. But if I ever find the men who did this to my granddaughter, I will kill them."

"I'll help you."

"Poor child," Jane murmured, turning back to Tess. "So many terrible things to remember."

Luke turned to Jane, compassion in his eyes. Poor Jane, she had had to live through so many terrible things of her own. But she had been right all along. Elizabeth *had* survived the kidnapping and now Jane had her granddaughter back. That was all that mattered. He smiled as he remembered how easily she had reeled him in on Wednesday after they had watched the Baldwin Security tape. A devious woman was Jane Cushman.

•   •   •

"And what will become of Tess?" she had asked on Wednesday.

"I think that I had better steer her into a less murky future."

"Good boy. I do trust that your intentions toward my granddaughter are honorable?"

"Strictly honorable," Luke assured her with a grin . . . which evaporated. "Granddaughter?"

"Yes, of course."

Feeling grim, Luke rose from his chair and did his best to loom over Jane. "I've danced to your tune long enough, Mrs. Cushman. Just what is going on? What do you know that I don't?"

Jane, far from being intimidated, smiled and patted his arm as if he were five. "I'll tell you in a moment, dear. But first, tell me something. What made you trust Tess in the face of that horrible video?"

Luke had searched his heart and answered slowly. "I love her. With all of the reasons not to staring me in the face, I love her. I trust myself. I trust my instincts. I wouldn't have fallen in love with another Margo. I've got too many defenses in place. I know Tess's heart. However good a con she is, she can't be the Jekyll and Hyde that miserable tape made her. It's not in her to be that unfeeling and cold. That's the only thing anyone needs to know about Tess."

Jane poured brandy into two glasses and handed him one. "I think a short engagement would be best."

Luke saluted her with his glass. "Very short. And now, Mrs. Cushman, will you please tell me why, in spite of all that you have seen and heard, you still believe Tess to be Elizabeth?"

Jane took her time, sipping her brandy, pale blue eyes twinkling at him, fully aware of his impatience. "First, there are a few small things, subtle things that no one but I would notice. There have been times when Tess thought herself alone and unobserved and she held her head in such a way or stood in such another way, and I was looking at Eugenie or John. She has their mannerisms, Luke. Certainly, Tess could have learned about the playhouse and Fred and the swing, but she could not have known how to tilt her head the way John used to do when he was lost in thought."

Jane's words were like a prizefighter's blow to Luke's midsection. "My God," he said, "you're right! When we've argued, something would nag at me and I didn't realize what it was until just now. When Tess gets angry, she looks like Eugenie, she *sounds* like Eugenie! The resemblance is uncanny."

"Yes, it is, isn't it?" Jane said with a smile.

"But there's more," Luke said suspiciously. "There has to be more. You were certain Tess was Elizabeth before she ever moved into this house. Come on, Jane Cushman, give!"

Jane had smiled a sphinxlike smile. "I'll show you tonight when we get home, dear."

Now the secrets were out and Luke stood watching over the woman he loved with Jane. Tess was white and still. She looked so fragile.

Kill the men who had done this to Tess? Who had stolen safety and love and happiness from her? Oh no. Slow torture wouldn't even be satisfying enough. Sitting in this child's room, he thought of the strong-willed happy child he had known, and the strong-willed haunted woman he loved, and he felt a ravening need to do something, anything. And all he could do now was wait.

The hours slowly passed. Neither he nor Jane felt like making conversation. Neither of them felt like eating. Finally, as the clock on the mantel began to chime three o'clock, Luke rose and walked over to Jane.

"You should go to bed," he said. "I'll watch over her."

"I told her I would stay."

Luke gripped her shoulder and made her look at him. "Jane, you're exhausted. Tess will sleep for hours yet. It's in the morning that she'll need all your strength and love. She still has a lot to get through. As you said, she has too many terrible things to remember. Go to bed, Jane. Take care of yourself so you can take care of her."

Jane sighed and rose stiffly to her feet. "Very well," she said. "But if Tess so much as stirs one toe, I want you to wake me."

"You have my word," Luke said, kissing her forehead.

Jane walked to the door and then turned back for a moment. "Luke?"

"Yes?"

"I'm very glad that you love her."

Luke smiled. "So am I, Jane. So am I."

For the next three hours, Tess did not stir and Luke's eyes never left her face. She looked so young, so helpless, like the child she had never had the chance to fully be. How he wished he had a magic wand that could give her back all that had been taken from her, but he could not. All that he could do was love her now and forever, giving her the life that she deserved and needed.

The clock on the mantel softly chimed six o'clock and suddenly Tess's eyes flew open. "Time to get up," she announced in a child's voice.

Luke was so startled that he laughed. "Is it?"

Tess frowned and slowly the cloud cleared from her blue eyes. She turned her head on the pillow. "Luke?" It was her own voice.

"Yes, my love?"

"I feel . . . so odd. Where am I?"

"In bed."

"I don't remember . . ."

"It's all right," Luke said, his long fingers smoothing the frown from her brow. "Don't try to force anything."

"I feel like I swallowed a bottle of barbiturates." Tess stopped and looked up at him. "Did I?"

"*No.*"

"Then why does my body feel so drugged?"

"You're still feeling the aftereffects of shock. Just relax and it will pass off soon enough."

"Shock?" Tess closed her eyes for a moment, her face tight with concentration. Then her eyes flew back open. "Luke! I—I—I'm Elizabeth!"

"Yes, my love, I know."

Tess jerked up into a sitting position and stared straight ahead. "I'm Elizabeth," she whispered. She began to shake so violently that her teeth chattered.

Luke sat on the narrow bed beside her and pulled her into his arms, frightened by how cold she felt, his stomach knotting as she continued to shake in his arms.

"Easy, my love, easy," he murmured.

"Oh God, Luke," Tess gasped, "the nightmare was real!" She uttered a sob that sounded as if it had been ripped from her. It was followed by another, and then another, until she was weeping uncontrollably in his arms.

He held her tight and crooned to her and rocked her and still the weeping continued. He knew that it had to be this way. He knew that twenty years of pain and terror were finally being released. She had to go through this if she was ever going to reach the other side of the violence acted upon her so long ago. And he hated it. And he was grateful that he could hold her when she needed that so much.

She wept for over an hour, as if drawing from a

twenty-year-old well of tears. Then slowly the crying calmed, her body lost some of its tension, her breathing became easier. Luke reached over and pulled several tissues from the box on the bedside table. He gently dried her tearstained face and told her to blow her nose. Then he held her close once again and continued to rock her, crooning words of love until Tess's heavy eyelids closed. Without a word, she fell into an exhausted sleep.

Moving carefully, Luke kicked off his shoes and got under the covers with her, holding her close, keeping the chill from her body with the warmth of his until he too fell asleep.

"I must say it is a good thing you two are engaged, or I might very well be outraged by such a sight."

Luke forced his eyes open and stared blearily up at Jane, who was smiling.

"What time is it?" he asked, his voice as low as hers had been.

"It's just after eleven. How is she?"

"Better, I think. She woke up around six, cried forever, and then finally fell back asleep. I didn't have a chance to come get you."

"So I see," Jane said. "Let her rest a little longer, but then she'll have to get up, I'm afraid. Isn't that awful Bert person coming at two?"

"Yes," Luke said grimly, "he is. Don't worry, Jane. I'll make sure Tess is ready in time."

CHAPTER

19

Tess woke to the sensation of being kissed on her forehead, her temple, her eyes, her nose, her cheeks. Only when she turned her head in silent request was her mouth kissed as well. She opened her eyes and met Luke's warm green gaze.

"How do you feel?" he asked.

For a moment, the innocuous question almost sent her into hysterics. But everything had already clicked into place in her mind and she forced herself to begin the new role she would have to play now.

"Nicely kissed, thank you," she said, stretching herself along the length of Luke's body. His warmth had no effect on the ice covering her soul. "I feel like I've slept for years."

"Just a few hours. You had a rough night."

"Tell me about it," Tess said, adopting a wry expression. "How on earth I am going to be Elizabeth after today I don't know. I've never been a real person before."

That Luke was startled was clear, but apparently he made the decision to go along with the tone she had set.

"Just be yourself and that will be Elizabeth," he said. "It'll come easily to you in no time."

"It's all very disconcerting, you know."

"You've got people who love you to help you over the rough spots."

Tess smiled, her lips brushing Luke's mouth for a moment. Then she sat up. "You're going to make me a wonderful husband. You do still want to marry me even though I really am Elizabeth, don't you?"

"Absolutely."

"Good. What time is it?"

"Eleven-thirty."

"Eleven-thirty?" Tess shrieked. "Bert will be here at two!"

"Calm down, calm down, everything's covered. My office sent a courier down Saturday with all the papers we need. You have plenty of time to shower, eat, and prepare yourself for whatever it is you've got planned. You do have something planned, don't you?"

Tess forced back the hysteria with every ounce of Cushman willpower she possessed. "Fishing will not help," she informed Luke. "Everything is top secret."

"I'm not just anyone, you know," he pointed out.

"No, you're not," Tess said, kissing him again. "You're the most wonderful man in the world and you are blocking my exit from bed."

Luke glanced at his leg thrown across both of hers. "So I am."

"If you would be so kind, Mr. Mansfield. I have places to go, people to see, things to do."

"Tess," Luke said, openly worried now, "we have to talk."

No, Tess thought, *I have to shriek and wail and keen for the next twenty years to rid myself of the pain twisting my soul.*

"Of course we have to talk," she retorted,

"that's what keeps marriages healthy and strong. But right now, I need to shower and get ready to see Bert."

Luke gripped her shoulders and forced her to look up at him. "Dammit, Tess, we have to talk now! I don't know what you think you're doing—"

"I am trying to get you out of my bed," Tess said, pushing at him. "You're the one who let me oversleep, now you have to pay the piper. Get up and out, Mr. Mansfield."

Luke went ballistic. "The hell I will!" he shouted. "I am not moving one inch until you tell me what is going on!"

Tess threw herself out the other side of the bed and stood glaring at him as fiercely as he glared at her. "Who are you to tell me what to do?" she demanded. "I am not your trained poodle. I am an independent woman and I intend to stay that way, married or not!"

"Dammit, Tess," Luke seethed as he stood and glared at her in return, the bed between them, "we're supposed to be engaged. We're supposed to love each other! Trust has to be a part of anything between us. It has to! But here you are planning something dangerous—oh yes, I can see it in your eyes so don't you dare try to deny it—and you aren't telling me anything! You're lying to me by pretending everything is all right when you and I both know this is probably the most devastating morning of your life!"

"How dare you *presume* to tell me what I feel and what I think!" Tess exploded as she marched around the bed and began pushing him toward the door with as much strength as she possessed. "You are not Edgar Bergen and I am not Charlie McCarthy. You will know what I feel when I tell you and not before. You don't know me, Luke Mansfield, you don't know anything about me. Oh, you've got the facts all right, but how about the truth that you keep harping on? How about the plain simple truth that I don't need you and I don't want you right now. What I want is a little privacy!"

Emerald eyes blazed down at her. "You don't want me? You don't need me? Fine! Play your little games with Bert and do your solo act as long as you like. You'll find out soon enough the only thing you'll win is loneliness!"

Luke stormed from the room, slamming the door behind him. She heard him stomp down the hallway and then suddenly stop. "The little she-cat was baiting me!" he gasped.

She cringed . . . and then jumped as he began to pound on her locked door. "Open this door, Elizabeth Aurora Cushman! You're not chasing me off that easily. Open this door and fight square, damn you!"

"I am going to take a shower now," Tess said tightly, arms wrapped around herself as she began to back away.

"You are very, very good at what you do, Tess. But don't try to railroad me again. I'm wise to you now. You may have got me out of your room, but no way in hell are you getting rid of me. Open this door!"

Tess backed into the bathroom, her hands over her ears, trying to block out Luke's voice. It didn't help. She could still hear him cajoling her into trusting him for these last few hours of her life as Tess Alcott and she couldn't! She loved him too much to put his life in any more danger than she already had.

She turned the shower on full blast, closed and locked her bathroom door, and then waited a little breathlessly to see if Luke would break down her bedroom door, come up with a key, or use a screwdriver to remove the hinges. One minute passed. Two. She almost let herself breathe again.

When five minutes had passed, she stripped off the pajamas Jane and Dr. Weston had put on her the night before, and stepped into the shower.

The moment the scalding water hit her, the first five years of her life flooded into her brain. The last day of those five years was there in stark clarity.

He was there. Hal Marsh, tall and skinny, red hair, bushy red mustache, and a smile so utterly terrifying that she had wet herself in his arms and he had slapped her hard, once, twice, the shock silencing her cries. No one had ever hit her before.

Hal Marsh.

After all these years to remember that monster. To see him as clearly in her mind now as she had twenty years ago.

In her bedroom.

Elizabeth. She was Elizabeth Cushman and Hal Marsh had lifted her from her bed . . .

"Stop it, stop it, stop it," Tess said through clenched teeth, her fist slamming repeatedly into her thigh.

There was no time to wrestle with the memories of that day, with the five years of memories lost to her until last night. No time to long for Luke's arms to hold her now and hold the terror at bay.

She had to cope with an entirely new identity for herself, her head felt ready to split open, her heart ripped to shreds, and Tess simply could not deal with any of it now. The present, the next two and a half hours, demanded all of her attention, all of her concentration, all of her cunning if she was going to successfully rewrite the script.

"Hell," she muttered as she turned her face into the hot water. She wanted to crawl into Luke's arms and hide there forever. She wanted to hold Jane's hand and make herself believe that she was holding her grandmother's hand. She wanted to see her parents one last time, hear their laughter, feel their love.

Her parents. Oh God, her poor dead parents. She needed time to grieve their loss, too.

Instead, she grimly reached for the shampoo and began to wash her hair.

Ten minutes later, a towel wrapped around her head, her bathrobe belted at her waist, her emotions precariously locked away, Tess marched out of the bathroom, listened carefully at her bedroom door (which was still intact), heard nothing, and pulled on her underwear. Then she sat down on her bed and picked up her bedside phone. It was answered on the second ring.

"Hello?" The voice was female and Irish.

"May I speak with Cyril Bainbridge, please?" Tess said.

"Cyril is taking a Valium right now. You're late, Tess. We've been going out of our minds!"

"I'm sorry, Gladys, things got a little out of hand here for a while. I'm planning a surprise party at two. Can you make it?"

"It'll be tight. But with a decent radar detector, we should make it, love. You made quite a splash in the news. Cyril and I are very proud."

"Thanks. Now, I don't want you joining the party until after I'm alone with Bert and signal you."

"You're not being reckless, are you, Tess? My nerves can't stand reckless just now."

Tess couldn't help but smile. Gladys had the steadiest nerves in the business. Tess only wished she had the same. "Everything is going to go like clock-work, Gladys, trust me." She cringed at the phrase and hurried on. "We've come too far for me to go suddenly stupid on you."

"All right, love. You know you can count on us. I'll tell Cyril he can finally lay off the Valium."

"Great," Tess said and hung up the phone with a smile. Cyril was the last human being on earth to put drugs into his body. Even aspirin was anathema to him.

Tess, on the other hand, was finding a bottle of Valium to be a very attractive idea.

Instead, she went back into the bathroom and dried her hair. Then she dressed in a full-length pale green satin gown that Grace Kelly might have worn around the house. She clasped the Farleigh around her throat, and stared at herself in the mirror over the bureau.

The Farleigh was staggering. It was made up of a quality of emerald you couldn't buy anymore. The twenty-two carat gold setting was simply designed to show off the dark emeralds. The combination was a little heavy around her neck, as if insisting that she be aware and appreciative of it every moment she wore it.

"You are Elizabeth Cushman," she said to her reflection.

Anger welled within her. Good. She needed anger now. It would get her through her newest charade.

She pulled her jewelry case from a dresser drawer, opened the false bottom, and pulled out the small automatic pistol she had stolen days ago from her grandfather's gun collection in the library. Really, the security system in this house was shocking. It was a good thing Solitaire was coming on Tuesday.

She checked the full clip and then slipped the gun into a side pocket. She stood in front of the bureau mirror and studied herself from every angle. The gown had been a good choice. The small gun was undetectable and she would be careful to have her hand in the pocket a good deal of the time.

"Show time," she whispered to her mirrored image.

She opened her bedroom door to find Luke lounging against the opposite hall wall.

"She emerges," he proclaimed in rolling accents, "like Venus from a half-shell."

Tess's hand dived into her pocket, her trembling fingers fumbling to hide the automatic. "Thank God you never became a poet," she managed. "We would starve."

"Oh, I think you're talented enough to keep us in Godiva chocolates for life. May I escort you to lunch, milady?" Luke asked, holding out his arm.

Tess stared up at him. What was going on? Why was he so pleasant when she had worked so hard to send him into a towering rage only thirty minutes earlier? What was he up to?

She tentatively placed her hand on his arm and he led her down the hall and then started downstairs, gaily discussing his blighted poetical career and his reluctant entrance into the law. She jerked him to a stop halfway down the stairs.

"Okay, that's it, I've had enough," she said grimly. "Just what in the heavenly name of Monet are you up to, Mr. Grim Reaper?"

"I had hoped for a pleasant conversation before lunch," Luke innocently replied.

"Brother," Tess muttered, "it's even worse than I thought."

"If a pleasant conversation doesn't interest you," Luke continued, "you might try telling me the truth."

"About what?"

Luke grinned down at her. "Yes, there are so many pieces to be uncovered, aren't there? But for now, I'll settle for the truth about why you really came to this house with your friend Bert."

"To con the Farleigh out of Jane, of course."

"Ah now, Tess, that's only half the truth and you know it. Try again."

"What is this, the Spanish Inquisition?"

Luke held his arms wide. "I haven't got a whip or a rack on me and my tone has been decidedly dulcet. Hardly the tactics of an Inquisitor, don't you think?"

"I think I want some lunch," Tess said, starting back down the stairs.

Luke quickly caught up to her. "It really is going to be exciting being married to you. A thrill a minute, probably. Getting you to accept compromise and a little help now and then will be the greatest challenge of my life. Did you know that fourteen years ago your friend Bert murdered Anna Mae Smith, also known as Violet? Strangled her with his bare hands."

Tess stopped cold. "What?" Bert had murdered the only adult who had ever been kind to her after the kidnapping?

Luke's smile was grim. "I thought that would catch your interest. The police are calling it an unsolved murder. I think they'll be happy to reopen the case when Leroy hands over his evidence."

Tess forced herself to shrug and continue walking down the stairs. "Bert has murdered nine people that I know of. Probably a lot more. He has little regard for human life."

"So why are you playing pat-a-cake with him today?" Luke demanded as they walked across the Grand Hall.

"The irony of using him as a witness to my ascension into Elizabethdom pleases me."

"Dammit, Tess, stop playing word games with me!" Luke shouted as he grabbed her arm and jerked her to a halt.

"How dare *you* accuse *me* of playing games!" Tess sputtered. "You've been stringing me along from the day I got here. You only decided to love me when you found out I'm really Elizabeth!"

Luke stared down at her in openmouthed astonishment. "Why, you pea-brained little dunce!" he sputtered, gripping her by both arms and shaking her a little so that she had to look up at him. "I loved you the first day you walked into this house and your blue eyes collided with mine. I loved you every minute of every day I thought you were only here to con Jane out of her millions. I loved you *in spite* of that damn video! *I loved you!* Heart and soul, body and mind. I don't care if even now you're running some sort of monumental con. *I don't care, Tess!* I love you and I want you and by God I am going to have you!"

Wanting to believe him was the hardest thing Tess had ever fought. "How could you love me in the face of that awful video?" she said in a small voice, the tears welling in her eyes. "It's impossible. The things I said about you ... about Jane ... How could you love me?"

Luke's fingers raised her chin so that she had to look up at him through a blur of tears. "I knew the heart of you, Tess, and I trusted that," he said gently. "You taught me to trust my instincts and a woman's heart. I knew you were incapable of being that hard, that cold. I knew you were acting for Bert's benefit, I just didn't know why. I still don't know why. I don't know why you agreed to work the con with him in the first place. This kind of job isn't your style. Does he have some sort of hold on you, Tess?"

She was silent a moment, though his gentle grip wouldn't let her look away. "You could call it that," she said at last.

"There must be ways to set you free—"

"I thought this con was the only way."

"I don't understand." Luke stared down at her, his green gaze tender. "Won't you tell me what all of this is about, Tess? Won't you trust me enough to tell me the truth?"

"My love was and is the truth," Tess whispered. "Every ounce of it."

"I know, my darling. But I want more. We are going to be married. That marriage won't stand a chance if we don't start trusting each other now. Tell me why Bert still has a hold on you. Tell me why you want to see him today. Trust me, Tess. Tell me."

She couldn't help herself. Staring up at him, the words started tumbling out of her mouth.

"Bert has used a lot of disguises and a lot of different names in his long and filthy career," she said raggedly. "The redheaded Hal Marsh was one of them. He's the man who kidnapped me."

Luke paled, even as his eyes darkened with rage. *"Bert?"*

"When you told me about Hal Marsh last night, everything splintered in my brain ... and I remembered. I remembered Bert scooping me out of my bed in the middle of the night, his hand over my mouth so I couldn't scream. Only his hand was so big, it covered my nose and I began to suffocate. By the time he started carrying me down the ladder he had wedged up against the house, I was so desperate for oxygen that I began to struggle. I even managed to break free, and took a header for the ground. That's all I remember about the kidnapping until I woke up a few days later. Bert was raging back and forth across the motel room. I had no idea who I was, where I was, or who he was. He soon put me straight on that score. He said he owned me. It was our first official introduction. A few weeks later he sold me to the Carswells."

"Oh, my darling," Luke said, but she wouldn't let him give her the comfort she longed for.

"When Bert bought me back six years later, he turned my miserable life into a living hell. I wasn't a human being to him, I was a tool. He used me"—Tess shuddered—"in the most hideous ways, Luke. But he made a very bad mistake. He trained me too well. When he finally dumped me, I was almost eighteen and all I could think about was getting my pound of flesh back. But I needed money and connections, so I kept working, for a while.

"That story I told you and Jane about turning myself in to WEB and working my time off with them? It was no story. It was the truth. And when I'd done my time, I told WEB about Bert. They were almost as eager as I was to see him behind bars. They gave me Blake Thornton and Diana Hunter, their best people, to help me nail him."

"This whole thing has been a double cross?"

Tess shook her head. "A double *con*. I'd been planning this job for years, Luke. I pulled strings Bert doesn't even know exist just to get him thrown out of South America, because I knew he'd eventually come back to his old hunting grounds and then I'd find some way of pulling a job with him, conning him when he thought we were conning some innocent mark, getting him to incriminate himself while under surveillance so he'd spend the next thousand years in jail. And you know what made all of that hard work worthwhile? Bert came to me!"

The oxygen left Luke's lungs in a hiss.

"And then, last night," Tess said, her voice tight with fury, "when I learned that *Bert* was the man who destroyed my life, a thousand years in jail just wasn't good enough anymore. An eye for an eye, a life for a life. He destroyed mine, I am going to destroy his."

"How?" Luke asked tightly.

"When he comes calling today, I'm going to teach him the life lesson he imparted to me during the seven years he *owned* me. He won't know if he's gonna live to see the next second, to draw another breath, to blink his eyes. That's not something a man like Bert can survive."

"Tess," Luke said, openly worried now, "what are you planning?"

With a smile, Tess took the automatic from her pocket and held it up admiringly. "Isn't it lovely? Small, but effective. I intend to show Bert just how effective."

"Tess, no!" Luke cried, grasping her wrist, trying to pull the gun away with his other hand. But Tess wrenched free. "You can't sacrifice your life to claim his!"

"Jail isn't good enough!" she shouted.

"It was good enough for the Carswells—"

"But this is the man who destroyed my life!"

"And you've taken it back!" Luke said urgently, grasping her shoulders. "You've got your independence, your career, your grandmother, your heritage, and *my love*. You have your own life now, Tess, with people who love you. You can't throw that away."

"You got to have your revenge on Margo Holloway. Why can't I have mine on Bert?"

"I had Margo Holloway arrested and convicted for the crime she committed," Luke grimly replied. "At no time was my life or the life of anyone I cared for in danger. And you know what, Tess? Even though I got my revenge, it didn't change what she had done to me. It didn't change how I *felt*."

"You don't understand," Tess said in a low voice. "This is all I've dreamed about, all I've lived for for over a decade."

"Dreams change, lives change," Luke pleaded. "You set out to con Bert, to throw him in jail, and instead you ended up with a new life and a love that will cherish you the rest of your life. Let your WEB agents put Bert in jail. There's no need for you to risk your life by confronting the most dangerous man I've ever known."

"There is *every* need," Tess growled.

Luke stared down at her, anger tightening his face. "Does Jane mean nothing to you, after all? Does my love mean nothing?"

"They mean everything to me!"

"Then why in hell are you deliberately throwing them away?"

"I'm not!"

"My God, Tess, can't you see that you are? If you use that gun today, you'll be throwing away everything you've ever cared about. You'll be choosing death over life!"

"I can't live a life of love and happiness if I haven't first gotten a little of my own back from Bert."

"Yes you can. You are capable of soaring to the heights, *if you choose*."

"Luke," Tess said wearily, feeling the walls going up between them and unable to stop any of it, "if you'd asked this of me yesterday or the day before, I'd have said yes without a second thought. But now I know that *this* is the man who ripped me away from everything safe, who killed my father, who scarred my mother and my grandmother. It is my duty to pay him back in kind."

"Tess, if you do this, then Bert wins. He *will* have destroyed your life and this time you will have helped him. Don't do this, *please*."

Tess looked sadly up at Luke. "In the beginning," she said softly, "there was Bert."

He stared down at her a moment and then roughly pushed her away. "I won't be a party to this stupidity and this blindness and this death wish. You want to confront Bert? Fine! You want to put a bullet in him? More power to you! But I'm not going to stick around to watch you destroy everything *I* care about. I'm not going to watch you throw everything away, including *me*. I'm not going to watch you devastate Jane just to get back at Bert. I'll send you a card once a year to whatever penitentiary they toss you in."

Luke threw open the front door and stormed outside, slamming the door so hard it sounded like a rifle shot.

Tess felt like a fighter pilot suddenly ejecting out of an alternative universe. Had that been *her* choosing a living death over life? Had that been her turning her back on everything she had ever wanted and loved most in this world? Had that been her driving Luke away? Had Bert finally succeeded in making her as ruthless as he? Had she deliberately lowered herself into his pool of slime? Had there been an ounce of sense in any of her arguments with Luke?

"No!" she yelled, diving for the front door. She ran out onto the front drive. "Luke!" she shouted.

But she was too late. His Jaguar had already spun around the last curve in the driveway and careened through the Cushman gate.

"Oh God," Tess groaned, "he's going to get himself killed before I can even apologize to him!"

She stood staring at the faraway gate for several minutes and then, with a troubled sigh, walked slowly back into the house. She stopped in the Grand Hall, unsure what to do first. Jane . . . her grandmother was waiting for her in the dining room. They had so much to say to each other. She gazed longingly at the hall leading to the dining room, then, with another sigh, began to trudge upstairs. She would finish what she had begun, tie up the loose ends, and then embark on her new life, hoping past hope that Luke would finally cool off and come back so she could grovel at his feet and beg his forgiveness.

Wearily she pushed open the door to her bedroom—*her* bedroom—and sat down on her bed. She stared at the phone for a moment, then gave herself a shake, picked up the receiver, and began to dial.

"Hey, Diana," she said when the car phone was picked up on the first ring.

There was a pause. "Don't you mean Gladys?"

"Not anymore. I have been contemplating my

life, doing deep intestinal soul-searching and I have
reached the conclusion that I am an idiot."

"What?"

"Terminally stupid. So, I've decided to change
the plan. I don't need to risk everything I've got,
including my life, on a piece of revenge. So, go ahead
and arrest Bert now. You've got everything you need."

Again there was a pause. "I'd be happy to
oblige you, love, but we've lost him."

"You *what*?" Tess shrieked.

"He found the tracker. I don't know how, but
he found it. He's ditched the Lincoln, he's ditched the
apartment. He's runnin' wild, Tess. Better keep low to
the ground for a few hours. We'll get him."

"*How* will you get him?" Tess demanded.

"We figure he made us and he's going to try to
get out of the country. Blake's heading to JFK. I'm off
to LaGuardia. Leroy Baldwin—"

"Baldwin?"

"He's on his way to Newark. He's also got his
agents out searching. We'll get Bert. Just keep your
head low."

The line went dead in Tess's hand. Keep her
head low? There wasn't a hole deep enough or a rock
large enough to hide under to escape Bert if he was on
your trail, and Tess had no doubt that if Bert had made
Blake and Diana, he'd made her, too. Her life wasn't
worth a glass emerald as long as he was free. Blake and
Diana and Leroy Baldwin, they were good, they were
fabulous, but Bert when cornered was the most dangerous animal on earth. He knew how to hide, he knew
how to keep his freedom, he knew how to exact his
revenge.

The question was, would he take out his
revenge just on her, or on Jane and Luke as well? It
would be like him, oh so like him, to make her twist on

the knife watching what he did to her loved ones before he took her life, too. Tess buried her head in her hands.

Oh God, she couldn't think! What should she do? Should she get out now? She had a few hiding places of her own, and if she was gone perhaps Luke and Jane would be safe. But if she left and Bert *did* come here, then Jane and Luke would be in absolute danger.

She couldn't let that happen. She would stay. She would stay and become Jane's watchdog. She was done running. Done hiding for her own purposes. She would stay and take care of Jane, if she needed it. She owed her grandmother that much, and so much more. Blake and Diana would catch up with Bert sooner than later. He'd never make it out of the country. The WEB agents were too good. She was overreacting, and badly, and it was time to retrench. There was no reason to alarm Jane, at least not now. She'd had more than a lifetime of worries. Bert would cover his own skin first, then seek revenge. There were days yet to be safe.

She walked downstairs, needling herself for being such a ninny and for causing Luke so much pain by starting that stupid argument in the first place, and vowing that if he didn't come back in the next hour, she would go after him and crawl on broken root beer bottles if that's what it took to get him back.

She was just crossing the Grand Hall when she heard the doorbell ring. "It's okay, Hodgkins," she called to the butler who was hovering near the staircase, "I've got it."

Her only thought was that Luke had cooled down much sooner than expected and come back. She ran to the door and pulled it open, ready to throw herself into his arms and never let him let him go.

"You're busted, babe."

CHAPTER
20

Tess's knees nearly gave out on her. Clutching the white door, she stared up at Bert disguised as Max Weinstein, feeling all of the blood drain out of her body. It was replaced by every survival instinct he'd ever pounded into her.

"Bert!" she hissed. "Quit fooling around and get into character. Hodgkins is standing ten feet away! Max!" she cried in a joyful voice. "What are you doing here so early? Come on in."

He hesitated just a moment before walking into the Hall, the benign Max Weinstein expression firmly in place. "A ... matter has come up, Tess, that I felt I must discuss with you in person. I hope I'm not intruding."

She could see the wheels turning in his brain. Did she know he'd made her, or didn't she? If she didn't, it would be so satisfying for him to lure her in for a little while before springing his trap.

"Hey, no problem," Tess said. "Mi casa grande es su casa grande."

She intended to keep him wondering just as long as she could. She needed enough time to get Jane out of the house. After that, it didn't really matter what went down. Survival at any cost no longer held any allure. The first priority was her grandmother's safety and Jane was not safe when Bert was within a hundred miles of her. Thank God Luke had already left the house.

"Hodgkins, get some brandy for Dr. Weinstein, would you? I think we'll go into the library. Oh! But first I really must just have a word with Jane . . . I mean, my grandmother. Luke and I had the most awful fight and I think it upset her. Just a second, Max."

She walked, without any sign of urgency, down the hall to the dining room.

Jane was seated at the dining table, sipping a cup of tea. Jane Cushman. Her grandmother.

"Hi," Tess said, her voice shaky in spite of herself.

"Hello, yourself," Jane said, her pale blue eyes warm and loving.

For one desperate moment, Tess wanted to throw herself into her grandmother's arms and weep. Ruthlessly she forced her emotions back behind their wall and smiled at Jane. "I'm sorry I gave you such a scare last night."

"That's all right, dear. I gave you a bit of a scare myself."

Tess made herself laugh and made it sound genuine. "You've got that right. I know we have so much to talk over, but I need a favor first."

"Certainly, my dear. What is it?"

Tess's expression was wry. "I'm afraid I started a totally stupid fight with Luke. He was right and I wouldn't let myself admit it and now he's stormed off and I'm so afraid he won't come back."

"That must have been some fight," Jane commented.

"It was awful. I know I'm the last person in the

world he wants to see right now, but I do so want to apologize and make things up. Do you think you could find him and tell him? He'd believe you. I'm not so sure he'd believe me just now."

"Don't worry about Luke, Tess. He adores you. He'll cool off sooner than later and come back—"

"But I can't wait!" Tess said, wringing her hands. "Bert is coming soon and I've got to know everything's all right between Luke and me or I just won't be able to finish what I started. Do you know where he might have gone? Could you go to him?"

Jane's blue eyes were twinkling with amusement at this display of the youthful pangs of love. "I have an idea where he might be," she said, standing up. "I'll go see if I can assuage his temper long enough to forgive you."

"Oh, thank you, Grandmother!" Tess cried and allowed herself to throw herself into Jane's arms and hug her tightly. It might be the only chance she'd ever have.

"We'll be back in half an hour, you mark my words."

"You're an angel," Tess said, kissing Jane on her cheek. She took Jane's hand in hers and began leading her to the breezeway connected to the garage. "Tell Luke I love him more than anything in my life, except you, of course. And tell him I think he's absolutely right and I'll do exactly as he says."

"Now don't go docile on me, Tess."

Tess chuckled. "It's just this once. He *was* right, you see."

"I'm glad to see the Cushman pride hasn't blinded you to the truth of a matter," Jane said, patting her cheek.

"Oh no," Tess said, opening the door to the garage. "I've also got the Cushman wits about me. They'll keep me in line, never you fear."

She watched Jane get into a Mercedes sedan and begin driving down the long estate road before she resolutely turned and headed back to the house, to the library . . . and Bert. She passed Hodgkins in the hall.

"Oh, Hodgkins," she said, stopping him. "My grandmother has just gone out on an errand and she asked me to ask you to begin an immediate inventory of the wine cellar, for the wedding you know."

"My records have never come in question, Miss," Hodgkins intoned.

"Of course not, Hodgkins," Tess said soothingly. "Grandmother is just a trifle excited about all of the wedding plans, and the dinner party and the ball must have made serious inroads on our stock. Let's just humor her, shall we?"

"Certainly, Miss Cushman," Hodgkins said with an icy bow. He turned with a glacial expression and began to walk toward the wine cellar.

"Oh, and tell the maids that Dr. Weinstein and I will be in the library and don't want to be disturbed for any reason," she called after him.

"Certainly, Miss."

When he was gone, she picked up the phone in the Grand Hall and hurriedly punched in Diana's number.

"Hello?"

"Bert's here."

Tess hung up and took a deep breath. She'd done everything she could to protect the people in this house, her house. Now it was time to see if she could survive Bert's rage long enough for Diana and Blake to come to the rescue.

Her hand closed around the small automatic in her pocket. She had never used a gun in her life and was no fast draw. Bert, however, was always armed and very used to firing a gun.

She offered up a silent prayer and strode into

the library, closing the door behind her. Bert was leaning against the Louis Quinze desk at the far end of the library. An empty brandy snifter sat beside him.

"What the hell do you think you're doing?" she demanded before Bert could say a word. "You're not supposed to be here until *two*. I haven't signed the papers yet. I don't have power of attorney, nothing has been transferred into my name. Nothing is set, nothing is safe, until I sign those papers!"

Bert studied her a moment. "Something came up that I felt I must discuss with you."

Tess swore with a perfect show of exasperation. "Are the cops onto us?"

"Not the locals, only WEB."

"*WEB?*" Tess shrieked. "We've got to get out of here! Screw the papers and the empire, let's go!"

She watched suspicion and uncertainty war in Bert's cold gray eyes. Had WEB been tailing him on its own account? Was Tess merely caught in the middle? Or had she organized it all? Where was safety and where was danger in this room with only two inhabitants?

Jane had driven ten miles when she suddenly remembered the high-tech revolution. She laughed at herself. She must be getting old after all. She pulled her Mercedes over to the side of the road, turned on her hazard lights, picked up her car phone, and dialed Luke's car phone number.

He didn't answer until the third ring.

"What?" he growled in an excellent imitation of a wounded grizzly bear.

"Luke, dear, wherever you are, pull off to the side of the road and stop your car."

"Why?"

"Because I want to talk to you."

"I don't—"

"Do it, or I sic Regina on you."

Muttering decidedly uncomplimentary imprecations, Luke barked at her, "All right, I've stopped. Now what the hell is it?"

"I am a messenger come to sue for peace between two warring factions."

"Have you been nipping at the sherry again?"

Jane chuckled. "Tess pleaded with me to chase after you—"

"She *what*?"

"—and to tell you that she loves you more than anything in her life, except me, of course, and that she thinks you're absolutely right and will do exactly as you say." Jane stared at her phone, which was silent. "Hello?"

"That doesn't sound at all like Tess," Luke said at last.

"That's what I said, but she assured me you *were* right. Were you?"

"Of course I was! But it's not like Tess to have anyone act as her messenger."

"Luke?"

His voice was tight with tension. "I've got a bad feeling in the pit of my stomach, Jane. I'm heading back right now and you . . . I think you'd better stay right where you are."

"Well, of all the absurd—"

The phone went dead in Jane's hand.

"If we're going to get away from WEB, we'll need cash. Lots of it," Bert said at last.

"Your Swiss bank accounts—"

"Have unaccountably been closed . . . by someone."

Tess's eyes widened with feigned horror. "Crud. WEB is onto you big-time, then."

"That *was* my impression."

Tess shoved her hands onto her hips to keep them steady. "Well, look, I've got the Farleigh. It's not cash, but it can bring us some soon. In the meantime, we've probably got enough money between us to at least get out of the country."

Bert suddenly reached out, his hand tangling in her hair as he jerked her painfully against him. "I don't want a companion on this little getaway. All I want is the Farleigh . . . and my pound of flesh."

"W-w-what do you mean?"

Bert's free hand slashed against Tess's face once. "Someone set me up! The Weinstein apartment was bugged!" He hit her again, harder. The world exploded in her head. "There was a tracker on my Lincoln!" He hit her again, sending her crashing to the floor three feet away from him.

Luke's car phone rang imperiously at him, once, twice. He grabbed it on the third ring.

"Jane, I don't want—"

"It's not Jane, it's Leroy. We've got trouble."

The Jaguar suddenly swerved. A white Mazda in the right lane blared its horn at him as he passed it.

Luke forced his hand to remain steady on the wheel. "What trouble?"

"I got a call from a WEB agent by the name of Blake Thornton about an hour ago. He and his partner have been tailing Bert for more than three weeks now. And they lost him about two hours ago."

"They what?"

"They began searching and then called me. Seems they know all about my work for you. They needed some fast, knowledgeable help and I was it. We figured your Bert was on his way out of the country. But I just got a call from Hunter. It seems Bert had some unfinished business. He didn't head for an airport. He's at the Cushman estate."

• • •

Tess's face was burning, her head ringing, from the minor beating Bert had just given her. She moved slowly, cautiously on the floor. She didn't want to give him any excuse to get rougher.

"Bert, what the hell is this?" she said, rising to her feet and staring up at him, the picture of baffled innocence. "I know you're tense about WEB—I'm scared to death, myself—but that's no reason to start beating up your best girl."

This time she had him. He didn't even try to hide his surprise. "Okay," he said slowly. "I'll cut you a deal. You give me the Farleigh and I'll let you get out of here alive."

"Thanks a lot. What about my ten percent?"

"You opted for the empire, babe, and you lost. That's your hard luck. I want the Farleigh."

Tess stared up at him a moment and then sighed heavily. "Okay. I can crack one of the wall safes and make off with something to make this job worthwhile. But tell me something first, Bert," she said, playing for time, hoping to distract him just enough. "Twenty years ago, when you were calling yourself Hal Marsh and kidnapped me, did you plan to resell me back to my family sooner than later?"

Bert stared at her. Then a slow, appreciative smile spread across his face. "So, you know."

"Yes," Tess said calmly.

"How long have you known?"

"Long enough. I was . . . um . . . surprised at first, but then I saw the humor in the situation."

Bert beamed at her. "Selling the real article as a fake. What a con! I tell you, Tess, I've lain awake at night just laughing."

"So have I, Bert, so have I. So what happened twenty years ago? Why did you dump me with the Carswells?"

"Ah, the damn job went sour from the start. You're the reason I didn't go into kidnapping full-time. God, what a mess! First you fall off the ladder and Jerry and I don't know if you're gonna live or die, then Jerry gets cold feet. Wanted to turn himself in, the bastard."

"Who was Jerry?"

"Jerry Burns, used to be an underbutler for the Cushmans. He was my inside man."

"So, did you ice the jittery Jerry?"

Bert shrugged his massive shoulders. "Sure. I'd always planned to, of course, just not so soon. There I was without a partner, a half-dead kid on my hands, and every cop and Fed in the country looking for me. You were so hot, there was no way I could ransom you for the million dollars I had demanded. So, I hid out for a few weeks, cut your hair, and then sold you to the Carswells for a thousand bucks. A lousy thousand bucks," he muttered, his gray eyes glittering as he glared at Tess. "I was expecting a cool million and you only brought me a thousand bucks. I figured you owed me big-time, babe, and I meant to get what was due me one way or the other."

Tess's stomach turned over. "Is that why you bought me back from the Carswells?

He smiled, grimly amused. "Oh, I'd figured a way to get my million out of you by then. I decided to give the cops five or six years to give up on the case, buy you back from the Carswells, and then ransom you to the Cushmans. But when Violet brought you to me in Charleston, you didn't recognize me. That's when my brain shifted into overdrive. I decided to sell you back to the Cushmans, all right, but only after you'd been trained, only after you were a good enough thief, a good enough con, to pull the job off and snare me a hell of a lot more than a million. And it worked. You did a great job, babe."

"Thanks, Bert. That means a lot to me. I have

just one comment." Tess pulled her WEB identification and badge from her left pocket, the gun from her right pocket, and grinned. "You're busted, babe! You have the right to remain silent. If you give up the right to remain silent, anything you say can and will be used—"

Bert stared at her. Then he laughed. "Very funny, little girl. You had me going for a minute."

"It's no joke, Bert. I really do work for WEB and you really are going to jail for lots and lots of years."

His gray eyes narrowed into murderous slits. "So it *was* you."

"The biggest and the best con I ever pulled," Tess said proudly. "You trained me well, Bert. You know all of those jobs we so fondly recalled during my prep time for this con? You were right: Weinstein's apartment *was* wired. Those conservations are on tape. You confessed to over thirty different criminal activities from theft to murder. My WEB associates have gathered the corroborating evidence for your stateside activities and, with a little reluctance from your former associates, they've found enough evidence on your Australian and South American drug syndicates to make even Noriega's defense attorney blanch. We've . . . er . . . convinced Mendoza to testify against you."

Bert went a little green at that.

"Now, I want you to very gently remove the thirty-eight from your shoulder holster with your left hand and set it on the ground and then kick it, gently, toward me."

"What thirty-eight?"

"Oh, give me a break, Bert. That gun is practically welded to your body by this point. Take it out, now."

Slowly, his eyes never leaving Tess, he removed the gun from his shoulder holster, set it on the ground, and shoved it toward Tess with his foot.

"Thank you."

Tess was pocketing her badge and ID when Bert leapt at her.

Luke nearly rear-ended Jane's Mercedes as his Jaguar screeched to a stop at the front door of the Cushman mansion.

He was out of his car and holding Jane's car door closed in the next moment. "Stay here!"

"Would you care to rephrase that?" Jane said icily.

"Bert's inside, dammit! He may be holding Tess!"

The blood drained from Jane's face.

Luke ran up the front steps, jerked open the front door, and looked wildly around. Where was she? Was she safe? Was she already dead?

A gunshot broke the silence.

Luke's heart slammed into his throat. The library!

He ran down the hall, drenched in cold perspiration. A second gunshot made his hand shudder on the library door as he pulled it open.

"Tess!" he yelled.

Bert had bent her backward over the library desk. Blood streamed from his shoulder as they fought for possession of the gun in Tess's hand. Luke's yell had distracted Bert long enough for Tess to knee him savagely in the groin. His bellow of pain was abruptly cut off. Luke had a hammer lock around his throat. Terrified and enraged, he could conceive of no greater pleasure than strangling Bert here and now. He swung him off Tess and into the center of the room.

Bert's face, what he could see of it, was turning purple as he gagged and gasped for air, struggling to get free.

"Luke, stop!" Tess screamed. "You're killing him!"

She was pulling at his shoulders. He shrugged her off. All he needed was a moment or two more and Bert's neck would snap.

Suddenly two hands grasped his hair and jerked his head back. "Don't you dare kill him!" Tess growled, her blue eyes burning into his.

Slowly Luke became aware of just what he was doing and about to do. With a gasp, he released Bert, who collapsed on the floor. He stared down at him, nearly dizzy with the rage and fear still churning within him. He had almost killed a man!

"Tess—" he said raggedly.

She slipped her arms around him and hugged him tight. "It's okay," she whispered. "I know the feeling."

"Are you all right?"

"I'm fine. Here," she said, pressing the gun into his right hand. "You'd better hold this. My hands are shaking so badly, I'm more likely to hit you than Bert if he tries anything."

"Thank God. Thank God you're safe!" Luke whispered hoarsely as he held her tight. He was shaking. Dimly he was aware of the warm tears slowly trailing down his face. "I was so scared that I'd lost you—"

"Never," Tess murmured, pressing her lips to his. "You are *never* going to get rid of me."

Bert groaned on the floor and struggled to his hands and knees. Instantly, Luke shifted Tess into his left arm and aimed the small automatic at him.

The precaution was not necessary for in the next moment three people, armed to the teeth, burst into the library. The first was a woman with thick black hair pulled back into a French braid. She had a forty-five aimed at Bert's head. The second was a man. He frightened Luke almost as much as Bert had. His hair was blond, nearly white. His eyes were an ominous black. He was tall, heavily muscled. His face was the hardest, coldest face Luke had ever seen. He too was holding a gun on Bert. The third person was Leroy Baldwin.

"Are we interrupting anything?" the woman inquired with a startling Irish accent.

"Think of it as a mop-up operation, Diana, and glad to have you!" Tess said.

"Why is he bleeding?" the blond man demanded, his soft Southern accent in chilling contrast to the hardness in his voice.

"I shot him," Tess replied. "Resisting arrest and all that."

"Where the bloody hell did you of all people get a gun?" the woman demanded.

"I stole it, of course," Tess replied. "There's a large collection of guns behind us and, as I've said more than once, the locks in this house are pitiful."

"Tess?"

Jane was standing in the doorway. She looked bloodless, her face aged a hundred years.

"Grandmother, I'm fine," Tess said, breaking free of Luke's arms to run to Jane and hold her tight. "The nightmare is over, I promise."

"I was so worried," Jane whispered.

"Me, too."

Suddenly Jane pushed Tess to arm's length. "Is that why you sent me off on that fool's errand after Luke? Bert was here and you were trying to get me out of the house?"

"He would have hurt you if he'd had the chance," Tess said gently.

"Fortunately," the blond man said, "he didn't and he won't." While the Irish woman covered him, he quickly and thoroughly frisked Bert. He removed a switchblade from a small holster on his calf and tossed it to the woman.

"Tess, who *are* these people?" Jane demanded.

"Oh, now where are my manners?" Tess exclaimed. "Allow me to introduce Blake Thornton and Diana Hunter, WEB agents and my able assistants on this job."

"What job?" Jane said.

Tess blushed. "It *is* time to explain, isn't it? I came into this house to con Bert. To catch him in the execution of a federal crime. I never knew I'd find you. I never knew I would endanger you. I was only thinking of my revenge, of seeing his face when I told him who the real mark was on this job. But as Luke so . . . cogently . . . pointed out, Blake and Diana and I already had enough evidence to have him arrested and jailed for the next thousand years. So, I told Blake and Diana to arrest him. Unfortunately, Bert had already slipped his leash and came looking for me. I had to be sure he didn't find you, too. And . . . there's one more thing, Grandmother. Bert has used the name Hal Marsh in the past. He's the man who kidnapped me."

"Kidnapped you?" Leroy Baldwin said, staring at her. "Do you mean you really *are* Elizabeth Cushman?"

Tess laughed. "Ironic, isn't it? I came to this house to get my revenge, and found my family instead."

"I love it," Diana stated. "I always said you were born with class, Tess."

"Thank you, Diana."

Suddenly Luke pulled Tess toward him. "What happened to your face?" he said grimly.

"Oh crud, has it started to bruise already?" Tess said, her hands going to her cheeks.

"Did that monster hit you?" Jane demanded.

"Only a little," Tess said gently. "I'm used to it. It's okay, Grandmother, really."

"No, it is not okay," Luke seethed, pulling her into his arms. "The next time we have an argument, *you* storm out of the house. Got it?"

"Got it," Tess replied with a grin. She glanced across at Diana. "What about Bert's stooges?"

"His so-called surveillance team is cooling their heels in jail," Diana replied as she holstered her gun. "I hate amateurs."

"This has all been a terrible strain for you, Diana, I know," Tess said.

Diana suddenly laughed and kissed Tess on her cheek. "You don't know the half of it!"

Blake handcuffed Bert and then, holding on to the cuffs, jerked him to his feet.

Bert bellowed with pain.

"If you're so delicate, you shouldn't be in the business," Blake advised him in a soft voice that sent chills down Luke's back. "You hurt a friend of mine. I don't like that. I'd like to make you pay for it here and now. But I'll let the justice system do it for me. Federal penitentiaries are notoriously . . . rigorous, you know."

Diana laughed.

"Federal penitentiary," Tess said with a happy sigh. "What a wonderful sound. It just rolls off your lips like music: federal penitentiary."

"You'll never even get me to trial," Bert sneered. "I've got connections—"

"Of course you do, Bert," Tess said soothingly. "Phil Larkin, Barry Kincaid, and the others. They're all in jail waiting for their own trials right now."

"We like to be thorough," Diana explained.

"And we wanted you very badly," Blake said in his chilling, soft voice.

"It is times like these," Luke said, holding Tess close, "that I wish I worked for the Feds. But don't worry, Bert, old buddy, old pal," he said as he directed his own chilling gaze at the monster. "I have friends in high places. Sometimes it pays to be a Mansfield. I'll make sure you get the prosecutor and the judge from Hell for your trial."

Blake eyed Luke with interest. "I like this man."

"So do I," Tess aid.

To Luke's surprise, Blake reached out and pulled Tess to him, hugging her for a moment and then releasing her.

"It was brilliantly done, Tess," he said. "You can be my group leader anytime."

"Thanks," Tess said softly.

"It's been a grand game, Tess," Diana said. "You're certainly the best con I've ever come across, and that's saying a lot. I can't wait to work the next job with you."

"Oh gee, Diana, I can't," Tess said. "I'm retiring from WEB. I'm going to be much too busy to pull any more jobs. You see, I have to learn how to run the Cushman empire . . . and I'm getting married very, very soon. Aren't I?" she said, looking at Luke.

"*Very* soon," Luke growled, pulling her back into his arms and kissing her hard. He looked up at Diana long enough to catch his breath. "Want to come to the wedding?"

"Wouldn't miss it for the world," Diana said with a grin.

Tess clung to him in a most pleasing and trusting manner. "You're first on the guest list, Leroy," Luke said.

"Consider the tux rented," Leroy said with a grin.

"I won't get married if you're not there, Blake," Tess said.

"You won't be able to keep me away," he said. "I love crying at weddings."

She smiled with open affection at the agent. "I

always knew you were a softie. That thirty-eight of Bert's that you pocketed is probably the same one he used to kill a fence by the name of Eddie Grafton seven years go. You might want to run it through ballistics."

"I love the way you work," Blake murmured. He and Diana led Bert from the room, Leroy trailing behind.

Taking a steadying breath, Tess walked up to Jane and pulled both of her aged hands into her own. Even across the room, Luke could see that Tess was shaking.

"I have an apology to make, but words don't seem enough somehow," she said. "I came into this house to con Bert, which meant conning you. Deceiving you. Using you. I didn't care about that. All I cared about was putting Bert behind bars. Nothing else mattered. That was unforgivable of me. Just because I've turned out to really be what I pretended is no excuse. I want to apologize for every lie, every deception, and for today's pyrotechnics. But today . . . Bert called the game. I had to finish the job I started."

"You are very good at what you do, Tess," Jane said, "and I am very proud of you. You are quite, quite forgiven and now I want you to fully accept what I am about to tell you: Welcome home, Elizabeth. Welcome home." She pulled her granddaughter into her arms.

EPILOGUE

"Your fuddy-duddy days are now officially behind you."

"Hallelujah!"

"You have a surprisingly good baritone, you know."

"You're too kind."

"I've never heard 'La Cucaracha' sung in the nude before. I was very impressed. And I know Grandmother enjoyed your performance tremendously."

"I sought only to please."

"Oh, you did," Tess said with a grin. "Your brother Joshua was especially vocal in his thanks to me, but I had to tell him it was none of my doing. *You* were the one who made such a silly promise."

"Trust me, if I had met you first, I never would have been so rash."

"It's best to be forewarned about these things. You should probably never play strip poker with Grandmother or me, either."

"I'll keep that in mind."

Tess laughed. "Are you really sure, Luke, that you want to live at the Cushman mansion? Grandmother would understand if we decided to live in our own house."

"The Cushman mansion is large enough to insure all the privacy we want for our married life and I'm not so cruel as to take you away from Jane after she just got you back. I move in after the honeymoon, Tess, and gladly."

"Sometimes you're just too wonderful. I don't know how I'll ever repay you."

Luke leered at her. "Oh, I'll find a way, *trust* me."

"I do. I do!" Tess said with a grin. "I like being married very much, you know," she said, sipping her champagne as she rambled around the huge hotel suite. She held up her left hand and gazed lovingly at the slim band of gold and the emerald engagement ring Luke had bought days before he had ever demanded she marry him. Such an impetuous man.

"I like that negligee very much, you know," Luke said with a grin. He sat on the king-sized bed, his back against the headboard. He was naked.

"Thank you. I was thinking of you when I bought it. You know, your father is really a bit of a darling, once he loosens his tie. But I may be prejudiced. As I recall, he was the best horsy I ever rode when I was three, and I had lots of grown-ups to compare him to. I trust that you will be just as good a horsy for our children as your father was for me."

"Our children? Are you pregnant yet?"

Tess frowned at Luke. "We have only been married for seven hours. These things take time."

Luke opened his arms invitingly. "I'm willing to give it all the time in the world."

Tess set her champagne glass down on a nearby table. "Eagerness is all well and good, and your eagerness is duly noted, Husband. But, if you will be so kind as to notice, *I* am still dressed."

"Not for long, Wife," Luke said as he slid from the bed and strode up to her. "Just two ribbons holding this thing together," he said, studying Tess from every angle. "How convenient."

Tess laughed.

"I must say that *I* was impressed," Luke said, gently tugging at the black silk ribbon on Tess's left shoulder, "with the way you and Jane were able to concoct a mammoth wedding on only three days' notice."

"We Cushmans are renowned for our organizational abilities."

"I wondered what it was," Luke said, studying the ribbon on Tess's right shoulder. He pulled it slowly. It fell apart. The black lace negligee it had been supporting slipped with a whisper of silk to the floor. "*Lovely.* It is true that the best things come in small packages."

"You always say the nicest things," Tess said, her arms going around Luke's waist as his warm lips nuzzled her throat.

"A Mansfield specialty," Luke replied and picked her up in his arms. "Allow me to demonstrate another Mansfield specialty," he said, striding to the bed. He set her down and quickly lowered himself beside her. "There is just one thing I think I ought to know before we consummate this union of ours," he said, his hands caressing her breasts as his teeth nibbled one sensitive earlobe.

"Yes?" Tess gasped, her fingers sliding across the muscles of his broad back.

"You know I would have been happy if we'd spent our honeymoon in a crate in the Mojave Desert, so don't think of this as a complaint. But why on earth did you want to spend our honeymoon at Niagara Falls?"

Tess smiled up at her husband, barely able to think straight as his hands caressed her. "Having lived